The Empress of the Latin Empire, Yolanda of Namurs, once a very minor French noble woman also known as Isabel of Oakhampton to the English members of her Norman family, has been murdered in the Empire's capital city, Constantinople. It is the year 1219 and her young son Robert is now the Emperor. His older sister, Elizabeth, wants to be his regent and, even more, to be the Empress as her mother was before her. There is mischief afoot because she is not the only one who wants the throne.

Today's Friends

Chapter One
We are surprised.

We were still anchored in Venice's great harbour when word of the deaths and possible murders of his father and the Latin Empress reached George Courtenay, the Commander of the Cornwall-based Company of Archers. It so distressed him that he wept when he heard the news. It also upset and greatly angered all the rest of us who had made our marks on the Company's roll. We were, in a few simple words, seriously pissed.

The death of one of our own, and the likelihood that he had been murdered, fell on the Company's fleet like a bolt of lightning on an old tree. It hurt us badly and we could do nothing to respond. What made it even worse, if that was possible, was that an English woman our Company had contracted to defend had been killed with him. A woman? Impossible. We were immediately filled with righteous anger.

As you might imagine, the murders and what would happen next quickly became the subject of every conversation. My mates and I talked about it constantly as we sat at our places on our galley's rowing benches or gathered for a drink of water at the scuttled water butt that was set out each day next to the door to our galley's stern deck castle.

News of the deaths swept through the fleet of Company galleys and prizes in the harbour at great speed as it was shouted from one galley to the next. We immediately began mourning our former Commander with many men making fiery declarations as to what they would do to those responsible. We also told each other numerous stories and tales that we had heard about him, including some that sounded to me as if they might even have been true.

One thing was absolutely certain and totally agreed by every man—the butcher's bill would be paid in the form of a very serious revenge of some kind. Unfortunately, we did not have a clue as to what that response might be or how it would affect us. And that, as you might also imagine, resulted in a constant stream of exciting rumours involving all kinds of actions that we might be required to undertake.

****** *Lieutenant Commander Harold Lewes*

"We need to get back to Constantinople as soon as possible."

George announced his decision when he returned, red-eyed and shaken, from the roof of the smaller of our galley's two deck castles, the little one in the front where he lived as he sailed about on the Company's business. He had been sitting alone up there for more than an hour whilst he digested the terrible news and made his plans.

Of course we would go back to Constantinople. And the sooner the better so far as I was concerned. George's young brother, John, and his even younger son were there along with hundreds of our Company's men. They might be in desperate need of a rescue or, God forbid, already dead or captured.

What George was thinking as he mourned his father, but never did say or needed to say, was fully and immediately understood by every man who heard the sad tale—we were going to find out what happened and put a great and terrible revenge on everyone who was involved.

George did not need to announce his thoughts and intentions to us, or anyone else for that matter. It was not necessary. We already knew the Company would respond in a way that would be horrible beyond words for everyone who was responsible or involved.

We had, of course, not the slightest idea as to what form the Company's revenge would take or upon whom it would fall. But that did not stop everyone from speculating as to who might have done the terrible deed and making claims and predictions as to what the Company was going to do to them as a result. The men constantly talked about the various possibilities as they stood together around our galleys' water butt and sat with their mates on our galleys' rowing benches.

As you might expect, and was always the case, some of the men claimed to know what was about to happen, and what we were going to do, because they or someone else overheard somebody else, usually a captain or lieutenant, say something.

In fact, the only thing we really knew for sure was that death, or perhaps even a more terrible fate, was in store for everyone who had participated in their murders. That something horrible would happen to whoever was responsible was as certain as the arrival of the sun each morning as it made its great circle around the earth.

We knew for a certainty that a great response of some kind was coming because the Company's articles, on which every one of us had made his mark, required that great and terrible acts of vengeance be laid upon everyone responsible for the death or injury of any man on the Company's roll or under the Company's protection.

It did not matter that George's father, William, had himself once been the Company's Commander and had returned to active duty when the Company's retired archers were called back to active duty to help defend the Latin Empire. All that mattered, at least so far as my crew and the rest of men in the fleet were concerned, was that the Commander's father was an archer on the

Company's roll. That was more than enough. The fact that the Empress who died with him was an important client of the Company for whom we had made a contract to protect would only make things worse for whoever did it.

For me the revenge would be personal and I would participate in it with the greatest enthusiasm. It was, after all, William himself who had promptly freed me from slavery when he bought the galley on which I was rowing. That was in the early days right after he and the handful of surviving archers stopped crusading and took enough coins off a murderous bishop to buy a couple of galleys to take them home. At the time I was a Southhampton man rowing on one of the galleys as a result of my cog being taken by Moorish pirates and being sold along with its crew to a French crusader turned pirate.

After William freed me, I immediately made my mark on the Company's roll as a sailor. During the years that followed we had sailed and fought together many times and become good friends. It was William himself who had given me the six stripes of a lieutenant commander and responsibility for all the Company of Archers' galleys and transports.

The murders of two people under the Company's protection would be more than enough to trigger a massive response even if they were not important. That was certain. What was also certain was that our revenge would be so fearsome that it would be remembered and talked about for many years, and then some.

Of course it would be most terrible. It had to be so it would be remembered forever—William Courtenay and the Empress were entitled to revenge and the Company had a reputation to protect.

In any event, instead of waving his hands about and making unnecessary announcements about what was going to happen to whomever was responsible, George quietly began giving orders. They were, at least initially, very much what everyone expected.

"Two fully crewed galleys will take a third of the chests with the ransom coins the Venetians paid us to Cyprus, and another fully crewed two will take a third of the chests to Cornwall. The rest of our galleys will sail for Constantinople with Lieutenant Commander Lewes's galley and another fully crewed galley carrying the final third.

"We will leave as soon as the fleet is ready to sail. Make it so."

We, the Commander's lieutenants, all solemnly nodded our agreement and muttered "ayes." It was the only thing we could think to do or say. Indeed, as the lieutenant commander in charge of the Company's fleet, I had so expected such a decision that I had already ordered the captains to recall their men and finish readying their galleys for an immediate sailing.

We were done with taking coins and prizes out of Venice, so leaving Venice and returning to Constantinople to find out what happened was what we would almost certainly do. Besides, I could have quietly called off or changed our preparations if the Commander had surprised me by keeping us in Venice for a few more days or ordering the fleet to sail to some other destination.

****** *Lieutenant Commander Harold Lewes*

All of our galleys rowed out of Venice's great harbour the next morning right after the sun arrived on its daily voyage around the edges of the world. George and I stood on the roof of my galley's forward deck castle in the early morning sunlight as my galley led the Company's fleet out of the harbour. My loud-talker and sailing sergeant were on the roof with us and so was my apprentice. The rowing benches were manned as fully as possible which was required by the Company's standing orders when one of our galleys was moving in a harbour. Keen-eyed lookouts were on both masts.

It looked to be the beginning of another fine late-summer day. There was not a cloud in the sky and it was already getting warm. The heat would be hard on our rowers if George decided we needed to hurry, particularly those who would be rowing on our galleys that were going out seriously under-crewed. I thought it likely we would hurry. That meant the two galleys sailing for Constantinople with full crews, one of which was mine, would leave the others behind whilst we hurried on ahead.

Not a word was spoken between George and me as we slowly rowed through the scummy waters of Venice's Grand Harbour and into the Adriatic to begin our long voyage. We just stood there together on the roof of the forward deck castle and listened to the familiar sounds of my galley's oars, the creaking of its ever-leaking hull, the voices of my sailors and archers as they went about their duties, and the periodic complaints of the live cattle and sheep on our deck with their legs cut so they could not move until we butchered them for food,

Distant voices and the sound of slowly beating rowing drums could also periodically be heard coming over the water from the other galleys in our fleet. Noisy sea birds, as usual, were circling overhead and periodically dropping poop on our decks. It was, in other words, in all ways a normal and peaceful scene despite the fact that we were leaving a port where we had recently fought a great battle and taken many prizes and ransoms.

I could not help but notice that the harbour was significantly less crowded than when we arrived about a week earlier. The almost-empty harbour was a mark of our recent great success in taking Venetian prizes. It made me want to smile, a feeling which I kept off my face and behind my eyes so George would not see it and misunderstand my thoughts. He himself was sad-faced and appeared to be deep in thought instead of being his usual keen-eyed self and constantly looking about.

An unexpectedly large number of Venetians were silently standing on the quay watching us leave, and there were empty berths and anchorages everywhere. As you well might imagine, a few of the watchers were saluting us with obscene gestures and not a one of them was waving and shouting out to wish us a good voyage.

Poor losers. That was what they were, I decided. So far as I was concerned, the bastards got what they deserved for helping the Greeks attack us at Constantinople and were lucky we did not sack the city—which, in my opinion, we should have done. I was tempted to return their obscene salutes but did not.

Some of our younger archers and sailors, however, were not so restrained, and more than a few added shouted insults to their gestures.

Venice's anchorages and the mooring berths along its quays were mostly empty. That was because the only cargo transports remaining in the harbour were the prizes we had taken and sold back to the Venetians. In fact most of our prizes had already either sailed away to be sold elsewhere or were on their way to Cyprus where they would be bought in to join the Company's fleet.

Our six coin-carrying galleys, including mine, were fully crewed as we passed through one of the harbour's entrance and entered the blue-grey waters of the Adriatic. Being fully crewed was important. It meant those of us who were their captains would have the rowing and fighting strength necessary to either run or to fight to protect the coin chests we were carrying.

It was also important in a bad way—because, as a result of fully crewing the six coin carriers, all the rest our galleys were so dangerously under-manned they had barely enough men to steer and set their sails. Every one of them was significantly short of men both because of our casualties during the recent fighting and because so many men had been taken from them to serve in prize crews and on the coin carriers.

It was clear to everyone that our under-crewed galleys would have to rely on their sails to get to Constantinople. And that raised the question as to whether George would order the two fully crewed galleys bound for Constantinople to hurry there at their best speed, or would all of our galleys remain together as a war-fighting fleet that would be able to move no faster than its slowest under-crewed member?

The unspoken question was soon answered by George—my galley and the other fully crewed coin carrier would sail to Constantinople as fast as possible. It would be hard on our rowers because of the heat, but it was the decision I and everyone else had expected. Besides, the sooner we got there the sooner we go ashore and enjoy the city's many delights.

Our fleet was seriously short of men even though we sailed with every available man; not a single man had run, and none of our seriously wounded and poxed men had been left behind for barbering. We even had a number of volunteers, mostly from among the foreign seamen on the prizes we had taken. More than two hundred of them signed on to help us row and work our sails. They did so in return for the promise of a couple of silver coins and various other undertakings.

Despite our new recruits, we were so short-handed that the captains, lookouts, and cooks would have to row if the majority of our galleys, those not carrying coins, were to get enough of their oars into the water to have any effect.

Normally our severely wounded men would have been left ashore in the care of well-paid local barbers and physicians to either be buried or to recover enough to either re-join the Company or honourably retire to one the homes provided by the Company. Not this time. Even those who were badly wounded came with us. They would live in our stern castles until they either recovered or died. Whether they did or not depended on the strength of their prayers, their mates who cared for them, and the sailmakers who sewed them up.

We had to carry our wounded and poxed men with us because we had no local shipping post in Venice to watch over them and we could not trust the Venetians to barber them properly or bury them with the necessary prayers if they died. We would bury those who did not make it at sea.

It also helped, as you might imagine, that all of our able-bodied men sailed with us; no one was foolish enough or desperate enough to desert in such an unfriendly port. The unhappy Venetians would likely have cut them down or enslaved them before the last of our galleys cleared the harbour.

Perhaps an even more important explanation of why no one deserted was that any man who ran would be giving up his share of the very substantial amount of prize money that would soon be distributed. No one knew for sure how much his share would be, but our takings out of Venice and its shipping had been quite substantial. Without a doubt it would be one of the biggest pay outs of prize coins in the Company's history, more than enough to enable a man to buy himself out of his contract with the Company and set himself up for the rest of his life.

Sailing on our under-crewed galleys did not worry the Company men who were sailing on them. Our lads were a cocky lot. Besides, even the greenest of our new recruits knew we had destroyed the Venetian fleet and that there was little chance that the Moors or anyone else would be brave enough to try anything in the waters between here and Constantinople.

Whether the Venetians liked it or not, and they clearly did not, the waters of the Adriatic now belonged to the Company of Archers and would for some years. There was no doubt about it, we would control these waters until the Venetians were able to recover from the losses we had just inflicted on them or the Moors refocussed their efforts away from the fighting in Spain and in the Holy Land.

It was true, of course, that some of the Venetian galleys had escaped. They might risk trying to re-take one of our prizes, particularly if the Venetians spotted it while it was sailing alone.

But would they try to take one of the Company's under-crewed galleys if they happened to come upon it? Probably not since they were not likely to know how few archers were aboard it. Indeed, or so we told each other, it was highly unlikely that any Venetian or Moorish galley captain who came across one of our galleys would attempt to find out how much fight it might have in it. To the contrary, he would almost certainly turn around and run for his life, and count himself fortunate to have escaped.

In the real world, it would be a cold day in heaven before a slave-rowed Venetian or Moorish galley could take a Company galley with even a handful of our longbow-carrying and pike-wielding archers on board. In other words, the prospect of meeting a galley or two of Venetians or Moors whilst we were sailing for Constantinople did not worry any of us.

An enemy fleet, of course, would be a different matter if it came upon one of our short-handed galleys whilst our galley was sailing alone *and* they knew it had only a few archers on board.

What *did* worry us at that moment was our Commander, George Courtenay, and what he would have us do when we reached Constantinople. We had absolutely no idea. He obviously would want revenge for his father's death, and rightly so. We all wanted that, particularly me who had been rescued by William from being a galley slave and had sailed with him for many years.

But would George be so blinded by his need for revenge that he would do something that would end up hurting himself and the Company? I certainly hoped not. But I was worried—it is well known that the murder of someone in a man's family can affect his thinking.

Chapter Two

Constantinople.

Our voyage from Venice enjoyed relatively favourable winds and came off without a hitch or the loss of a single man. The other galley carrying coin chests, Captain Thomas Richardson's Number Seventy-three, stayed with us when we charged ahead with continuous rowing and left the rest of the fleet following along behind. Our two galleys sailed together and sighted Constantinople's huge city walls in what seemed to me to be about ten days.

The other four fully crewed galleys that had sailed with us from Venice were not with us as we approached the great capital city of the Latin Empire. They had peeled off from us as soon as we exited the Adriatic in order to begin their much longer and more hazardous voyages to deliver the coin chests they were carrying to Cornwall and Cyprus.

The only stop we made during the entire voyage had been a very brief one when we finished rowing out of the Dardanelles Strait and came alongside the Company galley collecting the Empress's tolls. It was Captain Jackson's Number Forty-Six.

"What is the state of the city now that my father and the Empress are gone? Have there been any fighting or disturbances?" George immediately asked Captain Jackson.

"No Commander, none at all. The city and its taverns have been quiet; at least they were until yesterday morning when we came out to take our turn at collecting the tolls."

"Quiet as in normal or quiet as in the lull before a storm?"

"Normal I think. But I am not sure, Commander. Everything seemed normal when I was ashore and I heard nothing from my men and the merchants with whom I dealt. There were no cautions or alerts issued by the Commandry if that is what you mean. There was much talk about your father and the Empress, of course. But that was at the tavern and….."

At that the point the poor captain's voiced trailed off. He did not know what else to say, but felt he had to say something.

"I am truly sorry about your loss, Commander. Yes I am. Your father was good man. All of the men feel the same way."

****** *Lieutenant William Smithson*

There were only a few clouds in the sky as I watched the Commander's galley bump up against the quay that ran along the little strip of land that was the Company's concession. It was next to the towering city wall that kept our concession and its quay in the shade for a good part of every day. It was a warm late summer afternoon and everything appeared normal. A large and growing number of seabirds were hovering over us in search of food scraps and pooping on our deck.

One of the Company's three-masted ships was tied up along the Company's quay. It was discharging passengers so it must have been newly arrived. I did not recognize it. Perhaps it was one of our Venetian prizes that had recently been bought in to expand the Company's fleet of transports.

Our two galleys had, as usual, been seen by the Company's lookouts on the city wall and identified long before we actually rowed up to the quay that stood in front of the narrow patch of Company land between the quay and the city wall. The quay and our men's tents and lean-tos sheltering up against the great stone city wall beyond it were familiar sights. They had been there in one form or another for as long as I could remember.

As a result of our being seen by the lookouts on the wall above our concession, both Henry Harcourt, the Lieutenant Commander who had been left to command our forces in the city, and his number two, Major Captain Michael Oremus, had been informed of our pending arrival in time to be on waiting for us on the quay. They had not been on our great raid; they had remained behind to command those of our men who had waited in the city to help guard it whilst the rest of us put the Company's revenge on Venice.

A handful of men in Company tunics, almost certainly their guards and apprentices, were standing in a loose formation near the two men. They were red-faced and out of breath as a result of hurrying to meet us, but they were relaxed and standing casually on the quay as our galleys slowly rowed up to it and as our mooring lines were thrown to the waiting wharfies who quickly secured them.

No order had been given, but the proprieties of rank were observed. As a result, our galley had hung back to allow George and Harold, the highest ranking men in the fleet, to be the first to climb up one of the galley's hastily erected boarding ladders and go ashore.

"Our lookouts saw you coming," Michael said unnecessarily as Henry saluted and then reached out and gave the Commander a great manly hug. Of course he both saluted and hugged him; he was the Commander's honorary uncle after all, and had been ever since the Commander was a young boy of three or four years.

Commander Courtenay met his lieutenants on the quay as many hundreds of eyes watched intently from the newly arrived galleys and from the Company men who were already ashore. What we watchers were hoping to see was some sign of what might be in store for us.

All we saw, however, was four men talking intently and waving their hands about, but there was no gestures to indicate that earth-shaking news was being conveyed, or of the relief that would be apparent if there was danger in the air and we had arrived in the nick of time to save the day.

After a few seconds, a fifth man, a boy from the look of his size and the way he walked, detached himself from the little group of guards and hurried over to join them. He too got a warm welcoming hug from the Commander.

"The lad be the Commander's son, his name is also George," one of the men behind me said with a touch of sadness in his voice. "It were his grandfather the bastards killed," he added unnecessarily.

Perhaps most significant of all, at least so far as we were concerned, was that the half dozen or so archers who had accompanied Henry and Michael to the quay seemed relaxed and bored rather than tense and excited. The crews on the two arriving galleys, to a man, were relieved by the peaceful scene and many of them, surprisingly, were somewhat disappointed.

What was *not* present, that would almost certainly have been present upon our arrival at almost any other port, were the merchants and street women vying for our custom and the usual idle layabouts, wharfies, and unemployed sailors in search of a berth. That was because the quay and the sliver of land between it and the city wall were part of a Company concession that had been extracted from Greeks when they ruled the city and retained when the crusaders took it. Outsiders were not admitted through the city gate that opened into the concession unless they were there on some sort of Company business.

In other words, what my men and I saw was a relatively quiet scene. The only non-archers who were present were the sailors of the three-masted Company ship that was taking on supplies further down the quay and the passengers in the process of boarding it or already on board.

Some of the ship's crew and their passengers were on the quay next to the ship and on the ship's main deck. They were standing and watching everything that was happening just as we were watching Commander Courtenay and the men who had come to greet him.

Our fleet's arrival, it seems, had surprised the ship's crew and passengers and given them something to talk about. Seeing the men on the quay and the great city behind the wall in front of us certainly did the same for us.

****** *Lieutenant Commander Harold Lewes*

George greeted the arrival of his son, Young George, with a cheerful salute, a big smile, and a great hug. Then we listened intently as Henry quickly assured us that the Commander's young brother, John, was safe and the city quiet. John would have been with them, Henry explained, except he was away in the city delivering a routine message about buying more food supplies for the Commandry and for the wounded men who had been left behind for barbering.

"I sent him off to the market buy more supplies before we heard you were arriving," Michael Oremus explained.

But then the faces of Henry and Michael got deadly serious as they stood on the quay and briefly summarized what they knew about the sudden deaths of George's father and the Empress. It was not very much. In fact, we learned nothing new except that several extensive investigations were underway, big rewards were on offer for information, and that so far nothing of importance had turned up.

The Company's investigations, Henry said, had been organized with the help of several of the merchant associations from whom we did much buying of supplies and carrying of passengers. They had added their coins to the already-large rewards for useful information. He himself, Henry said, had immediately launched the investigation and taken personal command of it.

"There are a lot of rumours about poison and murder," Henry said as he looked at George cautiously.

"Or, of course, it might have been their time to pass as the Roman and Greek archbishops seemed to suggest when they presided over their funerals."

But then Henry fiercely added something with a touch of anger in his voice.

"I did not believe either of the archbishops' ox shite explanations for a minute when I heard them, and I do not believe them now; they were murdered and that is God's truth. We just do not know who did it or why. If we knew we would have already done for them."

Then Henry said something that surprised us.

"Helen be here."

"Helen? My stepmother?" George asked incredulously.

"Aye, she be arriving from Cyprus just before your father and the Empress died. Apparently your father sent for her. She is staying in the Commandry and is quite anxious to see you.

"She is well protected and safe, of course, with a half dozen of our steadiest men as her guards. And, her son John, your half-brother, is with her when he is not doing his duties as my apprentice. He and your son are with her a lot because both Michael and I are stationed at the Commandry."

"How is she holding up?" George asked.

"She was initially so distraught when your father died that I thought she might fall down and die herself. But now she is icy and angry, quite angry actually."

"So, is young Robert now the Emperor in fact as well as name? Or has a new regent been named to replace his mother?"

George asked the question of Henry as we turned to walk through the nearby gate in the wall and began walking through the city's narrow streets to the Wisdom of God Church where both William and the Empress had been temporarily buried,

"That seems to be a problem, a big one actually. Several men, including the Latin Archbishop who buried your father, have come forward claiming to be the boy's regent. So has the boy's older sister, your, uh um, good friend, Elizabeth, the Empress's daughter. She returned with the young boy who is her new husband as soon as she heard about her mother's death.

"She stole a march on the others by moving into the Empress's rooms and maintaining the Empress's court. Rumour has it that the boy's father sent them.

"And then there is the king of the Bulgarians, Otto, him what fought with us against the Greeks. He showed up a couple of days ago with quite a few of his men, a small army of them actually. Several others of the Empire's kings and princes have come to the city as well.

"You may have to sort them out and make sure the right one is on the throne and buys the Pope's approval."

"Me sort them out?" George asked incredulously as he stopped walking and turned towards me. "Why me?"

"There is no one else to do it, is there? And the Company needs someone on the throne as the boy's regent who will honour the Company's contract to collect the tolls. You, for instance."

Chapter Three

A big surprise.

Our first destination was the burial field in the sheep pasture next to the city's huge Wisdom of God Church, the one which was now known by its Latin name as the Hagia Sofia because its Greek priests and bishop had been replaced by Latins who answered to Rome. The church's burial field was, I had been told, where my father and the Empress had been temporarily buried in unmarked graves.

According to Henry, they would remain there until something more appropriate could be built for them. And they would be resting in good company as the Company's dead from recent war with the Greeks and other skirmishes and poxes were buried there including Aron who built the ribaldis and his betrothed. It was my only consolation and it was not even close to being enough.

The Hagia Sofia was thought to be the grandest and largest building in the world. Immediately next to it stood the smaller palace that was the traditional residence of the exiled Patriarch of the Orthodox Church and was now occupied by one of his underlings, the "Metropolitan" who was in charge of the Orthodox Church in Constantinople and the surrounding countryside. The even finer "Great Palace" of the emperors was just beyond the church. The large and ornate building that housed the old Roman baths was nearby and so was the City huge central market with its many lanes and stalls.

According to Company legend and the stories I heard from my father and uncles who were there, it was from the Patriarch's palace whilst the crusaders' were sacking the city that my father and his men had "rescued" the great relics of the Orthodox Church, including the gold-covered head of John the Baptist and two of his gold-covered right hands that had baptised Jesus.

Those were the priceless relics, including several additional copies of the two right hands made for my father by London goldsmiths that were some years later sold by the Company to various princes. The princes, in turn, used them to obtain the Pope's favour by donating them to the Church. In essence, the relics reached Rome in a way that had greatly enriched the Company and enhanced the worship of God.

At the moment, the Patriarch's palace was *not* occupied by the city's Pope-appointed Latin archbishop. That was because, in an effort to keep peace in the city whose residents were mostly Orthodox, the Orthodox Church's "Metropolitan," the man who led the Orthodox faithful in the city when the Patriarch was absent, was allowed to continue living in it with his personal priests and servants.

As you might imagine, the Latin Archbishop was a prime suspect in the murders. That was because he and his priests had been extremely unhappy with the Empress because she had refused to order the city's Orthodox churches, and thus the priestly employments and coins they generated, to be turned over to the Latin Church.

What would ultimately happen to my father's body, according to what Henry told me as we walked to the Hagia Sofia's burial yard, was up to me. The next emperor or his regent would decide about the Empress's.

My initial view of my father's grave moved me to tears. It was an ugly mound of raw dirt that had been dug out of a burial hole next to his and piled on top of his hole. Apparently a new empty hole was readied at the time of each burial with the dirt from digging the new hole being used to fill in the hole with the newly deposited body. Already there were a line of dirt mounds beyond my father's with a newly dug empty hole at the end of the line. The church was nothing if not efficient in such matters.

I knelt next to the little mound of raw dirt and prayed for some time. My son and brother and my lieutenants and guards knelt behind me. No one said a word and they remained kneeling until I stood. I think they were a bit embarrassed by my great heaving sobs. I was not; I had loved him dearly.

******

My eyes were still wet and puffy as we walked through the city streets back to the Commandry from the burial ground. Later I realized that the number of guards seemed to have somehow grown while I was praying beside my father's grave. Perhaps someone had sent for reinforcements for some reason. I meant to ask, but I never did.

It was an hour or so before the sun would finish passing overhead. The streets were crowded with women doing their last minute shopping, street merchants constantly calling out in an effort to sell all kinds of things off their hand carts, and with men returning home from work. Horse carts and two-wheeled carts carrying people and goods were everywhere standing in the street or moving about. There was no sense of danger so we walked with our swords sheathed and our longbows unstrung and slung over our backs.

We walked informally and carefully through the crowds without using a marching drum. Mostly we weaved our way through the crowded streets in a line that was two men across except where we had to split apart into a single file to get around a pile of shite or a stopped or slow-moving cart.

It was particularly necessary to walk carefully to avoid stepping into the piles of poop that had been dropped on to the street stones by the horses and deposited on them by the neighbourhood people and those who were walking on them. It had not rained for several days if the sizes and smells of the piles were any indication.

As usual the city's great numbers of cats were everywhere prowling about or sleeping. And also, as usual, they were above it all and totally ignored us as we passed. They were always that way according to the local people.

A few people stared at us as we passed, but most either paid us no attention or briefly looked at us out of the corner of their eyes as we walked past them. I had the feeling that some of them knew who I was. Or perhaps the looks of sympathy I saw were all in my imagination because I wanted to see them.

I was still shaken by what I had seen—a great pile of dirt with my dear father somewhere underneath it. It was still hard for me to believe.

******

We had no more than walked through the Commandry gate and entered its little bailey when the door to the Commandry opened and Helen came rushing out with a look of relief on her haggard face and her hair all wild and flying about. What struck me was that her hair had turned grey since the last time I had seen her several years earlier. She ran across the bailey to embrace me with her arms wide apart and tears running down her cheeks.

"George, thank God. I was afraid they had killed you too." She sobbed as she choked out the words and held me tightly. My lieutenants and my son instinctively moved back a couple of paces to give us a bit of privacy.

"Here now," I said as I held her and patted her gently on her back. "Please tell me all about it. What happened?"

"I got here on a galley from Cyprus and stayed with your father in his room. And the next day…"

It was about then, as I looked over her shoulder, that I saw that every man in the bailey was looking at us expectantly.

"Wait. We should talk privately. Do you have a room?"

"Just your father's," she sobbed.

As I consoled her, I wondered why he had not taken her to the Great Palace; then I remembered. It is always hard for a man to deal with two women at the same time if they are rivals for his dingle and affections.

******

The story that emerged a few minutes later was neither enlightening nor encouraging. My father, Helen said, had sent to Cyprus for her and was most happy and enthusiastic to see her when she finally arrived.

"But he seemed terribly upset about something. He was his usual self at first. But then he had trouble sleeping despite all of his .. um.. exercise. He got up in the middle of the night and paced about. It was not like him at all. I asked him what was wrong, but he would not talk about it. All he said was "something is going bad here." *Going bad?*

"Did he say what it was?"

"No, but I got the impression it had to do with the Empress."

"Well, that is not much of a surprise. Everything and everybody in Constantinople depends on the Empress and revolves around her. *And so does the Company even though we are also fetching substantial amounts of coins from elsewhere.*

"At least, everything depended on her and revolved around her until she died. Her death changes everything. Now what will happen in the city in the days ahead, including whether the Company will continue to prosper here, will depend on who takes her place as her son's regent."

We sat and talked for some time. Helen alternately laughed and cried as she told me stories about her early days together with my father and how they first met in

Syria when she was a young slave and the man she thought was her father had given her to my father as a gift.

"My mother really wanted me to be with a good man, you see, and made sure her owner agreed. And, oh my but your father was a good man. And then he married me in the church and dear old Uncle Thomas bought a dispensation from the Pope so your father could have more than one wife and would never have to use a tavern woman. That is when I sent a message to my mother and suggested that she get her master, my father, to send my two sisters to him as well."

"Oh God how we loved him." And then she covered her eyes and wept and sobbed.

It was heart breaking and I laughed and cried with her as she told me stories about their early days together that I did not know.

After an hour or so my younger brother, John, came hurrying in to join us. He was Helen's son and all wide-eyed with excitement and relief at my return. I had forgotten how young he was. And, although I said not a word, I once again wondered why Uncle Thomas had ordained him so young and sent him out to join the Company as an apprentice sergeant.

Perhaps what counts with God is the quality of a priest's Latin when he gobbles his prayers and asks the faithful for their coins, not his age and experience. I will have to remember to ask Uncle Thomas. One thing is sure—neither my brother, John, nor my son, Young George, are old enough or strong enough to stand in a Company battle line and fight; they would endanger the men on either side of them and probably get themselves killed.

The sun was setting when I realized I was getting hungry. So I finally left after promising to visit Helen every day and to keep her informed. My brother stayed behind to attend to his mother.

As I left, I gave some orders to the archer who was on guard at the end of the hall.

"Tell your sergeant to make sure the lady always gets a proper meal with some meat and bread and at least one bowl of wine every morning and evening. And make sure no one bothers her."

It was probably and unnecessary order, but he nodded anyway and cheerfully repeated it back to me and agreed that he would carry it out. Then I went in search of Henry and Michael to get more information as to what had happened and who was responsible.

******

Henry and Michael were sitting at the long table in the Commandry's hall with my son, Young George, and Harold Lewes. Erik, the great hulking commander of the Empress's Varangian Guards was sitting with them. My son, Young George who was increasingly being called "George Young," was there because he was Michael's apprentice. Harold's wide-eyed new apprentice, Archie Smith, was there also. Archie was the red-haired son of a Yorkshire smith who had somehow gotten into the Company's school. He had been in Cyprus with Yoram.

Good, I thought as I came through the door and saw Erik. He, more than anyone else, was likely to know what happened. And then another thought came into my head. *Did he and his men do it so he and the Varangians could take over, or could they have done it for someone else whom they preferred to serve?*

"Hello Erik, it has been a while," I said as he stood up and we gave each other great manly hugs and back pats as only men who have fought side by side together can properly do.

As we embraced it suddenly struck me that Erik smelled most foul—which surprised me because I knew that Erik usually changed his tunic and visited the city's old Roman baths every week or so. On the other hand, perhaps it was me; I had not been near a bath for several months. *Yes, I decided as we let go of each other and I sat down; it is me.*

"I am so sorry for your loss, George. Your father was a fine man. My men and I respected him very much. He will be missed. I came here to tell you that. And also, of course, to congratulate you on your great victory over the Venetians and to tell you what I know of the tragedy."

"Thank you, Erik. I appreciate your kind words. Might you be free to talk after we finish eating," I responded. "I have many questions as you might imagine."

After a moment of reflection while everyone at the table stared at us and listened intently while trying to appear as if they were not, I changed my mind and made a suggestion that surprised many of my listeners. *Why did I change it? So I could talk to Henry and Michael first.*

"No, perhaps even better, if you find the idea agreeable, we could go to Roman Baths and talk after we break our fasts tomorrow morning, eh? I have been aboard a galley for several months and truly need a good watering."

"Of course, George, of course. Talking about things whilst we water ourselves is a good idea. But please know that my men and I are continuing to make strenuous efforts to find out about your father's death and that of the Empress. I will certainly tell you everything we have discovered. If you are agreeable, I will come here and we will walk together to the baths. Would an hour after dawn be good for you?"

Of course my suggestion that we talk at the baths caused eyebrows of my listeners to rise and disappointed them; they wanted to know what Erik and the Empress's guards thought had happened and many of them believed that bathing weakened a man.

****** *George Courtenay*

The food in the Commandry's great hall was a wonderful change after several months of eating on a galley. There were slices and joints of sheep and goat meat piled on wooden platters as well as warm loaves of bread in the new French round style and shredded onions, olives, and turnips cooked in butter and covered with melted cheese. It went down well with dates, good red wine, and slices of apples and oranges.

No one said a single word about my father and the Empress or of anything related to their deaths. I did not mention them because I wanted to talk to Henry and Michael in private, and no one at the table was brave enough to talk about the tragedy for fear that it might upset me. As a result, we spent the entire dinner talking about Company matters such as the prices we were paying for supplies, the cargos and passengers we were carrying, and the state of the various Company men who had been wounded earlier in the spring war against the Greeks.

Harold and I ate and drank much too much and then, finally, belched our appreciation, gave a good scratch to the lice around our dingles, and walked out into the bailey with Henry and Michael to relieve ourselves and talk privately. It was a nice August night without even a touch of chill in the air along with the usual wisps of smoke from the cooking fires of the city's families in the street in front of the bailey.

"Cornwall is probably already starting to get cold and rainy," Michael observed over his shoulder as we stepped into the bailey and he pissed against the bailey wall in the designated low spot where it would run out into the street. "But at least it is peaceful according to the word that came in on one of our transports last week."

Harold agreed about Cornwall as he and I stepped up on either side of Michael.

"Aye, and the seas between Lisbon and England will be getting rough about now. I hope our galleys with the coin chests will be able to get across before the weather in the Atlantic turns too foul to sail. I would hate to think of the coins we took out Venice going down in a storm or having to spend the winter in Lisbon."

"Alright," I said to my lieutenants as I pulled out my dingle and stepped to the wall next to Michael to pee. "No one can hear us out here. Tell me everything you know about the deaths of my father and the Empress."

****** *Lieutenant Commander Henry Harcourt*

It was the first time George had heard the details about his father's death, and they were not pretty. Dying of being poisoned is a terrible way to go. Painful for sure. As you might imagine, Michael and I tried to be as gentle as possible when we told him what we knew.

"According to the servants who found them in the morning, they were in the Empress's sleeping chamber.

She was hanging half out of the bed; your father was on the floor stretched out towards the entrance door.

"The Empress's bed was all torn up as if she, uh, had been thrashing about. Neither of them was wearing any clothes and both of them had wild looks in their eyes and some kind of frothing, like the foam on a newly dipped bowl of ale, coming out of their mouths.

"Neither had any new wounds from being hit or cut. I looked myself to make sure, and so did Michael and the Empress's Greek physician. They were almost certainly poisoned."

"How long had they been dead before they were found?" George asked.

"From the way the servants described them, it sounded as though it had been some hours. They were already getting stiff."

"And the guard at the stairs?"

"There were three that night. Two Varangians and one of ours, John Shoemaker. And they all three swear that at least two of them were always awake and alert at the foot of the stairs, and that no one passed them coming in either direction once the Empress retired. Erik believes them and so do I."

"Could someone have come from one of the other rooms in the upper hall, my father's for instance?

"The guards say not. They could see the door into the Empress's chambers from where they stand at the bottom of the stairs. They swear they neither saw nor heard anyone once the Empress retired.

"On the other hand, there is a door between the Empress's rooms and the room next to it where your father often stayed.

"What is interesting is that your father was with his wife in her room at the Commandry earlier that night. He must have walked or ridden through the city to get there. Yet no one saw him in the city. The men on guard on the staircase below the Empress's chambers all swear he did not enter."

"But he obviously did," George softly mused. "How did he do it? And why was he in her chambers if had just been with my stepmother?"

****** *George Courtenay*

My lieutenants and I drank bowls of wine and talked until late in the night. Many reports and rumours had reached their ears about the death of my father and the Empress. We talked about them all.

The list of the possible murderers of the Empress turned out to be quite extensive. It included Erik and both the city's Latin Archbishop and a man, called the Metropolitan who directed the priests serving the city's Orthodox believers.

It also included the Patriarch and the Pope himself, each of whom might have arranged it because he wanted to install one of his favourites. And then, of course, there were all of their religious followers and the members of their entourages who might have seen removing the Empress as a way to curry favour with God by supporting their superiors.

Unfortunately, there were many other names on the list such as the father of Marie's young husband who had led the Orthodox army against the Empress and the various kings and princes of the Empire's states who might have seen becoming the new emperor's regent as a step towards the throne for themselves.

The King of the Bulgarians was a particular possibility. When we were fighting together against the Greeks he had made no secret of his ambitions and his unhappiness that a woman was making the Empire's decisions.

None of the princely suspects was in the city at the time, or so my lieutenants said, but they all had palaces and retainers in the city. On the other hand, a number of them had come to the city immediately upon receiving the news, probably to protect and advance their interests.

And that was just the list for the Empress. My father's list was even longer because it included almost all of the men on the Empress's list and just about every one of the Company's major competitors as well as the French king, and any number of Moorish princes and merchants. And, of course, there was a lot of overlap. The Venetians and the recently defeated Greeks and the Orthodox Church, for example, had undoubtedly hated them both.

In the end, the list of people who might have wanted one or both of them dead was so long that it boggled my mind. Some of the people on it had names I had never heard; others I knew because I had met or knew of them because we had taken prizes or customers from them. The problem was that the names on the list included people who might well have had a reason to kill just one of them and got the other as well.

"There are so many possibilities that I cannot get my arms around them," I said when they my lieutenants finally finished telling me all the rumours and speculations they had heard and naming and telling me about everyone who might have had reason so kill my father and the Empress. It was a long list.

"Your father and the Empress were, uh, close as you know; perhaps the food or drink was intended for one and got them both when they shared it," Henry suggested.

"If it was poison, it was most likely delivered to them by the Empress's servants or someone with whom they recently met. The servants have been questioned closely by the Varangians, but have not yet been tortured.

"So has everyone who visited either of them in the days before they passed away. They all deny being involved. Moreover, no one on the list has fled the city as they might if they were guilty. To the contrary, many have hurried here in hopes of advancing themselves"

What it all boiled down to was that there was a long list of possibilities such that my lieutenants and I did not have a clue as to who had done it or why—just a lot of suspicions and many suspects.

"Alright, that is what the Varangians and the Empress's chancellor have done and discovered. What have we heard and done?

"We too have closely questioned all the servants and we have also offered a big reward for information, a huge reward as a matter of fact—a thousand gold bezants. So far there have been many false tips from people seeking the coins, but nothing that sounded useful in any way."

"We can torture the servants, of course, but then they will all confess and point to everyone they can think of in an effort to save themselves. And besides many of them came out with the Empress as her personal servants and are likely to be ruined by her death. As a group, they are not likely to have caused it. An individual, however, can always be gotten to in some way or another as you well know."

"What about the servants of the nobles and religious leaders?" Michael asked. "We could grab some of them and see if they have heard anything."

"I think that is what the Varangians are doing," Henry offered. "But, if they are, it has not yielded any useful information, at least none so far as we have been told. You will no doubt learn much more about the Varangian's efforts when you meet with Erik in the morning."

Chapter Four
The Varangians.

Erik arrived early. As usual, he arrived alone without any bodyguards. He did not need them—one look at the Erik walking along the street carrying his big battle axe was enough to scare away anyone short of a small army.

I knew him as quite an amiable fellow. Most people did not. They hurried to get out of his way when they saw him coming and, after he passed, many made the sign of the cross to thank God for keeping them safe.

It was not just the big axe Erik carried with him wherever he went, it was also his size and the scar on his heavily bearded face that gave him such a ferocious appearance. At almost six feet I was a head taller than most of my men, and Eric was at least a head taller and two stones heavier than me. As a result, he looked as ferocious and fearsome on the street as he truly was in battle. I knew that for sure because I had seen him use his axe when we fought against the Greeks.

Erik's commitment to guarding the city and whoever was on the throne was in his blood as his father and grandfather had both been Varangian guards before him. His men were reported to adore him.

On the other hand, it was possible that Erik thought he could guard the city and throne better if he himself was the Emperor who was sitting on it. One thing was certain; I could only hope that he saw me and the Company as useful allies, not as potential rivals whose galleys were no longer needed to collect the tolls and help protect the city.

Strangely enough, it was because I knew Erik that I did not fear going alone with him to the baths. He was too smart for that—if he did attack me whilst I was with him, it would be known who did it and the Company would never rest until he paid the price by being killed most horrible along with everyone who helped him.

On the other hand, if Erik was involved in an effort to seize the throne and feared I was similarly inclined, my death would be at another time and place such that the blame would fall on someone else other than Erik and his Varangians.

******

I was sitting with Michael Oremus and just finishing the breaking of my nightly fast when Erik arrived at the Commandry the next morning. He was early.

"Hoy George."

"Hoy Erik. Have you broken your nightly fast? You are welcome to join us."

"Thank you, George, but no thank you. Your offer is much appreciated, but I always get up before dawn to eat with my men who have spent the night in the city. It is one of the ways by which I keep in touch with my men and learn about the latest news and rumours."

"That sounds very wise of you, Erik, it truly does."

I said it sincerely and meant it as I pushed my plate back and got ready to stand up to go with him to the baths. Everyone around the table nodded their agreement, even my young brother and my even younger son. They were there as apprentice sergeants and nodded instinctively when their betters did.

Erik beamed at my compliment and the response of the archers. "It is something I learned from my father when he commanded the Varangians and I was just a young recruit."

A moment later I took one last swig of morning ale and swung my leg over the bench to stand up. Henry looked at me from across the table and mouthed the question "guards?" I shook my head and stood up.

My leaving alone with Erik meant they would hold him responsible if anything happened. Even Erik understood. He nodded his acceptance to Henry and gave an agreeable little shake to the axe he was holding.

******

"Your men are right to be concerned," Erik quietly offered as we made our way out of the hall. "Someone has done this thing and we still do not know who or why. My men are angry. They liked the Empress and were sworn to guard her. Her death has made all of us look weak."

A moment later he added, "and your father's death too, of course."

We continued talking as we walked down the street towards the old Roman baths. People and carts, even horse carts, tended to move out of the way if they saw us coming. Quite a few, particularly the small merchants peddling from carts, extended friendly greetings to Erik.

"The people seem to like you," I suggested.

"They like the peace we maintain and the thieves and rioters we chop; we Varangians they do like not so much."

We talked as we walked and the great columns of the Roman baths were in sight after a brisk twenty minute walk. They were standing there as they had been for almost a thousand years. That was right after man was created by God and life began.

Chapter Five
We meet again.

"Mother wanted me to be my brother's regent until he came of age. I know she did because she sent for me when she realized she was dying. I hurried as fast as possible but, unfortunately, I arrived too late. She was already gone when I got here."

Elizabeth was looking at me intently and speaking with a great sadness and hesitation in her voice. Without actually saying so she was asking me if I wanted her to continue with her tale. I nodded my agreement. We were in the Empress's chambers where my father and Elizabeth's mother had died.

From the looks of the personal possessions that were scattered about and the way the servants had hurried out when I arrived, it was clear that Elizabeth had moved in and taken over the three rooms traditionally occupied by the Empire's rulers—the outer room where the Emperors and their regents received their supplicants and conducted their Empire's business, the middle room where they slept and received their lovers, and the inner room where the Empire's treasury was kept in great coin chests. It had been that way for centuries, both under the Empire's Byzantine Greek emperors and now under the new Latin emperors.

"I first met Helen, your stepmother, the day after I arrived. We met when we went to the church at the same time to pray for their souls. The poor woman was distraught most terrible such that it is hard to believe that she could have murdered them in a fit of jealously.

"I am told that you just visited your stepmother. Is she better now, or is she still totally distraught as I have heard? So am I for that matter, distraught that is; I am still numb. The whole thing is hard to believe. I keep thinking I will wake up and find that it was a bad night dream."

"And how would you be knowing that I just came from visiting Helen? And why are you suggesting she might be involved, eh?"

How would Elizabeth know I had just visited Helen? That was the thought that instantly came into the space in my head behind my eyes. It left immediately, however, because Elizabeth continued to hold on to my hand and look longingly at me. It was about then that I realized she had sent her servants away and there was no one else in the room.

I promptly forgot about Helen. It was only much later that I realized that Elizabeth had very smoothly added Helen's name to the list of suspects.

As Elizabeth continued to stroke and play with my hand, I suddenly realized that I had not been with a woman since she had been in my bed several months earlier. That was just before I led my men to Venice to take our revenge and Elizabeth, already the widow of a crusader, was rushed into a peace-making marriage with the much younger boy who was the heir to the Epirus throne.

Then Elizabeth's face changed right in front of my eyes and there was fear and uncertainty in her quavering and anxious voice.

"My situation is desperate. That is why I immediately moved into my mother's rooms where the Emperor or his regent are supposed to live—so no one else would be able to move into them and claim to be the new regent or, God forbid, the new emperor."

Then she took a deep breath and continued in a quavering voice.

"I fear for my life because it is well known that my mother wanted me to take her place as my brother's regent and protect him. But many other people also want to be Robert's regent and some of them are also determined to get the throne for themselves. My mother's death has changed everything; it has given hope to all of them."

What I did not do was share what I was thinking— you may not end up being Robert's regent, but whoever does will not change the Company's agreement to collect the tolls, not if my men and I have anything to say about it.

That was what I was thinking as Elizabeth continued holding both my hands and talking softly so no one could hear us. For some reason, as she did, I my thinking suddenly changed when I realized how long it had been since Elizabeth and I had known each other—and how good it had made us both feel when we did.

As a result, my thoughts and concerns began to rapidly change as I sorrowfully nodded my head in agreement with Elizabeth's words. It had, after all, been several months since I had been alone with a woman, and that had been Elizabeth herself.

"It will be up to God who is Robert's regent, of course," Elizabeth whispered. She said it as she moved up against me to get even closer so no one could hear us. "God will tell the Pope whom he wants as Robert's regent until he comes of age. I do hope God will choose me, or you, so that Robert is not replaced and killed."

She was looking into my eyes intently as she slowly said "or you" with a great deal of emphasis. I was as stunned when she said it as I had been when Henry had suggested it earlier.

"Me?" I exploded. "Surely you jest, Elizabeth? You know I would not set aside my position in the Company just to be your brother's regent for a few years."

"Yes, I know. But someone must be the Regent and you could do it and still be the Company's Commander until Robert comes of age. If it cannot me, it must be you. One of us must hold the position if your Company is to keep collecting the tolls.

"Besides, who knows—something might happen to Robert and my husband, and then you could be the Emperor and I the Empress."

Elizabeth had looked at me intently as she said it and appeared to be relieved when I repeated my unwillingness to leave the Company. Then she pressed herself up against me and began playing with the knot that tied my tunic together around my neck.

After a few seconds, she sighed deeply and explained the problem as she saw it. *And continued rubbing her breasts up against me as she talked. It was very pleasant. She spoke so softly that I had to hold her close up against my chest in order to hear her.*

"Unfortunately there are only a few chests of coins left in the treasury, and certainly not enough to buy the necessary prayers from the Pope as my mother did with the help of your father.

"Of course, my new and dear father-in-law, the King of Epirus, could loan my husband and me enough coins to pay for the Pope' prayers for me. But I doubt that he will since he wants to be the Emperor himself. In fact, he is just as likely to buy the Pope's prayers for himself to become Robert's regent—so he will be well-placed to become the Emperor if Robert dies or is killed."

Her concern for her brother touched me. It was also something new. In the past, according to my dear father, she had not had any use for him at all. On the other hand, it was totally understandable; they were family after all.

Elizabeth paused for a moment and then continued.

"My mother only wanted the best for me. Now she is gone and I am left with only my brother to take care of me when he is old enough to become Emperor, and my husband, of course, when he grows up. *And neither is of much use or ever will be.*

"My husband, Michael, is a dear boy. He thinks he has already got me with child. I had to help him get started, of course, but he was a fast learner."

Whoa. That was fast.

Elizabeth was still holding my hand and looking at me intently. Suddenly she stepped into my arms and held her chest tight against mine. She wiggled her breasts to get even deeper into my arms and then gave a big and satisfied sigh and continued. I held her close against me; it felt deliciously good.

"Oh God I have missed you," she said softly. A moment later she brushed her hand against my now fully alert dingle and gave me an order with a strained intensity to her voice.

"Put the bars on the doors so no one can come in. I need to show you something."

Keeping everyone out of her rooms was a fine idea in view of the thoughts that had begun swirling about behind my eyes. So I quickly rushed to do as she ordered. As I did, Elizabeth added to my excitement with even more encouraging words.

"We do not have to worry about the servants or anyone walking in on us. Jeanine, my personal maid, is outside the door with orders to turn everyone away. If anyone asks, she will tell them that we are meeting to discuss improving your Company's contract to collect the tolls and protect the Regency.

"Besides, so what if someone thinks we are getting to know each other again? I have taken over as Regent and I can do whatever I want."

"And your husband?"

"No need to worry about him. He has gone off to spend the day in the city playing with his little friends. Besides, he has his own rooms on the other side of the palace."

With that she stepped once again into my arms and began rubbing up against me once again. But then she suddenly stopped.

"I want you to look at something before we .. " Her voice trailed off. And then it strengthened and she told me what exactly she wanted me to see and do.

A moment later I felt terribly let down and disappointed—because what she wanted me to look at, whatever it might be, was not anything close to what I had hoped it would be a moment earlier. It was a great wooden chest that stood on its end with its back against the wall in the corner of the room, a chest that was taller than most men.

Elizabeth opened the door to the chest and motioned for me to look at its contents. It was filled with a collection of her mother's tunics and robes. They were hanging next to one another on wooden pegs.

"Look," she said as she pulled some of the clothes aside and pointed at the back wall.

I saw nothing.

"Do you see the long crack in the wood along the side, George? And also across the top? And the heavy strip of wood that runs all along the back of the chest. I think it is a door that opens into the wall and the strip of wood is the bar that seals it from being used."

Elizabeth told me about it with the same happy and excited sound in her voice that had made me think of other things a few moments earlier.

"My mother told me there was a way for someone to get in and out of her sleeping room without anyone knowing. But she never told me where it was or how to use it. All she told me was that one of the old Byzantine emperors must have installed it in the early days when the Great Palace was being built.

"Maybe that is how your father would come to visit her when they did not want anyone to know."

She made the suggestion with a shy little smile that clearly implied we might be able to use it ourselves.

"Or maybe it is how their murderer got to them without anyone seeing," I said grimly as I pushed aside the clothes and my dingle went limp.

******

It was easy to lift and set aside the wooden bar that kept anyone from using the door to enter the Empress's room, if that is what it was. But it took quite a while to find the secret to opening the secret door so I could get though the back wall of the tall clothes chest. We finally did—when I was twisting and pulling on the pegs with clothes hanging on them.

We found out how to open the door by accident when the wooden back of the chest suddenly swung open. It happened when Elizabeth was steadying herself by touching the back of the chest whilst I was playing with one of the clothing pegs which somehow seemed to be different from the others.

The back of the clothes chest suddenly swung open like a door. Beyond it in the darkness I could make out what appeared to be a very steep and narrow stone staircase. For some reason it surprised me that it ran both up and down. The air in passage smelled musty and unused.

"Oh my God!" Elizabeth said softly. "Where does it go?"

"We will need a couple of candle lanterns for light," I said as I pushed past her and returned to the Empress' sleeping room. "We can use those that are here in the Empress's sleeping chamber."

There were five candle lanterns in the room including two that used the oil of whale fish instead of reeds filled with bees wax. There were also a large number candles in various bowls and metal candlestick holders. None of them were lit.

That there were so many lanterns and candles in the room was not surprising. It was, after all, occupied by the Emperor or his regent and was one of the biggest of the Great Palace's many rooms. And, of course, being as it was still daylight and the day was warm, none of the candles were lit.

The unlit lanterns and candles turned out to be one of several problems. The first being that the servants who lit the lanterns and candles every day did not do so until the sun began to go down. Then they lit them with a candle fetched from the kitchen.

"Go to the door and shout down to your servant that you need a candle so you can melt some wax to put a seal on a parchment," I ordered as I closed the front of the chest so the Empress's clothes and the opening into the passageway could not be seen.

"But there is no seal. I could not find it."

"It does not matter. Just do it. It is just an excuse that is believable."

It would also suggest to everyone that we were not in Elizabeth's chambers behind closed doors so I could lift her skirts and get into knowing her again in the biblical sense—which I was determined to do as soon as possible.

I looked at the lanterns as we waited for the fire to arrive. It was at that point that the second problem became apparent—the lanterns in the chamber were very ornate and heavy; it would be nigh on to impossible to carry them up and down the steep steps that through the narrow passage way.

"Shite," I muttered as I tried to lift one of the lanterns. "These will not work. They are too large and heavy. If we cannot get a regular candle lantern we will have to use candles and hope they do not blow out."

******

It seemed to take forever before a young serving girl scurried up the stairs to the Empress's room and knocked on the door. Elizabeth and I spent the time touching each other in a way that suggested it would not be long before we once again began getting to know each in the biblical sense.

I could hardly contain myself and tried to manoeuver Elizabeth towards the Empress's great bed. Elizabeth, however, was having none of it. She pushed me away and told me to wait.

Finally there was a knock on the outer door. I opened it to admit a hesitant young servant girl who very carefully went out of her way not to look at me even out of the corner of her eye as she entered.

"Light a couple of the candles so the Regent can melt wax for her seal on our new agreement," I ordered the girl.

I was pleased with myself for suggesting that Elizabeth and I had reached an agreement that needed to be sealed. It was an explanation the girl would almost certainly mention to the palace's other servants when they asked her what I was doing in Elizabeth's rooms.

A moment later I realized that I had just recognized Elizabeth as her brother's regent. Had I just been tricked into doing so? It somewhat bothered me, but not for long. There were more important things to think about.

"Light one more candle and then run back down the stairs and send someone to fetch a couple of additional candle lanterns. They must be small enough to be moved about if the Regent decides she needs more light elsewhere in her chambers."

I gave the order to the serving girl when she had finished lighting one of the candles. She still had not looked at me, not once. Someone, probably the Empress or my father, had trained her well. I spoke in the crusader French that people are starting to call English. It was the language of the palace and the Empress's court.

Elizabeth nodded her approval at my having taken charge and the orders I had given. Or perhaps she was pleased because I had acknowledged her as Robert's regent. I had no idea. But I knew that servants had ears and the word would spread that Elizabeth was in command and making decisions as her brother's regent, and that I had recognized her as the regent. It did not particularly worry me at the time.

Chapter Six

We go exploring.

An out of breath servant arrived about five minutes later with two unlit candle lanterns. She was immediately sent away and the door once again double barred. Only then did I use one of the burning candles to light both lanterns.

As soon as the lanterns were lit, I blew out the candles, picked up my unsheathed sword from where I had leaned it against the wall next to the door, and carried it and one of the lanterns to the big clothes chest. It was time for us to see what we could see. As you might imagine, I was getting more and more excited.

Elizabeth hurriedly picked up the other lantern and ran after me. We left the door to the middle room open.

It did not matter. No one could get into Empress's chambers because the outer door was barred shut.

I took neither my longbow and quiver of arrows nor the galley shield I usually carried in addition to my sword when I was walking in the city's streets. They would be of little use since I would need at least one hand to carry the lantern and the other a sword. I left them in the corner of the middle room.

For a brief moment I had thought about bringing the shield and carrying it slung over my shoulder. But I instantly decided against bringing it because I only had two hands and both would be busy holding my sword and the lantern. Under my tunic, as was my practice whenever I was not with a woman or waiting for one, I was wearing my chain shirt and had a hidden knife on each wrist.

The door to passageway was still partially open because Elizabeth had suggested that we put some of the Empress's clothes on the floor of the chest so the secret door would not be able to shut behind us. It was a good idea and I nodded my appreciation at the clothes and used my foot to move them into a slightly better position. I did so as I pushed the hidden door all the way open.

****** *George Courtenay*

I entered the secret passage holding my lantern up as I high as I could get it.

"Down or up?" I asked Elizabeth as I cautiously stepped out of the chest and on to the stone floor of the staircase. I was holding the lantern up high so I could see. She was right behind me with the other lantern.

I made a decision without waiting for her response and started down.

The winding stairway was dark and the stone steps were narrow and showed signs of being worn down from years of people scuffling up and down on them. The stairs curved to the right as stairs traditionally do to make them more defendable since most men are right-handed.

The passageway seemed increasingly cool and damp as we descended even though the walls were dry when I touched them. We had to walk somewhat crouched over in order to avoid hitting our heads on the low stone ceiling, at least I did. Elizabeth being shorter was able to walk upright most of the time.

We held our lanterns in front of us and as high as possible as we went down slowly down the steps one step at a time. It was necessary to avoid hitting our heads or falling because we missed a stair step. Elizabeth stayed close was behind me. After I had gone down only three or four steps I stopped and drew my double-edged short sword.

There was no particular reason I drew my sword, but it somehow felt right to do so. I held it in my right hand and used my left hand to hold the lantern and touch the ceiling so I would not hit my head.

It was difficult to walk despite the lanterns. Every so often I scraped my knuckles from holding the lantern too high or banged my head from not holding it high enough. The ceiling was very low and the stone steps were uncommonly steep and narrow. The stairs curved tightly to the right such that one man with a sword could easily hold them against an army.

Elizabeth walked close behind me. She was almost too close so I very tersely ordered her to walk carefully and two steps further back. It was necessary in order to prevent her from bumping into me or tripping me. I had, after all, no idea how far I would tumble or where I would end up if she did.

We were going very slowly and cautiously because we did not know where we were going or what we would find along the way or when we got there. I was pleased to be wearing my chain shirt and wrist knives under my tunic. Wearing them was a family tradition.

After what seemed to be about sixty or seventy steep and winding stone steps, the passageway levelled off and became relatively flat. I was not sure, however, that it was actually flat. To the contrary, I had the impression that we were continuing to descend as Elizabeth and I slowly made our way along the passage. Our lanterns made strange shadows on the wall and ceiling as we walked.

I did not know why, but I somehow had the feeling that this part of the passageway was even more ancient than the stairs. Later, when I had time to think about it, I decided that the tunnel was probably an escape tunnel had been built at the beginnings of the city. That was probably right after God created the earth many hundreds of years ago.

The existence of an old tunnel under the Great Palace was not surprising. Every prince or noble with a somewhat reasonable mind, meaning no more than half of them according to my Uncle Thomas, had at least one such secret way to escape from wherever he was living. That was because a secret way to escape was necessary when things went totally wrong and one's prayers and indulgences failed.

Our company was no exception. We had at least one tunnel either in place or under construction for every of the Company's fortresses and shipping posts. Indeed, every one of our major holds such as our castles in England and our Cyprus fortress already had two or three secret ways to escape from it and more under construction.

Of course we had secret tunnels and other ways to escape; the world was a dangerous place and would continue to be so until Jesus returned and there was peace on earth. Hopefully, of course, that would not be for a few more years so we would have enough time to fill our coin chests before people no longer needed us to protect them or carry them away to safety.

Our immediate problem was that Great Palace was so much older and so much larger than any of our holdings and that there was no knowing how many tunnels and escaped routes it might have acquired over the years—and every one of them could have been used to secretly enter the palace and kill my father.

But where did the tunnel from the Empress's room lead and, more importantly, was it used by whoever murdered my father?

******

Elizabeth and I came to a side tunnel in the passageway after about three or four hundred paces of walking in the darkness holding our lanterns out in front of us. It was an even smaller tunnel that branched off to the left and it too seemed to descend and been little used. More importantly, however, and just beyond entrance to the smaller tunnel I could see an opening in the wall that turned out to be the entrance to another staircase.

We stopped in front of the smaller tunnel whilst I tried to decide which way to go. I also stopped because I suddenly felt a great urge to piss. Accordingly, I handed my lantern to Elizabeth and pissed against the tunnel wall. It was right after I finished pissing that we heard the scurrying of little feet ahead of us in the darkness.

Mice or rats for sure. Where are the city's numerous cats when you need them? And why have they not been able to get in and take these?

Barely had we resumed walking and taken more than two or three steps when suddenly, for a few moments, there were very faint and indecipherable voices somewhere in the distance. We both instinctively stopped walking and froze.

"Shh,"

I gave the order quietly and unnecessarily as we stopped and listened to the distant voices. They faded away a few seconds later. There was no way to know where the voices were coming from or how far away they might have been. As you might imagine, we stood still and waited silently for quite some time after they ended.

"Wait here," I finally whispered to Elizabeth. "I am going to see where these stairs go."

"Stay here alone? Not on your life. I am coming with you," she quietly hissed back at me in a quavering but determined voice as she returned my lantern.

"Alright then. But be damn quiet and watch where you walk," I whispered.

I did not really need to order Elizabeth to be quiet, of course, but I did; and it somehow made me feel better to know that I was in control of something even if it was only Elizabeth.

******

I climbed the new stone stairs very slowly, one step at a time, in an effort not to make even the slightest noise. The stairs were narrow and set in a winding stone staircase that wound tightly to the right in order to make them more defendable against anyone attempting to climb them. They were just like the stairs that came down from the Empress's sleeping room. *Of course they were; they were probably built at the same time.*

My sword was pointed up the stairs and my lantern held high as I climbed. As I did, I realized that the dusty stairs I was slowly climbing were totally empty just like all the rest of the passage. We had seen nothing on any of the stairs or in the tunnel, not even the faint smell of long ago piss or shite.

In fact, the only thing we had had seen in the tunnel so far were the tracks of people who had left a record of their passage by walking in the heavy layer of dust that covered the floor of the tunnel. I had seen many an escape tunnel, but this was the first one that was totally empty of such things as old tools and broken ladders.

The emptiness of the tunnel was strange and somehow seemed to be significant. But I had not a clue as to why that might be.

****** *An unknown scribe*

George and Elizabeth held their lanterns high and out in front of them as they worked their way very slowly up the tightly winding stairs. Suddenly, there was a small wooden door in the side of the wall even though the stairs continued upward. They stopped when they reached the door. Whatever was on the other side, if anything, was totally silent.

"Shh," George said as he held his lantern up. What he could see, and it was not much, was that the door was very much like the door to the Empress's bedroom. At least he thought it was. He could not be sure because he had not looked closely at the *back* of the door to the Empress's chamber.

In fact, he had not looked at the back of the door in the Empress's chest at all—they had used clothes from her chest to hold it open. It was a bad mistake and George realized it as soon as he saw the door in front of him. How did it open? And was it barred like the one in the Empress's clothing chest?

George very carefully and quietly put his lantern down on one of the stone steps that continued upward. Then he gently pressed his ear against the door and listened. Elizabeth held her lantern up so he could see. After a while, he shook his head. Nothing.

He was still listening more than a minute later when an impatient Elizabeth moved up next to him and began running her hand along the top of the wooden frame that held the door. Suddenly there was a "click" and the door moved a couple of inches. They both gasped and George instinctively brought the point of his sword closer to the door. Nothing happened.

They waited silently for several minutes before George slowly pushed the door open. It opened into another clothes chest and this one's front door was open so that they could see all the way into the empty room beyond the chest. It was dimly lit by light coming in from around the edges of the shutter-covered wall openings and barred entrance door. And it looked familiar.

"I think this is my father's room," George said so softly that no one heard him.

A moment later, despite the dim light, he was able to see the bar on the room's main door. No one could get in. At that point, he decided it was safe to climb into the chest and on into the room. He was immediately struck by the room's somewhat foul smell. It was as if its bedding had gone mouldy and its piss bucket had not been emptied for some time. Probably both, he decided.

Getting off the stairs and into the room was easier said than done. The door to the passageway was too small, much smaller than its counterpart in the Empress's chest. But he managed to squeeze through the doorway and was soon all the way into the room. Elizabeth was right behind him.

"Yes, this is his room. I recognize his old tunic and his extra pair of sandals. And there are his wrist knives and his his sword and chain shirt and his longbow and quiver. He must have left them when he went to visit the Empress."

It was about then that the reality of what George was looking at struck him. His father had gone to visit the Empress and left his chain shirt and weapons behind because he did not expect danger to be waiting for him.

Moreover, the door to the outside hallway was still barred as his father had undoubtedly left it—which meant no one could have come in to use the secret passageway to get to the Empress's chambers and kill him. Another entrance must have been used.

Chapter Seven
We march to the palace.

Commander Courtenay was accompanied by his usual guard of four archers when he left the Great Palace and walked back to the Commandry that afternoon. He was, they later commented to each other whilst visiting a local tavern, lost in thought and walking fast with a look of determination on his face. Something was up and the four of them spent the rest of the evening drinking bowls of wine and speculating as to what it might be.

Something being in the wind, they all agreed, was nothing new for the Company or its Commander. Indeed, they also agreed and assured each other sagely as they sipped their wine; it was to be expected because of the Venetian raid and the recent deaths of the Commander's father and the Empress.

It was, however, what the Commander did when he reached the Commandry that ended up truly surprising everyone. He walked into the great hall where two of his lieutenant commanders, Henry and Michael, were working on the Company's accounts and records with the help of their apprentices, and began giving orders that brought both men to their feet with a flood of questions.

"I need Lieutenant Richmond and a dozen or so good swordsmen here tomorrow first thing in the morning right after they have broken their nightly fasts. They cannot be too tall or be afraid of being underground in mines and tunnels. Men who have had experience working in mines would be the best.

"And here is something important—only you two, and Harold because you will be taking some of his men, are to know about the tunnels and that it would be best if the men were miners and not overly tall. It is an important secret that they will be going into the tunnels so the three of you will have to choose the men yourselves and not tell them or anyone else why they were selected.

"Oh, and we need to send someone to the market to buy a couple of dozen easily carried candle lanterns. If anyone asks, they are to say we need more light in the Commandry at night when we are working late."

It was, and there was no doubt about it, an unexpected order with unexpected requirements. Lieutenant Richmond was thought to be one of the Company's very best swordsmen. He had, for instance, proved his fighting ability to Commander Courtenay in a battle at the Athens slave market to free some captured British sailors. But swordsmen who were "not too tall" and "all seasoned fighting men; no young ones or apprentices?" George's two lieutenants clamoured for an explanation.

"Clear the room," the Commander ordered. "And you three," he told their wide-eyed young apprentices, his son, his younger brother, and Archie as he pointed at them, "are to go to the market right now and buy two dozen candle lanterns for use here in the Commandry. Buy only small ones that a man can easily carry from one place to another with one hand.

Normally George would have sent his own apprentice to fetch them, but he still had not selected an apprentice sergeant to replace the man who had recently been promoted to be the lieutenant on one of the captured Venetian galleys.

"And one more thing—you three are never to discuss what you just heard or anything about the lanterns or tunnels, not even with each other, or even hint to anyone about them or anything about the men or how the men and lanterns might be used. It might endanger our men if word gets out."

Everyone hurried to obey. After supping with his lieutenants that evening and explaining his plan, George took one of the lanterns that had been fetched from the market and walked back to the Empress's palace to spend the night. His four guards went with him and then continued on to visit a particularly friendly tavern. They would accompany him back to the Commandry in the morning.

Sometime later, at the tavern, the most junior of the four guards commented as to where he thought George intended to spend the night. And he would have been right. Had anyone been able to get through the barred door to the room of George's father that night, he would have seen the room to be empty with only George's chain shirt and wrist knives on the bed and an open door in the upright chest where his father had hung his clothes.

****** *Lieutenant Harry Richmond*

I was having one of my black days when all I could think about was losing Anne and my old life in Grimsby. Then everything changed. A courier from the Commandry was rowed out to my galley, Number Seventy-one, on which I was serving as Captain Blacks's lieutenant. He brought a message to the captain ordering him to have me report to the Commandry first thing in the morning with my sword and a galley shield.

Captain Black did not tell me why I had been summoned. More than likely he did not know. But he knew something was up because I was supposed to bring a sword and galley shield and leave my longbow and arrows behind. He also knew I was the best swordsman in the Company and had several times been given special assignments because of it. I had spilled a lot of blood carrying them out and was a lieutenant as a result.

The captain promptly agreed to let me spend the rest of the day practicing my swordsmanship with some of the better swordsmen in our crew. We had to use practice swords, of course, but they were better than nothing.

The prospect of action! What else could it be? It excited me and totally changed everything by letting me think about something other than what I had left behind in Grimsby. I spent the rest of the day sharpening my sword and practicing against the three most useful swordsmen in my galley's crew.

Early the next morning I was among the first few men in my galley's food line. That was when I found that Captain Black had once again shown me that he is a good man. During the night he had moved our galley to the quay. I am sure he did so in order that I might get ashore quickly.

In any event, I was fully ready despite a somewhat sleepless night and was able to present myself at the Commandry gate a few minutes after dawn. I was immediately allowed to pass through the gate and enter the Commandry's bailey. To my surprise and pleasure, I found a dozen or so other men reporting in at the same time who were also carrying swords and shields.

What was most encouraging of all was that every man waiting in the bailey with me was a veteran chosen man or sergeant with a sword on his belt and multiple battle dots on his tunic. I recognized several of them as useful swordsmen and was particularly pleased to find that I had the highest rank among them. There was the usual pre-battle sense of tenseness and good fellowship in the air. It was wonderful.

Our curiosity was great and every man's spirits were high as we filed into the Commandry's great hall a couple of minutes later. They got even higher when we were each given a bowl of wine and Commander Courtenay told us what we would be doing. What we heard certainly surprised us.

"Men, you are here because each of you is an experienced fighting man who knows how to defend himself with his sword and shield if he is attacked.

"This is the situation we face: There are tunnels under the Empire's Great Palace, how many we do not know. We also do not know where the tunnels lead or who we will find at the other end of them. What we do know is that one of them comes up to the room in which the Empress and my father were killed.

"What we are going to do is search the tunnels to see what we can find. Our problem is that we may surprise innocent people when we come out of the tunnel entrances. They may think *we* are invaders or robbers and try to fight us off.

"You have each been selected because you are known to be steady men and very good with swords and shields, men who can be counted on to be steady enough to defend themselves *without* killing the innocents and friends who do not understand what is happening and think they are being attacked.

"So here is the order of the day: We are going to search the tunnels and you are to defend yourselves and your mates if we are attacked, but you are not to make any effort to kill or seriously wound anyone unless it is absolutely necessary."

****** *Lieutenant Commander Henry Harcourt.*

"I may have white hair, George, but I am still your deputy and battle advisor when the Company fights on land; so I am going with you and your swordsmen and that is the long and short of it."

Those were my indignant words after we heard the details of George's plan and I realized he did not intend to take me with him. I leaned over the table and shook my finger in his face as I said them. And as I did I thought of something and added it to my argument.

"Besides, you need me because you have already made a mistake by forgetting something *we* will need when *we* are in the tunnels." I emphasized the word "we."

"Alright, Uncle Henry, alright. It is your right; I surrender; you can come. And what, pray tell, do *we* need that I forgot?"

"*We* need to take a couple of heavy axes or large hammers with us in case we come to a door or wall that needs to be broken down, eh?"

George just looked at me for a moment whilst he thought about what I said. Then he broke into a smile and nodded.

"Damn, Uncle Henry, you are right. We are likely to need one. I should have thought of that." A moment later he began giving the first of many orders. The first was to my apprentice, his younger brother and the oldest of the three apprentices.

"John, you and Young George and Archie are to run to the market and buy a couple of big hammers or axes. They have to be heavy enough that we can use them to batter down a door. And you are not to say a word to anyone, not even to each other, about why you are buying it or who you are buying it for. Do you understand?"

"Aye Commander, not a word to anyone," John said solemnly as Young George and Archie nodded their agreement.

We watched them go. No one said a word until they cleared the hall.

"A log from the market's wood lot would probably have been better," Harold suggested.

"Your father used one in Alexandria when Moors tried to kill him years ago. Henry and I had just joined the Company when it happened. That was right after what was left of the Company's archers stopped crusading and got into the trade of carrying passengers and cargo.

"Four of us grabbed the log by the stubs of its branches and swung it against the door. It worked quite well."

And then we had to listen as Harold once again told the tale of how the door of a couple of murderous Moorish merchants had been battered down in the middle of the night with a hurriedly trimmed log. Harold had been there because he was the pilot of the galley George's father had been sailing on and could speak a bit of the Moorish gobble; I had been there as one of the fighting men William, George's father, had taken with him.

It had happened when George's father led some of our men in a night time raid against a couple of Moorish merchants. That was many years ago in the Company's early days right after its survivors had stopped crusading and had somehow acquired a couple of galleys and began using them to earn coins by carrying refugees and cargos.

William, George's father, went after the Moors because they had hired assassins who tried to kill him on Alexandria's quay. The assassins almost got him because he was foolish enough to climb on to the quay without carrying a weapon or wearing his chain shirt. I had come to his assistance and he had marked me for it. As you might imagine, going out in public unarmed was a mistake that William never ever made again.

What Harold did not mention was that Moors had good reason to be unhappy with William, George's father, and try to kill him—because he was the Commander of what was left of the Company and we had just taken a couple of their transports as prizes and brought them into Alexandria to sell.

It had to be done, the capture and subsequent tossing into the sea of the assassins and the Moors who had hired them. The Company was just getting started in the carrying of passengers and cargos; we would not have been able to attract custom if people thought the Company was so weak it could not defend its own people. Besides, the Moors deserved it and revenge was required by the Company's charter.

****** *Lieutenant Harry Richmond*

Commander Courtenay's words both inspired me and depressed me. What we were to do was certainly different from how we usually spent our days. That was good since it took my mind away from Anne and Ramsgate. What was depressing was that it did not sound like there would be much chance of the serious fighting that I constantly craved.

We filed out of the Commandry's hall and formed up two abreast in the bailey. Two of our twelve swordsmen were given great long-handled hammers to carry in addition to their swords.

Our round galley shields were slung over our backs as we set off for wherever we were being led. A small horse-cart led by a couple of apprentice sergeants followed immediately behind us. Its cargo was covered by an old sail.

Just before we got underway the Commander ordered the men with the hammers to put them on the cart and cover them with the sail. I caught a glimpse of the cart's other cargo as they did. It was candle lanterns with their candles already in them. The Commander obviously did not want the lanterns seen. But why?

We left as soon as the hammers were safely stowed away and covered. The Commander led the way.

At the Commander's request, I called the chants as we marched behind him from the Commandry to the Great Palace. We marched in a column of twos. There was no drum, but the cadence of my calls and the men's chanted answers were more than enough to let each man put his foot down at the same time as everyone else. It was a nice morning and the sun was not yet scorching hot.

Fortunately, the city's streets were not yet crowded. Even so, our passage was periodically hindered by the women along the edges of the street cooking their families' morning flatbreads and the gaggles of children gathered around them. There were also a number of carts parked along the side of the streets and moving along them.

The women and children we passed eyed us with great interest, and some of the older children began following us and trying to march with us. Great clowders of cats were everywhere either sleeping or begging for food and arguing over the scraps that were sometimes thrown to them.

People walking in the streets tended to give way and carts were often pulled aside as we approached. As you might imagine, the Commander led us down the middle of the streets in an effort to avoid the carts, the cooking fires, and the poop.

After a while, we came upon a trio of axe-carrying Varangian guards, their great battle axes in hand, standing on a corner watching the activity on the streets around them. They pulled themselves to attention and saluted as we passed. The Varangians were friends and allies so we returned the courtesy and smiled at them. I had always wondered how it would be to fight one of them.

Our line of march was entirely in the city's Latin Quarter. The people we passed seemed quite friendly, no doubt because they thought we would always fight on their side because we gobbled crusader French and made the sign of the cross correctly. Children, mostly young boys, were constantly joining us and pretending to march until they got sufficiently bored and dropped away.

After about twenty minutes we were on a fine cobble-stoned street that took us past the huge Wisdom of God Church, the big one which the local people called the "Hagía Sophía," its Latin name, even though they were not sure what it meant because only their priests spoke Latin.

Beyond the huge church, the street continued on into an open park-like area with grass and big trees. Among the trees were several small ponds and a number of statues. Beyond the park was a building with two floors that was almost certainly the barracks of the Varangian Guards. And just beyond the barracks stood the high wall that surrounded the Great Palace itself and its park-like bailey.

The gate to the Great Palace's bailey was swung open by a pair of Varangian guards as soon as we approached it. Arrangements had obviously been made and we were expected. A long line of horse carts and man carts were waiting to enter. Their drivers and pullers watched as we marched past them. A few of them smiled and nodded, but most of them just looked at us impassively.

Commander Courtenay led the way as we marched into the palace's bailey. A huge giant of a Varangian was waiting for us in the middle of the bailey. He was holding a great axe but greeted the Commander with a big smile and a great flourishing bow of welcome with wide-spread arms. The Commander smiled back and bowed similarly. It was clear to all of us that we were among friends.

The Varangian and Commander Courtenay talked briefly, and then the Commander led us to one of the more distant entrance doors on the far side of the palace. The big Varangian came with us. I had seen the palace from the city wall when we were fighting off the Greeks, but never up close. It was made of stone and it was huge with many shuttered openings in its walls that could be opened to admit day's light and then shut to keep out the dangerous night airs.

We waited again when we reached one of the doors and the Commander and the Varangian talked again, but not for very long. When they finished, the Commander walked back to us and we were given a short break and told to piss and poop near the bailey wall. To my surprise the bailey's pissing spot was not in a low spot such that it would run out. The empire was clearly not as advanced as the Company in such matters.

When we finished pissing, the two hammers were returned to the men assigned to them and every man including the Commander was handed one of the unlit candle lanterns the cart had been carrying. Then we all marched into the Great Palace itself.

I appreciated the piss break. It was something an experienced captain or commander lets his men do before he sends them into a fight. I found it quite encouraging. Perhaps it meant there might be fighting.

Chapter Eight

We are surprised several times.

Commander Courtenay and the big Varangian led us into the Empress's palace. They entered first with the lieutenant commander and one of the two hammer carriers right behind them. The swordsmen and I followed them. The two apprentices remained with the now-empty horse cart.

I had no idea what any of my fellow archers thought about the Great Palace, but it certainly impressed me. It was by far the biggest and grandest building I had ever been in. The door we entered suggested the grandeur and importance of the palace. It was not the main entrance but, even so, a man did not even have to duck his head to enter.

Stairs running upwards and two Varangian guards were immediately in front of us as soon as we came through the entrance door. The stairs were certainly not built for defence; they did not curve and were so wide that people walking up them down them could easily pass each other at the same time.

Immediately off to the right after we entered we could see into what appeared to be a hall with several groups of people sitting and talking on benches set against several wooden tables; to the left was a long corridor. The people sitting on the benches stopped talking and stared at us in surprise.

We did not stop. Our leather sandals made loud click and clacks such that we sounded like a horde of locusts as the Commander and the Varangian led us up the stairs. When we reached the top we turned left and walked a few steps down a long hallway which was lighted by the sun streaming in from a number of wall openings all along it. There was another axe-carrying Varangian standing next to a big and ornately carved door. The door could be seen by the two Varangians at the bottom of the stairs.

Somehow, without being told, we knew that we were approaching the entrance to the Empress's private rooms, the rooms where everyone says she and the Commander's father were murdered.

We entered through the door to the Empress's chambers and without slowing down walked straight through the first room to an open door on the far side of the room.

The first room, the one we initially entered and walked through, was huge. It was almost as large as our Commandry's hall. It had a chair sitting on some kind of raised deck at the far end and there were all kinds of woven sails with many colours covering the wooden floor. An exquisitely carved wooden table and a row of sitting stools with backs on them were lined up against the wall on the left.

Colourful sails of some kind and sizes were also hanging close together, one after another, on all the walls. Some of them had designs and outlines of horses and people and faces on them. My mates and I could not help ourselves; we stared at the room in open-mouthed surprise as we passed through it.

On the far side of the first room there was an open door that was the entrance to a second room. The second room was large, but nowhere near as large as the first. Even so, it was one of the biggest rooms I had ever been in. It was at least three times the size of our galley's stern castle.

The second room had a very large string bed, a finely carved table with drinking bowls and a pitcher on it, a piss pot under a stool in the far corner, three sitting stools with backs on them, and a large chest against the wall that stood as tall as a man. There was also a second small table with a sitting stool next to it and a writing quill and parchments on it.

Brightly coloured sails and fur blankets covered the bed, the floor, and most of the walls. I saw everything in the room up close and had plenty of time to do so because that was where we halted.

There was a door in the far wall of the second room and another door on the wall to the right. Both of the doors were closed. My first thought on seeing the closed doors was that breaking them open was why we had brought the big hammers.

But I was wrong; we did not begin by breaking down one or both of the closed doors. Instead, a lighted candle was produced and one after another the candle lanterns we were carrying were lit.

When the lanterns were all properly flamed, the Commander drew his sword, uttered the command "no talking and watch your heads," and, to everyone's great surprise, he entered the upright shipping chest with his sword in one hand and a candle lantern in the other.

Those of us who were near him watched as he stepped through a large hole in the rear of the chest.

The Varangian moved to follow the Commander but was elbowed aside by the lieutenant commander. He, the Varangian that is, just shrugged and became the third man to walk into the upright chest. I was the fourth.

We had all drawn our swords when the Commander drew his. Our shields, however, were still slung over our backs. The Varangian was the only man without a sword or shield; he carried, instead, a great axe. And from the ease with which he had been carrying it, it was likely that it never left his hand, even when he was sleeping.

My candle lantern and those of the men in front of began making strange shadows as we too ducked our heads and moved slowly and cautiously through the upright chest and into the narrow stone passageway that lay beyond it.

It was instantly obvious in the flickering light that we had stepped on to a narrow and winding staircase that ran both up and down. The lights in front of me went down the stairs so I held my lantern as high as I could and followed them. No one said a word. It was surprisingly cool.

My thoughts as I stepped out of the chest and smelled the cool and musty air were that I was pleased to be where I was and about to do whatever it might be that I was about to do—and glad I had peed in the bailey.

We proceeded down the stairs in the flickering light. It was so quiet and we walked so carefully that I could hear my heart pounding and the sounds of the men breathing and the scuffling of their feet. No one including me was walking with big strong steps. On the other hand, there was no feeling or scent of fear in the air, just excitement and anticipation.

It did not take long before we reached the bottom of the stairs and began walking along a flat rocky surface. We were in a tunnel that was so low that we had to crouch over to avoid banging our heads and the shield slung over our backs. Even worse, it was so narrow that we could only walk in a single file with our heads leaning forward. It was the first time I had ever been in a tunnel.

Most of the tunnel seemed to be carved out of rock. But not all of it; every so often we came to a section where the sides and roof of the tunnel were made of carefully stacked stones and rocks.

After a bit of walking, and more than a little banging our heads and the top of our shields on the tunnel roof, we came to an even smaller cross tunnel.

The Commander whispered an order to me.

"Lieutenant, remain here with the men I do not take as our rear guard."

It was an understatement to say that I was disappointed.

"Aye Commander, I am to stay and command the rear guard," I whispered back. "But begging the Commander's pardon, I respectfully suggest that I am the best swordsman in the Company and should be forward with you."

And then, God bless him, the lieutenant commander walking behind me spoke up.

"Lieutenant Richmond is right George," he whispered. "He should be up front with you. Sergeant Livingston is a steady man and senior. He can walk last and command the rear."

"Oh aye, that sounds reasonable. Make it so."

Thank you Jesus and all the saints.

******

The Commander went first and led us down the side tunnel. I squeezed past the men who had been walking between us until I was right behind him—with my sword in one hand and a lantern in the other.

We walked and walked and walked. It seemed like miles, probably because I had to walk bent forward and periodically banged my lantern hand because I was trying to hold it as high as possible, and, less frequently, my head and shield. It did not take long before I had absolutely no idea how far we had come or which direction we were walking.

The tunnel seemed forever and we got thirstier and thirstier as we walked and crawled, at least I did. At times it looked as if the tunnel itself had been hacked out of solid stone; other times the earth must have been less solid because large stones had been stacked in curved arches to prevent a collapse.

We had long ago sheathed our swords so we could hold an empty hand up to feel the ceiling when it got lower. It was the only way to protect our heads and shields from constantly bumping them on the uneven ceiling. And all too often they did despite our efforts.

Suddenly the tunnel came to an abrupt end. We came upon it so unexpectedly after walking for so long that I took a couple additional steps and stepped on the Commander's heel when he stopped. I quickly apologized and begged his pardon.

And I was not the only one who hit the man who had unexpectedly stopped in front of him—behind us we could hear a string of muttered curses and quiet apologies as some of the men walking behind us bumped into each other when the man in front of them unexpectedly stopped after more than an hour of constant walking and periodic crawling when the tunnel roof was too low.

"We must have missed something," the Commander said when we while we were holding up our lanterns and examining the end of the tunnel in disbelief. There was a more than a little sound of frustration in his voice.

One of the men behind us spoke up.

"It may have been my imagination, but I think my hand touched a piece of wood aloft a while back. We went right under it. It could have been covering some sort of hole in the roof."

"How far back?" someone asked. I think it was the lieutenant commander.

"About five minutes ago" was the reply shouted from somewhere behind us. "Someone else added, "I think I felt it too."

"Everyone turn around and start walking back the way we came," the Commander ordered. "And everyone hold a hand up to touch the roof." A moment later he added, "And do not bunch up. Give the man in front of you enough room."

We moved out smartly, or at least as smartly as one can move when walking hunched over like an old crone. Sure enough, a few minutes later there was a shout from somewhere ahead of us.

"Here, by God; I think I found it. There is wood here for sure."

"Commander coming through," the Commander shouted. "Everybody hold their place and let me squeeze past. And stop your damn talking."

Chapter Nine
An interesting find.

It did not take long for George to squeeze past the men in the tunnel and reach what we hoped was the tunnel's exit. What the Commander saw and felt in the flickering light was a blackened piece of wood. It looked as though it had not been disturbed for a long time. It also looked as if it were too narrow to be hiding an exit.

"Perhaps it is a hole for letting in fresh air?" Someone suggested. "Or a deliberately small exit hole that could be dug out in an emergency."

Commander Courtenay thought for a moment, and then made what turned out to be a very bad decision—he poked at the wood with his sword.

There was a loud "crack" and, a moment or so after the sword touched the wood, it gave way. It fell apart and dropped a great mass of wood and dirt and rocks onto the men standing below it.

There was a moment of chaos and startled screams in the sudden cloud of dust and the darkness, and then a great scramble began to dig out those who had been buried. We may never have been in a tunnel before, but we knew we had to dig them out before it was too late.

Not all the men and lanterns were covered by the downfall, just the Commander and the man who had been next to him who had been directly under it. There were still lanterns and men on both sides of the downfall. Those of us who were closest began digging frantically even before the dust settled and they stopped coughing and choking.

The survivors nearest the downfall attacked the pile of debris with our bare hands and threw whatever we grabbed behind us. Those who were further away from the fall then passed it back deeper into the tunnel.

Several of the archers were on the palace side of collapse, but most were trapped on the dead-end side of the fall. They all instantly understood what was at stake and worked desperately. They used their hands like dogs using their paws to try to dig a fox out of a hole.

"Holy Shit," said one of them as he saw in dimly lit dust what he had grabbed and was about to put behind him for the next man to push even further back into the tunnel. It was a skull. He threw it behind him and kept digging with his bare hands.

Lieutenant Richmond

There was one man between me and the dirt and rocks that had fallen into the tunnel. I coughed and the dust blinded me but I set my lantern down behind me and moved up next to him. We began desperately digging into the pile of dirt and sticks with our bare hands.

Suddenly I felt a sandaled foot. It seemed to be twitching and trying to move. I grabbed it with both hands and pulled. The sandal came off but nothing moved. I threw it behind me and kept on grabbling and throwing rocks and sticks and handfuls of dirt,

The man next to me was a sergeant by the name of Hardy from Galley Forty-five. He and I were on our knees and frantically pulling away rocks and pieces of wood from around the leg. We grabbed hold of it and pulled again. And again nothing happened. A moment later we uncovered another leg. So again we dug our hands into the debris and pulled more rocks and wood away. We pulled again. This time there was some movement.

I braced my feet as best I could, and grunted hard as I gave another great pull. Still nothing. I moved backward and knocked over my lantern as I moved to get my legs out in front of me and got my feet firmly up against some kind of rock that was sticking out from the side of the tunnel.

Sergeant Hardy, although I did not know it at the time, was doing the same thing. I pulled again with all my strength on one of the legs while Hardy did the same and pulled on the other. Somewhere along the way we had both shrugged off our shields so we could move more freely.

It worked. We both went over on our backs as the Commander's body popped out of the dirt and rocks like the plug in a foot archer's water flask. Hardy and I were both flat on our backs when the Commander's body came free and landed on top of us. He was gasping great deep breaths and coughing in the dust-filled darkness. So was I, for that matter, but nothing like the Commander.

"Help," he croaked as he took in great gasps of air and coughed each time he did. "Help." The tunnel was full of dust and it was totally dark except for some flickering light from a candle lantern somewhere behind us

There was not much we could do to help him. So we shouted at the men behind us to "pull him off of us and further back."

A moment later he was pulled off of us. Then we sat up and returned to once again desperately trying to clear away the rubble from the collapsed tunnel. I did not know until much later, but I had bloodied the back of my head when I went over backwards and hit the rocky floor of the tunnel.

It did not take long before Sergeant Hardy and I could hear someone doing the same thing on the other side of the pile of debris. We redoubled our efforts. Less than a minute later, about the time that I realized that everybody in the tunnel was shouting orders at everyone else and my hands were hurting most terrible, we broke through.

Thank you Jesus and all the saints.

****** *Lieutenant Commander Henry Harcourt*

The sudden collapse of the tunnel came as a total surprise and caused a great cloud of dust to surround us. It immediately became impossible to see what had happened because of the dust and because of the loss of some of the lanterns.

There was a moment of silence and then much swearing, coughing, and shouting. I lifted my tunic to protect my eyes. They had instantly become full of dust and grit.

"Jake and the Commander were under it when it fell," someone shouted from somewhere ahead of me. *Mother of God.*

"Stop talking and dig them out, goddamn you. Dig them out. Hurry, lads, faster, faster."

I shouted my orders as I put my lantern down and tried to push my way past the men in front of me. Everyone was coughing and shouting similar orders at everyone else.

I got past a couple of men and then, whilst still having a severe coughing fit, began being hit in the face with dirt and stones being thrown back into the tunnel by the men in front of me. They had thrown off their shields and were using their bare hands in an effort to clear away the debris, and throwing it behind them as they did.

"Stop panicking and do your duty," the man I was trying to pass snarled at me as I tried to get around him to reach George. He said it whilst pushing and throwing debris behind him at a prodigious rate. It was not an order I wanted to hear.

The man who had shouted at me and prevented me from passing him was a stocky red-bearded sergeant by the name of Sam Keene. I vowed to look him up and put him in his proper place if we survived. Of course I would remember him; he had embarrassed me in front of the men by keeping his head whilst I was losing mine.

****** *Sergeant Samuel Keene.*

We was all coughing and digging and shouting at first. The dust was still most fearsome, but it had lessened by the time we pulled Jake and the Commander free and cleared away enough of the fall to be able to see and talk to our mates on the other side. It was about then that I realized my eyes and hands hurt most fierce. And every time I took a breath my chest hurt too.

I stopped my desperate pawing at the downfall and fell backwards in exhaustion as soon as I felt the hand of someone digging on the other side of the fall. A few moments later someone pulled me further back into the tunnel and took my place.

It was about then that I screamed from the pain. My hands began to really hurt and so did my chest. The pain was worse than after the Moor stabbed me a couple of years earlier and knocked me off the boarding ladder.

In the distance I could hear someone shouting to "go get water and sleeping skins to put them on."

Sleeping skins? They must be mad. This is no time to sleep. We have got to get out of here. I started to say something, but nothing came out. And then I think I remember bumping along the floor of the tunnel.

I woke up when I was being pulled into the fancy room where we started and someone holding my head up for a drink. There were people talking and moving about but they were so blurry in my eyes that I could not see who they were.

All of a sudden someone began pouring a bucket of water on my eyes and trying to give me a drink from a bowl. That helped and for some reason I tried to sit up. What I remember most was having dirt in my mouth and spitting it out along with some of the water. Then my hands began burning like they were in a fire.

"My hands. Pour some on my hands," I managed to gasp." Someone did and then I was so tired I somehow went back to sleep. At least that's what old Peter Pewter from Galley Seventy-eight told me when my hands gave me a great pain and woke me up.

It was quiet when I woke up. And it was a different room. "Water," I croaked as started to sit up. It was about then that I realized my tunic was gone and my hands were burning and felt heavy. "Water for God's sake."

A tall man with a robe covered with all kinds of symbols sewn on it came over immediately with a bowl. He and a serving girl helped me sit up and drink from it. It was wine with a strange taste.

It was about then, when I held up my hands to help guide the bowl to my mouth, that I first realized my hands were heavy because they were wrapped in some wet and dirty rags that smelled like olive oil. I looked at them in surprise when I finished drinking. My hands hurt underneath the rags.

"Olive oil?"

"Yes, oil pressed from the olive. Your hands are wounded from digging with them. Olive oil will sooth the pain and help them heal faster. It is well known that this is true. Sacrificing a white chicken and certain prayers are also helpful.

"I am the Empress's Greek physician, Apostolos of Nicea. You and several other English men are in my care. You are in the Commander's room in the Great Palace. He is still being attended to in the Empress's rooms."

"Will he survive, the Commander?"

"Oh, I should think so. He did not stop breathing for very long—thanks to you I am told. Now lie back and let the girl pour water on you to wash off the dirt."

Chapter Ten

We get ready to return to the tunnels.

Three days later we tried again. Commander Courtenay had recovered whilst residing in the room next to the Empress's. The Regent, for that is how the Empress's daughter, Elizabeth, was now styling herself, had insisted on him remaining there so that help could be summoned available "in the event he suffers a relapse."

Elizabeth had been quite busy ever since she moved into the Empress's rooms. She was now issuing orders, making decisions, and requiring everyone in the court of the late Empress, meaning the foreign ambassadors and the courtiers who were there for the free food and gossip, to address her as "Your Majesty" if they wished to remain.

George was in surprisingly good spirits when he addressed the new and larger group of sword carrying archers Henry had brought in to accompany him. He met them in the palace's great hall in the early morning before the free-loading courtiers arrived.

It was a fully recovered Commander who met them. He had stopped coughing soon after being pulled out of the tunnel and had been taken in a horse cart later that afternoon to the city's baths to get rid of the dust that had continued to vex him until it was washed away.

It probably helped that the new Regent had been extremely solicitous of his health; she had ordered that he remain nearby in the event he suffered a relapse and she was needed to direct the efforts to revive him. Fortunately the room next to hers was available as the Regent's young husband, who had begun residing there, had been sent back to Epirus with what the Regent described as "a very important message" for his father.

****** *Lieutenant Commander Henry Harcourt*

Not all of the swordsmen in the original party of tunnel explorers were going with George on his second attempt to investigate the tunnels. Two of the original men had severely damaged their hands digging him out and another had been allowed to beg off and return to his galley. The excused man had reluctantly made the request on the grounds that the mere thought of being in another cave-in gave him the shaking and sweating pox.

More than enough new men had been added, however, such that the second party of tunnel explorers was substantially larger than the first. It was also better equipped in that every man was carrying a hastily acquired small water skin, some cheese, and a piece of chicken that had already been burnt and was ready to eat.

What no one was carrying this time was a shield slung over his shoulder. That was because we had found in our previous trip through the tunnels that the shields stuck up too high such that they would periodically scrape up against the tunnel's ceiling—and ceilings, we had also found, can collapse.

Our second tunnel search began late due to a well-intentioned idea gone wrong. George, learning from his near-fatal recent experience, had initially required that every man enter the tunnel with a long line of ships' rope tied to each of his ankles. The idea being that in the event of another cave-in, the men walking behind someone caught by in the downfall could be located and pulled free using the rope that trailed out behind him.

It was a splendid idea, except that it did not work. What we quickly learned was that the men walking behind one another in the dimly lit tunnel were constantly stepping on the ropes trailing out behind those in front of them. This, in turn, tended to trip the men whose ropes were stepped on such that they ended up being constantly inconvenienced and periodically falling to the ground.

The last man was not yet in the tunnel when the search was temporarily called off so the ropes could be removed from everyone except for the lines attached to one man, an archer by the name of David Black from Galley Thirty-two. Black had volunteered to walk well ahead of the main party carrying a lantern with ten paces of line trailing along behind him.

As you might imagine, no one, not even Henry, was brave enough to remind George that it was him walking in the middle of the tunnel searchers who had poked at the roof and caused the collapse, not the man who had been walking at the very front, who had been caught in the collapse of the tunnel's ceiling.

George's explanation

George later admitted to himself that he had been lost in thought as he started walking down the secret stairs to reach the tunnel. He had been the second man in the line of tunnel explorers behind the lantern-carrying volunteer. The Company's best swordsman, Lieutenant Richmond, his sword drawn, was walking immediately behind him. All three of the men were carrying lanterns as were all the other men behind them.

He had been lost in thought and not paying attention when he stepped on line and tripped the leading man. That was because of what Elizabeth had proposed when they were lying exhausted in bed the previous night was so breath-taking and unexpected, and so unwanted—that they become the Empire's Emperor and Empress.

"Robert is not up to being the emperor and everyone knows it," she had proclaimed. "All he wants to do is take his falcons hunting. He is not even interested in the servant girls, for God's sake.

"How long would he last as Emperor when he comes of age? Not long and we both know it. Then everything will be lost including the Company's contract to collect the tolls and help defend the city.

"We must act while we still have a chance."

My rejection of her offer had so angered her that I found it best to return to my room next door. Fortunately it was after we had gotten to know each other so I had a good night's sleep. And, of course, it was a mistake to reject her out of hand. I should have waited and done it more smoothly.

I tried to see Elizabeth and make peace the next morning when I woke up. I knocked softly on the door into her room and then tried to gently push it open. No luck. It was barred. I knocked and tried the door again after I finished pissing in my room's piss pot and putting on my chain shirt and wrist knives. There was still no answer so I went down to the main hall to break my fast.

Elizabeth was eating at the head of the table when I arrived. And, to my astonishment she waved most friendly to me. I, of course, acknowledged her with a smile and a bow. I did not take the empty space on the bench next to her that was usually occupied by her husband. It might have started a rumour.

When I was finished breaking my fast with morning wine and burnt bread with cheese, I went down to the bailey meet the men who would be accompanying me in the morning on my second attempt to explore the tunnels.

Elizabeth's barring of the door between our rooms would not be a problem. The day's tunnel explorers would use the main door into her chambers to reach the tunnel entrance. Indeed, very few people, mostly her long serving and loyal personal servants, were aware that I was "recovering" in the room next to hers such that we could "visit" each other when her boy husband was safely away.

Of course, I could have just as well stayed in my father's room at the other side of the palace and used the tunnel to visit her just as my father apparently had visited her mother. Staying next door had, however, made it easier for us to "know each other" in the biblical sense, something I enjoyed and hoped to continue, but only for so long as it did not permanently attach me to her.

****** Lieutenant Richmond

My fellow tunnel explorers and I spent what was left of the day of the tunnel collapse taking care of our injured mates and getting cleaned up. Getting cleaned up was a problem. Neither I nor any of the other men had ever been so fouled with dirt and dust. Worse, the bones and foul things that dropped on us seemed to have come from a cemetery such that most of us smelled like we were already dead.

No choice was given to us in the matter of getting the dirt and stench of death off our bodies and clothes. The Commander himself got up from the bed where he had been temporarily placed and marched us down to the city's baths. When we arrived, he led us into the water and told us to wash ourselves as he was doing.

We even had to get all the way under the water to get the dust out of our beards and hair. It was a scary ordeal even though, in the end, thank you Jesus and all the saints, it did not end up affecting us as badly as we feared it might. What we had all feared, of course, was that watering ourselves would weaken us when we were with women.

After we finished getting the dust and the smell of death off of us, we were each given new tunics and some liberty coins according to our ranks and informed that we would be staying at the Commandry until further notice. We were also told that we would likely be returning to the tunnels "probably on the day after tomorrow."

We were then given a liberty for that evening. The only requirement laid on us was that we had to stay in the Latin Quarter. That was not a burden because the quarter had numerous taverns with public women we could use to make sure that the bathing had not weakened us.

It was both a fine evening of drinking and a great relief to learn that I had still not come down with the weakness pox as a result of being watered. I came to the conclusion that I had likely dodged an arrow and escaped being weakened after spending some time with a slender young tavern slave with little breasts and strange eyes. She probably came from the land of dragons on the other side of the great desert.

Fortunately, watering ourselves seemed to have had just the opposite effect of what we feared, at least that was case if even half the stories I heard from my fellow swordsmen that evening and the next morning were true. The effects were so encouraging that several men announced they were thinking about watering themselves again sometime.

One thing was sure even though we did not think about it whilst we were out carousing—by the time we returned to the bailey everyone in the city knew we had been in the tunnels and would be going into them again.

******

Several things happened on the day after the cave-in whilst we were idling about in the bailey and trying to recover from our previous day's experiences and drinking. For one, the Commander came out to see how we were doing. He gathered us around and told us that several companies of archers had been sent out from the city that morning to try to find the graveyard that was the site of the tunnel collapse. The Commander also told us something we had already heard from Lieutenant Commander Harcourt—we would be making another search of the tunnels in the morning.

Early in the afternoon we were joined by several dozen additional sword-carrying archers from the men stationed in the city. The new men, we were all told by Lieutenant Commander Harcourt who came out to greet them, would be accompanying us on our next tunnel search.

One of the new arrivals was a lieutenant. Seeing him bothered me greatly until I remembered he was junior to me.

The new arrivals were all long-serving veterans as we were. Even so, they sat with us in the shade and were wide-eyed as they listened to the stories we told them about what we had seen and heard whilst we were in the tunnels.

Our stories were what you would expect—about strange misshapen creatures we had vaguely seen in the dim light and the screams and other noises we heard in the darkness, and how several of our men had themselves suddenly screamed and disappeared never to be seen again.

The new arrivals were all veteran fighting men like us. Even so, many of them were clearly horrified about our descriptions of what we had heard and seen in the tunnels.

Our stories got more and more farfetched as we described how the remains of dead bodies had dropped on us—and then went on to describe sounds and screams we heard that could have only come from hell, which was obviously under our feet and so close that we might breakthrough and drop into it. A couple of the new arrivals actually trembled when they heard about the snake-like scales and black mould that covered the slimy creatures we had seen, the ones that fed on the dead bodies when freshly dead bodies were not available.

Finally, of course, the wide-eyed new arrivals realized we were funning with them and began telling stories of their own.

That evening we "tunnel rats," as those of us who had been in the tunnel were now beginning to call ourselves, all went out together to drink in the courtyard of one of the local taverns. The new arrivals came with us and were allowed to pay for the wine we drank in exchange for being allowed to sit with us and hear more of our increasingly farfetched stories and speculations.

By then, of course, even the most gullible of the new arrivals had come to realize that we had been telling them tall tales and having great merriments at their expense—and all but one or two were relaxed and reassured. The wine, of course, helped immensely.

Later that evening, as we sang chanties and walked drunkenly back to the Commandry, or perhaps I should say "lurched," I realized that I had not thought about Anne and Grimsby for several days. It was a fine thing to be among men who respect you. Living in the Company amongst such fine fellows was not at all like living in Grimsby.

Chapter Eleven
Once more into the tunnels.

It was early on a fine early September morning when we once again marched from the Commandry to the Great Palace for another day of tunnel searching. It was two days after our first tunnel search. It seemed to take a few minutes longer to march there this time, perhaps because there were more people, carts, and feral cats in the streets.

On the other hand, our walk was a bit easier this time because an early morning rain had washed away most of the accumulated poop such that we did not have to walk with extraordinary care. Moreover, at least for me, the possibility we might be about to again do something dangerous made it an even finer morning despite my sore head from a second night of serious drinking and girl-poking.

****** Lieutenant Richmond

"You and the lads were right about this place, Lieutenant," one of the new swordsmen muttered in a barely understandable dialect from the South of England after we had arrived at the Great Palace and walked into the Empress's room. "I never see nuffink like this in my whole life."

It was a significant acknowledgement as the sergeant who made it had claimed to have been in most of England's great holds and houses because he had driven a coach for one of London's biggest moneylenders until his master ran off with someone's coins.

The door to the big upright chest with the pegs holding the Empress's skirts and tunics was closed when we entered the room. The Commander himself opened it and led the way through the door into the tunnel. That was right after each of us was given a candle lantern with its candle already lit and two lines that were each about a dozen paces long.

The purpose of the lines had been explained to us before we left the Commandry—they would be tied to our ankles and dragged along behind us on the floor of the tunnel. They would then be available to be used to pull the man free if the tunnel ceiling came down and covered him. It certainly might have saved us a lot of trouble and grief if we had been wearing them a couple of days earlier so it sounded like a good idea to me. In any event, it was the Commander's idea so we all commented on how much we appreciated them.

An ambitious sergeant from our first exploration, David Black, led the way into the tunnel with the Commander second and me third. Behind me came Lieutenant Commander Harcourt. Our ankle lines trailed out behind us as we walked.

Black claimed to have been the son of an Oxford scribe who had to run for some reason such that he had ended up being birthed in Leicester. It was a lie, of course, but the man was one of the few archers who could scribe and, or so I had been told, did so with a particularly fine hand and used more words than most men even knew.

Our problems with the ankle lines became apparent almost immediately when the Commander somehow stepped on one of Sergeant Black's ankle lines as Black was walking down the stairs with his lantern held high.

The Commander probably stepped on the line because he could not see it in the flickering light cast from his lantern, or perhaps he was not looking because he was thinking of other things. In any event, it happened just as Black was moving his foot downward towards a lower stone step. Black's foot suddenly being unable to move forward whilst in the middle of a step caused the Leicester man to stumble and fall down four or five stairs to the bottom of the stairwell.

Black fell hard and bloodied his head, and was pained enough to yelp and swear as he did. But he was not badly stunned or hurt from his mishap and quickly got to his feet and apologized to the Commander even though he was not at fault. His lantern, however, did not survive hitting the rocky tunnel floor. Its flame went out and could not be relit.

The result of the fall was a sudden stoppage of our forward progress and much shouting and commotion because no one knew what had happened or what had caused it. Finally, a lantern from one of the men at the back of the line was passed forward for Black to carry and we started walking again.

A minute or so later there was a similar mishap somewhere behind me, and then another. There was no doubt about it; lines trailing along on the tunnel floor behind a man are hard to see when the light is uncertain. And it was made more uncertain by the walkers' spending most of their time looking for rocks hanging down from the ceiling that their heads might hit.

The Commander finally gave up.

"Everyone sit down and take off your ankle lines. They are slowing us down and causing more trouble than they are worth," he said. He shouted it loudly so all the men strung out behind him could hear.

"What should we do with them?" a voice asked from somewhere in the rear.

"Put them next to the wall so no one trips over them. We will gather them up later when we come back this way."

****** *Lieutenant Commander Henry Harcourt*

We resumed our march and a few minutes later came to the entrance of the side tunnel we explored so disastrously a few days earlier. Right beyond it was a narrow staircase stone stairs. To my astonishment, we walked past the stairs and kept going.

Ignoring the stairs surprised me; surely they must lead to somewhere we needed to know about. *Later I learned that the stairs led up to what had been his father's private room in the palace and that William, George's father, and then George himself, had stayed in the room and used the tunnel to visit the Empress's sleeping room. But by then, of course, it was too late.*

The tunnel continued on past the stairs for some distance. After what seemed like thirty minutes or so of walking we came to a fork in the tunnel. After a moment's hesitation, George made a decision and we continued down the tunnel to the left. I had absolutely no idea which direction we were headed and, so far as I could tell from the comments of the men walking around me, neither did anyone else.

I found myself increasingly tired and my knees ached so badly that I would have stopped if I had been walking alone. When this is over I am going back to Cyprus and tend to my wife and garden.

We walked in the tunnel for some time until we came to three stone steps that led up to what was clearly a trap door. We stopped.

"Quiet. No talking. Everyone be quiet."

The order was whispered from man to man as those of us at the front of the little column held up our lanterns to better see it. Nothing could be heard. All of a sudden, there was a sound of someone walking on trapdoor above of us. And then we heard the faint and muffled sounds of a woman's voice and a dog barking. We could not make out the woman's words but she did not sound agitated.

We held our breath and waited. Nothing. In the dim and flickering light I saw George slowly draw his sword from is sheath. Lieutenant Richmond saw him do it and immediately put down his lantern and drew his sword. I immediately did the same. And then the men behind us began copying us even though no order had been given. The drawing of swords rippled down our little column like a wave in the sea.

Someone in the rear started to say something and was immediately drew a quiet "shush" from several of the men around him. It immediately became so silent in the lantern-lit tunnel that I could hear my own breathing and that of the men on either side of me.

****** *Lieutenant Richmond*

Commander Courtenay started to reach up to try to lift the wooden plank above the stairs. I gently stuck out my arm to block him and shook my head. He saw my arm in the flickering light of the lanterns and stopped.

Then he nodded his head and stepped back. It had become totally silent above us.

I could have easily reached up and tried to push the plank up a few inches to see what I could see. But I did not immediately do so because it would have left me in a bad position to use my sword if there was an enemy above me.

What I needed was to be able to deflect any weapon that might be waiting stab or slash me. Accordingly, instead of touching the wood plank that was clearly an exit from the tunnel, the first thing I did was slowly and cautiously climb up on to the first of the three misshapen stone steps until both of my feet were firmly on the step and my sword was in position.

When I was ready I began slowly pushing the wooden plank of the trapdoor up with my empty left hand. As I did I kept the point of the sword in my right hand aimed straight at the end of the wooden plank where I intended the first opening to appear.

My thinking was simple—if someone was waiting up there to stab or slice down at me, I intended to use my sword to slip through the opening to turn away his blade, and then let it continue on to stab into him as deeply as possible. If that succeeded, I would try to hurry through the trapdoor and put a wound on anyone who was with him. Normally, of course, I would have tried to kill everyone but the Commander said we needed prisoners to question.

The problem was that I did not know on which side of the trapdoor someone might be standing and, thus, where the thrust would come at me. So I held my point only as close to the trapdoor as I could get it and still have my blade in position to turn aside a blade coming at me from where I expected the trapdoor to first rise.

When I was ready, I took a deep breath and used my left hand to slowly push up on the middle of the wooden plank in such a way as would cause it to rise at one end. Something was weighting it down. But I kept pushing. It was heavier than I expected. But I increased my pushing until there was a slight and very strange sucking sound as the plank gave way and began to rise.

Initially the wooden plank, for that is what it was, only went up enough to provide me with about an inch of opening at one end. That was all I needed to get my first look at what was outside the tunnel exit. What I saw was nothing.

There was no one in sight so I shifted my hand slowly lifted the plank higher and higher until there was an inch or two of open space all around it. Still nothing. Then, all at once, I became aware of a somewhat foul smell and then, a moment later, the familiar sound of an animal snorting. *Damn. Yuck.*

I turned my head down and whispered my news very softly.

"Pigs. It is a pig sty, Commander.

"The opening comes up in a pig shed with a low roof so only pigs can get under it. There is no one about except some pigs.

"Wait. Yes there is. I can see a woman. It must have been the woman whose voice we heard. She is walking this way to see why the pigs are excited and moving about."

"Come down. Let me look," the Commander ordered in a similar low whisper.

There was silence in the tunnel as I stepped down whilst still holding up the plank and the Commander slowly reached up to join me in holding up the plank, and quietly climbed up on to the first stair to take a look. A moment later he lowered the plank and stepped down.

"Then he held his finger up to his lips in the age-old order for silence and whispered a decision that only the men nearest to him could hear.

"Shh. Everyone be quiet. We will leave the exit undisturbed since it is not likely to have been used to get into the palace. Pass the order on to the man behind you to turn around and for everyone start pulling back."

Something George did not say out loud at the time, but later discussed with his lieutenants in some detail, was that the escape exit through the pigsty would also be a good way for the Company to secretly get men into the city if that should ever become necessary. They would be able to find pigsty because he had seen a useful landmark, the distinctive dome of an Orthodox village church.

Chapter Twelve

The Big Eye and more dead archers.

We bid farewell to the pigsty and marched back the way we had come. The men who had been bringing up the rear were now leading. Our rear guard led the way until we came to where the tunnel had forked and we had turned off to the left.

Being in the tunnel had somehow gotten easier. We were getting used to walking in it and becoming more and more relaxed, at least I was. Somewhere along the way David Black had taken off the lines that had been attached to his ankles when he was walking out in front of us.

When we reached the fork in the tunnel we stopped for a few moments to put fresh candles into our lanterns and piss against the tunnel wall. I took advantage of the stop to take a swig of water and finish off my cheese and chicken.

At that point, Commander Courtenay had us squeeze past each other and return to our original marching order. A few minutes later I was once again walking in the third position immediately behind the Commander and David Black who had remained as the first man in our column.

Lieutenant Commander Harcourt was right behind me and trying not to step on my feet. This time we took the other fork, the one that branched off to the right. It was not long before the tunnel forked again.

****** *Lieutenant Richmond*

We came to another set of rough stone stairs leading upward only a few minutes after we stopped for a piss break and to restore our original marching order. The Commander stopped at the stairs and held up his lantern to look at them.

A moment later the Commander drew his sword, held his finger up to his lips to order silence, mouthed "quiet; pass it on" to me, which I did. Then he gestured for Sergeant Black to climb the stairs.

I, of course, immediately drew my sword when the Commander did and so did everyone else; the distinctive sound of swords being drawn from their sheaths rippled down the line of men behind me. No one said a word.

David Black and his lantern led the way as we began slowly and quietly climbing the winding staircase. It wound in tight circles to the right and turned out to be quite long. We had either been further below the city than we realized or it was taking us to a floor above the ground in a big building, or perhaps both. We had no idea

In the flickering light I watched as David Black's lantern suddenly stopped. He had come to a landing at the top of the stairs and could go no further. Commander Courtenay held his finger up to his lips and motioned for David to move back and for me to come forward and join him.

David and I pulled in our stomachs and eased past each other on the narrow stairs. What I saw as I got past David and reached the Commander was a low and narrow wooden door at the top of the stairs. The stairs stopped at the door and the ceiling in front of the door was low. We had to bend our heads to stand in front of the door and look at it. There was barely room for the two of us.

The top of the doorway was even lower than the ceiling and it had a very narrow width. We would have to bend our heads even more and turn sideways to get through it. It was definitely a defensible door and it was set in a stone wall. There seemed to be some sort of black mould on the wall stones around the door.

Commander Courtenay was holding up his lantern and inspecting the door as I joined him. I promptly held my lantern up and did the same. As I did I became aware of the smell of the beeswax candles drifting up from the lanterns below me.

There was silence on the other side of the door and on the stairs. The only sound I could hear was the periodic faint scuffling of our men's sandals as they moved around on the stairs below me and a choked off sneeze from someone who had gotten too much dust and candle smoke.

I watched intently as the Commander put his lantern down and motioned for me to do the same. When I finished putting it down, he began gently pushing on the door to see if it would open. My sword was ready in case someone was waiting on the other side. The door did not yield.

Suddenly, to my surprise, the Commander handed me his sword and held up his lantern to closely examine the door. I took it and then was further surprised to see that he had a knife in his sword hand and was gently moving its blade up and down in the crack between the wooden door and the door frame around it. *Where did the knife come from?*

Commander Courtenay spent quite some time exploring the gap between door and the doorframe. Sometimes he could move his knife up and down in the gap; other times he could not. At first, I did not understand what he was doing, but then I did—he was trying to learn how and where the door was barred and if it was anywhere joined to the wall in which it was set.

******

"Sergeant Perkins is to come up very quietly; pass it on."

The Commander leaned over whispered the order down the stairs. He did so as soon as he finished probing the door. His knife, I suddenly realized, had somehow disappeared. One moment it had been in his hand, the next moment it was gone.

It did not take long before I could see a sturdy-looking sergeant making his way up the stairs towards us carrying a great long-handled hammer. I knew him slightly. His name was Perkins and he had been walking not too far behind us. There was a great deal of tension in the air by the time he reached us.

More orders were whispered.

"Everyone is to move down four steps to make room at the top to for the hammer to be swung. Pass it on."

And then the Commander whispered an order that I appreciated.

"Lieutenant, you stay here with me; Sergeant Perkins you come up and stand behind the lieutenant. Wait there but be ready to step up and take the door if we step down to give you room."

The order was given so softly that I barely heard it.

"Lieutenant, Sergeant Perkins, listen closely, lads," he whispered into our ears when Perkins reached us.

"There are two bars on the door and no hinges. The lieutenant and I are going to try to lift the bars off using our knife blades. We will try the top bar first.

"If we succeed and the door falls down, Lieutenant Richmond will go in first. I will go second, and you, Perkins, will have to go third and bring your hammer in with you so none of the lads who follow us trip over it. David will come in behind us. Do you both understand?"

We both understood, at least I did, and whispered our "ayes."

"But here is the thing, Sergeant Perkins. You will have to batter the door down with your hammer if Lieutenant Richmond and I are unable to lift the bars off. If using the hammer becomes necessary, I will give you the order and the lieutenant and I will step down a couple of steps to give you enough room and hold up our lanterns. But be damn sure not to hit us or anyone else when you start swinging that thing."

****** *Lieutenant Richmond*

It seemed to take forever for the line of men below us to move down the required four steps. I held my knife in my left hand and used it to explore the door to find the whereabouts of both the bars so I would be ready. My sword was held tightly in my right. The Commander was on the left side of the door; I was on the right.

"We will try the upper bar first. If we cannot get it off, we will try the lower bar," he whispered. "Aye," I whispered back.

In the dim lantern light we inserted our knives into the crack between the door and the stone wall, and raised them until we could feel the wooden bar on the other side. Then the Commander nodded at me and we slowly began to lift the bar using our knife blades.

It was a heavy bar to lift one-handed with the end of a knife, but we got it higher and higher until it was free and fell forward. The loud noise as the bar hit the floor on the other side of the door was enough to wake the dead. Some of the men standing below us jumped and moved about.

The Commander and I did not hesitate for a second. As fast as possible we moved our knives to get them under the second bar and begin lifting it. It seemed to be heavier but, finally, it too came up.

There was another crash on the other side as the second bar hit the floor. It seemed like it took forever even though it could not have been more than three or four seconds. Both the Commander and I had felt the bar come loose and had begun pushing on the little door as soon as it did. The unhinged door tipped over into the room on the other side from where we were standing with a loud crashing sound.

I did not hesitate when the door went over in front of me. I instantly lowered my head and turned sidewise to go through the now-empty door opening with my sword and right arm leading the way—and then charged across the fallen door towards the middle of what appeared to be some kind of large hall. I was the first man into the room. The Commander, Sergeant Perkins, Lieutenant Commander Harcourt, and David Black were right behind me.

******

We instantly realized we had come into an astounding place the likes of which none of us had ever seen. The ceiling was quite high and there was a huge and unblinking great eye covering most of the wall area on the left side of the room. Just beyond the middle of the room there was a raised area with some sort of a large chair on it.

Near the chair was an upright book holder similar to what one would see in a church. It was where a priest might stand when he was gobbling at his flock about what God wanted them to do and the need for more tithes and such if their souls were to be saved. But it was clearly not a church for prayers and money-raising as there were no crosses and not a mosque because there were no rugs.

The great eye watched over the hall. There were wall openings all around the room to let in light and some sort of long painted screen, almost a wall, behind the raised area. There was a long wooden table without benches along the wall opposite the eye. Several unlit lanterns were on the table, but nothing else.

I took everything in with one glance as I moved over the fallen door and into the room. Nothing made sense so I did what any man would do under the circumstances—I shifted my sword to my left hand and made the sign of the cross with my right.

I was still making the sign of the cross when the long painted screen at the end of the room was suddenly pushed over and a great shouting as a band of armed men carrying spears and clubs charged over and around it to get at us. There were more than a dozen of them and they had been hiding behind it and waiting for us. Their loud shouting and attack was a complete surprise.

The fighting that followed did not last long. I managed to turn aside the spear of the first man to reach me and slash him in the neck with my return stroke. But the next spear got me and pushed me to the floor before I could get my sword back down to turn it aside. And then I felt several others push into me and hold me down when I tried to get back on my feet.

Strangely enough, I did not feel anything even though I could not move when I tried to get back on my feet. For a few seconds I listened to the shouting and tried to understand what was happening and what was being said. But it was all so confusing that I quit trying.

Instead I somehow began thinking of Anne and could see her quite clearly. She was alone and reaching out to me. I was very pleased. And look at that—our roof needs a visit from the thatcher.

Chapter Thirteen.
We are surprised.

Sergeant Perkins, the hammer man, was the third man into the room. He and Lieutenant Richmond had hurried in behind the Commander. Lieutenant Commander Henry Harcourt was the fourth. One or two of the men who came through the door behind them also made it into the room before the ambush began. The archers had all gone through the door ready to fight, but the surprise assault that fell upon them was too big and they were ill-prepared for the fight in that they did not have even small shields to turn away the attackers' spears.

The result was inevitable: the handful of surprised men who made it into the room were instantly overrun.

Only one of them escaped, a short and very strong two-stripe chosen man by the name of Billy Bishop from Ramsgate.

Billy had been the only name Billy ever had until he ran away from home and made his mark on the Company roll. The apprentice sergeant doing the scribing to record Billy's enlistment had asked him a few questions about himself and, upon hearing that Billy had once been an altar boy for the Ramsgate church, announced that the Company already had at least one Billy Church so he had a choice between being on the Company roll as Billy Bishop or as Billy Priest.

Being ambitious and knowing the difference, Billy had chosen to be a Bishop. What he never told the apprentice sergeant or anyone was that it was the church's priest he had been running from when he went for an archer. Someday he had promised himself at the time, he would return to Ramsgate, tell the priest he was a bishop, and kill the bastard. It was a young boy's dream and long forgotten.

Billy had been the sixth man in the archers' tunnel column and was just stepping into the room when the unexpected attack began. He had somehow kept his wits about him enough to step backwards through the door when he saw the spear carriers coming at him. Even so, he had been speared in the thick part of his leg above his knee as he did. That happened because the man behind him was still trying to move forward and blocked him from getting back through the doorway soon enough.

The thrust of the spear helped push Billy back through the doorway. The spear was somehow pulled out of Billy's leg as he scrambled backwards through the door. And then the direction of the spear's push and the wound in his leg caused Billy to fall off to the side of the door as soon as he went through it.

Billy quickly dragged himself up against the wall next to the door to escape the several spears that instantly began being poked through the door opening—and became a Company legend as a result.

From where he fell bleeding against the wall next to the door, Billy had watched and listened to the leaderless shouting and chaos amongst the leaderless rank and file archers on the steps below him. He could not see them in the dim and flickering light, but he could hear enough to know exactly what was happening.

Several spears were soon being stabbed through the open doorway in an effort to clear away any of the archers who might have been front of it. One of them just missed Billy as he scrambled towards the wall next to the door in a desperate effort to avoid being stabbed again. He was seriously wounded and he knew it even though the pain had not yet started.

A second or two later, and seeing nobody immediately in front of the doorway because all the archers except Billy were on the stairs below it, one of the attackers started to come through the door.

No one will ever know if the enemy spear carrier was trying to come through the door just to look or if he really intended to attack the men on the stairs—because Billy crouched and waited until the attacker stuck his head out, and then put all the strength of his archer's strong arms into a slicing two-handed swing of his sword to the back of the man's neck.

The sight of the man's head rolling down the stairs in the dim light so distracted the archers gathered on the stairs that one of the archers stumbled and took down two others as he fell. It was, the men later agreed, as if a carved wooden ball had been bowled on the village green.

As you might imagine, the men who fell on the stairs quickly recovered and scrambled back to their feet with their swords at the ready—and Billy was thereafter known as Billy Bowles until the bolt of a Genoese crossbow took him some years later.

Billy's end came when he was a lieutenant serving on one of the Company's transports. By then his son, Andrew, had joined the Company and made his mark using the name Bowles. Andrew ended up marrying a merchant's daughter and returning to England, whereupon over the years that followed his descendants became quite well known as useful courtesans and parliamentarians.

The other thing Billy did on the day of the attack on the tunnel searchers, however, turned out to be much more important in terms of how the Company reacted to the attack in the days that followed and the Company's future—he remembered seeing the Commander go down fighting and he remembered seeing the big eye on the wall.

Lieutenant Commander Henry from Harcourt

The end of my time in the Company came when I followed close behind the hammer carrier as he went through the door behind George and Lieutenant Richmond. We went in fast as soon as the door bars were lifted and the door at the top of the steps fell into the room. The man coming up the stairs behind me was so anxious that he stepped on my foot and damn near tripped me.

It was right after I came through the door when it happened. Some sort of low wall on the far side of the room was pushed over and a great gang of men rushed over it shouting their battle cries. I barely had time to get my sword up and start to move towards the Commander when the first spear got me. And then a couple of others did as well and pinned me to the floor.

Oh dear God, they got George too... Maybe I can ... Oh no. .... My poor wife, she will have to ....

****** *Commander George Courtenay.*

The long screen running across part of the other end of the room was suddenly pushed over towards us and a great mass of attackers came running over it to get at us. They had been in place hiding behind the screen when we entered. There was no time to form any kind of defensive position before the first of them reached me. I did not have time to do more than a hurried side-step to avoid the point of the first spear coming at me before, out of the corner of my eye, I saw the shadow of something coming towards the side of my head.

It must have been a hard knock for the next thing I was aware of was that I was on the floor and there was a lot of loud shouting all around me. There was only one thing to do so I did it—I kept my eyes closed and played dead.

All I knew at first was that I was face-down on some kind of wooden floor. After a while the shouting and sound of fighting stopped and I could pick out some of the voices—they were gobbling in Greek. At least it sounded like Greek to me.

But then I heard someone standing above me say something in crusader French. From the tone of the voice, it sounded as if he was giving an order.

"Tell them that this is the valuable one. See all the stripes on his tunic." ... "Yes, I am sure it is him. Get him out of here." ... "Hurry before the English can launch a counter attack."

My eyes remained closed as, a few seconds later, I felt someone take my sword and begin rummaging through my coin pouch. A moment later I was literally picked up off the floor and thrown over someone's shoulders.

I was almost six feet tall, well fed, and wearing a chain shirt under my tunic that added to my weight; so my carrier must have been a very strong man. He carried me down a flight of stairs, leaned against a well to rest for a few seconds and catch his breath, and then walked a short distance before taking a deep breath and giving a great heave that dumped me into the bed of a horse-drawn wagon.

My head banged so hard when I landed that I grunted in pain and became confused for a few moments. But I was also as surprised and pleased as a man might be under such trying circumstances—because the men who captured me had been in such a hurry that neither the man who carried me nor anyone else had thought to search under my baggy-sleeved tunic.

A great jumble of fears and ideas flooded into my head. Sooner or later they would search me, and probably sooner because I was wearing a rusty old chain shirt that someone would inevitable want for himself or to sell. And when they did search me they would find my wrist knives—which meant, I quickly decided, that I needed to try to escape as soon as possible while I still had weapons to assist me.

Three or four men immediately jumped in the wagon with me. I knew they did because the wagon bed rocked as each of them climbed aboard, and several of them stepped on my legs. Someone shouted an order, and there was a reply. Almost immediately a wagon driver-sounding command was given in what sounded like Greek, a whip cracked, and we lurched forward.

The wagon must have been in an alley because it was quiet and smelled most foul. But we soon turned left and moved out on to a regular city street. I knew we were on street because I could periodically hear street noises and the clickity-clack sound of the wooden wheels as the wagon bounced over the cobblestones.

At first no one in the wagon said a word, but then they opened up and began excitedly gobbling to each other in what was almost certainly Greek, although I could not be sure because I cannot gobble it myself. What I was sure was that my head was banging up and down against the wooden wagon bed like a galley drummer rapidly beating out a command.

I did not try to open my eyes and put my head up to look about. It would have been rather difficult since someone had one of his sandals firmly planted on my neck. It was my hope, of course, that my guards thought I was badly wounded and would leave me alone until I could escape. And that, I had already decided, was something I needed to try to do sooner rather than later.

Although I could not see, the men in the wagon must have been sitting on benches on either side with me in the middle. I knew that because their Greek-gobbling voices were on both sides of me and they were all above me. Unfortunately, I could not understand a word of whatever it was that they were saying.

Finally! Whoever had his foot on my neck took it off. I decided it was time to make my move before it was too late. What I intended to do was suddenly leap to my feet and go straight over the side of the wagon—and then run like hell.

I blinked my eyes in an effort to get a quick look at where the men were sitting so I would know where to go when I made my move. What I saw was more than a little disheartening —a couple of tough-looking men were grinning at me as they leaned towards me whilst holding their knives a few inches from my throat. I was, it seemed, not much of a mummer.

Goddamn it; they were expecting me to try.

After about ten minutes, the wagon turned off the cobblestoned street and came to a stop. A couple of men dropped the tailgate of the wagon, grabbed me by the legs and pulled me out.

I narrowly avoided being dropped on my head by opening my eyes as they did and mumbling "I can stand. I can stand" and trying to slide off so that I would land on my feet

My captors did not understand what I was saying, but they did seem to understand that I was willing to walk. They promptly decided, quite rightly, that it would be easier for them if I walked so they would not have to carry me. About all I could do to help myself escape as I walked was make a few deliberate staggers and missteps to suggest that I was too weak to be a threat.

What I saw as I walked was that the wagon and I were in the small bailey of a somewhat run-down walled compound such as might be the home and work yard of a carpenter or a cart wright. I had that thought in my head because there were stacks of wood and wagon wheels piled about and several carts and wagons that looked to be under construction. There were no men at work, but several women and their children were standing together in a little group looking at us.

I made no effort to look around and deliberately stumbled because I wanted the men who brought me to think I was no threat to them because I was still woozy and unsteady on my feet. It was not difficult because, as I realized when my feet touched the ground, I really was a bit unsteady. I was also quite thirsty.

******

"You English are not so tough," said the heavyset man in broken crusader French. He said it after I was roughly pushed into a cell-like small room and he had followed me into it. The room was dark because there were no wall openings. It also smelled as if people had been sleeping in it for many years.

It was not a prison cell was my first impression, at least I did not think it was. If anything, it was more like a monk's cell in a monastery or the sleeping quarters of a couple of apprentices.

The gobbler and the two men who came in with him had their swords drawn. I could see them by the light of the open door behind them. They were obviously ready to cut me down if I gave them any trouble or tried to escape

"We killed some of your men and took you easily," the heavyset man continued with a rather arrogant tone in his voice.

"And it is lucky for you that it was so easy for us. We were supposed to kill you. But you need not worry about that, at least not for a few more days. They told us you were valuable so we are going to get a ransom for you in addition to killing you."

He said it with a great roar of laughter and satisfaction in his voice. The men with him smiled and nodded their agreement when he turned to them and told them what he had said. The dejected look on my battered face probably encouraged them.

The speaker's appearance and speech gave me no idea who he was or what he was. So far as I could tell he was a Greek. He carried a sword but his clothes were not those of a merchant or priest. My initial thought was that he might be part of a church protection gang or a successful artisan such as a carpenter or mason.

"Who paid you to kill me?" I asked. "And how did you know I would be there or that I would be in the room where you could get to me and not still in the tunnel?"

He laughed when I asked him. And then he turned to the men with him and gobbled at them for a few seconds. And they laughed too.

It was about then that what he said suddenly hit home. *"We killed some of your men."* Who? Uncle Henry? Oh my God. What will I ever tell his wife? And who else—the lieutenant and Sergeant Perkins, the hammer carrier?

What also hit me about then was the realization that my captors had let me see their faces. That was when I knew for sure that they were going to kill me even if a ransom was paid. They had to do so because I could identify them.

My head was spinning with despair as my laughing and soon-to-be-rich captors left the room with big smiles on their faces. A moment later I heard the distinctive sound of the door's bar being dropped into place. I was a prisoner.

******

I was not alone in the darkness for very long. Suddenly I heard the bar on the door being lifted. A moment later, light flooded into the room as the door was pulled open. I could see a ragged young boy in the doorway. A man carrying some sort of club was standing behind him.

Taking great care to avoid me, the boy slunk into the room and grabbed up some filthy bedding that had been piled in the corner. He rushed out of the room with it whilst looking fearfully over his shoulder at me.

The door was immediately closed behind him and barred once again. The only good thing about the visit was that the room began smelling better after the boy removed the bedding —and I felt like kicking myself in the arse for not trying to make a run for it while the door was open.

Chapter Fourteen

Chaotic times and the great search.

The archers on the tunnel staircase had been caught by surprise when the fighting started, and then again when the head rolled down the stairs. Some had tried to push their way forward to join the fight and a few were overcome with indecision. The latter just stood there because they did not know what to do. In so doing, they blocked the way of the would-be fighters who were trying to move forward.

It was chaos with everyone was shouting orders at everyone else both amongst the surviving archers and in some kind of foreign gobble on the other side of the door. The headless body of the attacker Andy ha chopped lay halfway through the doorway pumping blood onto the doorway floor and the stairs below.

It did not take long before a semblance of order returned. The archer closest to the door, a sergeant, loudly announced what he was going to do and the men on stairs below him, for lack of anyone else to tell them something different, went along with it.

The sergeant's name was Harry Fletcher. His mother had been a Christian refugee from Syria and had helped feed her family when they reached Cyprus by carving and fletching arrows for the Company.

"Andy is wounded. I am going stay here with him and try to hold the door. Whoever is at the arse end of the column should run back to sound the alarm and get reinforcements. The rest of you can do whatever you damn well please."

With that announcement, and staying carefully to one side so a spear being poked through the door opening would not take him, Harry Fletcher cautiously climbed up to the top of the stairs and squatted next to Andy. He had just become the archers' decision maker.

"Where did the bastards get you, Andy?"

What Sergeant Fletcher was really asking, of course, was how bad are you hurt and can you continue to help hold the door?

"In my leg, Harry. A spear. It hurts like shite and I am bleeding out. But I can hold on for a while until you can get a sailmaker to sew me up."

"Scooch over closer to the wall so I can get past you, lad. I will take over guarding the door. You do whatever you can for yourself until we can get someone up here to help you.

"Hoy to the last man on the stairs. Take two lanterns and run back for a sailmaker and his needle. Andy needs some sewing." ... "And tell them to send up some flower paste as soon as possible. ... "And tell the reinforcements to hurry."

"And you there, Jack," he said to the next man down on the steps. "Get up here careful-like and see to Andy. He needs a bit of help with his leg."

With that, Sergeant Fletcher crawled over Andy to get next to the door opening. He raised his sword high with both hands as he did—ready to bring it down hard on anyone else who was fool enough to come through the door.

Suddenly, just as Sergeant Fletcher was moving into position, there was movement on the other side of the door. The headless body of the man lying in the doorway was grabbed by the feet and pulled back into room on the other side of the door.

It did not take long before the doorway was empty except for a puddle of blood. There was a lot of what was obviously swearing and shouting as the men who had attempted to pull their fallen mate to safety saw his that his head was missing. Then some kind of loud order was given and the shouting and swearing began to die away.

Sergeant Fletcher was not a fool as he crouched in the dim light provided by remaining lanterns and the open door. He understood what the absence of the sounds of fighting and the effort to retrieve the headless body meant—that the attackers were in full control of whatever was on the other side of the door. And that meant the Commander and the archers who had gone through the door with him were either dead or captured.

He also understood that if the attackers were going to try to get through the door and have a go at the survivors on the stairs, it would happen soon.

******

It became increasingly quiet, both on the stairs and in the room where the fighting had occurred, as Sergeant Fletcher waited with his sword ready to chop down on anyone who tried to come through the door. It might have been his imagination, Fletcher thought, but it sounded as if their attackers were leaving.

After a few minutes of silence, Fletcher announced what he intended to do.

"Jack, get ready to climb over Andy and take my place as soon as I move. I think they might be gone. I am going to chance a look when you are ready." ... "and you lot down the stairs get your arses ready."

The sergeant waited a moment for Jack's "aye" and a couple of mumbled responses from the stairs below him; then he carefully and very slowly began extending his head in an effort to look through the doorway to see what he could see.

Less than a minute later he was sure. All he could see from the doorway were the bodies the attackers had left behind when they retreated. They were all wearing archer's tunics. A puddle of blood was all that remained of the headless body.

"I think they are gone. No one is here," he shouted. *No one alive that is.*

"Everyone stay where they are. I am going to go in to check it out."

And with that the sergeant very slowly and cautiously slipped into the room. He moved quickly from body to body before he said anything more. When he looked back towards the tunnel entrance he saw Jack's head peering around the edge of the doorway to watch him. He also saw the big eye painted on the wall, but was so engrossed in checking out the fallen archers that he paid it no intention.

"They are all dead. All of our lads are dead." He shouted less than a minute later, and then he added "keep the doorway clear. Stay ready; no one is to come in or block the doorway until I finish my looking."

Of course the sergeant wanted the doorway clear. In the event anyone jumped out at him, he intended to run back and dive through the doorway to safety. He would take his chances on the hard stone stairs. He had quickly decided that a possible broken head or arm was better that than getting stabbed and killed.

There were two doors out of the room. One big door was in the corner of the room. A small one was in the wall opposite the big eye. The small one had a bar on it to prevent anyone from entering; the big one did not; its bar was on the floor next to the door.

Sergeant Fletcher moved cautiously to the big door and, as he did, he decided to open it and see what was on the other side. Before he opened it he took a deep breath and double-checked to make sure he had a clear path from the door he was about to open to the doorway to the tunnel on the other side of the room.

As he later told anyone who would listen, if there had been danger waiting on the other side of the room's one regular-sized door he intended to run to the tunnel doorway as if the devil himself was snapping at his arse and dive through it.

******

Sergeant Fletcher was no fool. Before he opened the door he took off the rope around his tunic that held his sword sheath, personal knife, and purse, and tied it with a good sailor's knot to the two hooked pieces of beaten iron upon which one end of the doors' wooden bar would normally rest to keep the door from being opened. He gave the line a little slack, but not much—just enough so the line would not be pulled tight until he opened the door a couple of inches to see what he could see.

Fletcher's reasoning was simple. His tunic rope would take the place of the door's wooden bar if someone tried to push his way into the room. It would let him open the door slightly before it stretched tight, but it would prevent the door from opening any farther. What he hoped, of course, was that the line might not be broken or cut until he had time to snatch up his purse and run to the tunnel entrance and dive through it to escape.

The sight of the bodies of the dead archers in the room had affected him greatly. He had already decided that if he was chased he would dive through the door and take his chances on the stone steps on which he would land.

When he was ready, Sergeant Fletcher took a deep breath, got a good grip on his sword, made sure his purse and other possessions were where he could instantly grab them, and turned his body as much as he could towards the tunnel entrance. He wanted to get the fastest possible start towards it if there was a danger waiting.

Only when he was totally ready did he begin using his free hand to push on the door until it opened a crack.

The door opened a crack. *Nothing.* He pushed it open until his tunic rope was tight and it could open no more. *Still nothing.*

What he saw was a small and totally empty compound whose entry gate was wide open. Beyond the gate was a busy street in which he could see walkers and carts going in both directions. Best of all, he saw that no one was in the compound or even looking into it.

Fletcher immediately shut the door and put the wooden bar in place to lock it. He and the surviving "tunnel rats" would live, he realized as he breathed a great sigh of relief, to fight another day.

Chapter Fifteen
The aftermath and a search.

The first messenger ran through the tunnel with his sword sheathed and carrying a lantern in each hand to light his way. He made good time and stumbled into the Regent's room in the Great Palace to sound the alarm to the astonished Regent and her equally astonished guards. The result of his arrival would later be charitably scribed as "all hell then broke loose and there was great confusion."

A small party of archer reinforcements, every archer then at the palace, all six of them, set out immediately for the scene of the fighting with the messenger and his two lanterns leading the way. At the same time messengers sent by the now somewhat hysterical Regent galloped through the city streets to the

Commandry and to the Company's concession with the news of the ambush and fighting. As you might imagine, the fighting and need for reinforcements grew to almost epic proportions as the story passed from man to man.

The initial reinforcements, all six of them, every man a veteran archer, followed the first messenger back to the scene of the fighting as fast as possible. On the way, they met the man who had been subsequently dispatched to fetch a sailmaker to sew up Andy Bishop's leg and damn near killed him before they recognized him as a fellow archer.

Erik, the Commander of the Varangian guards, had not accompanied the tunnel explorers on their second day. He was, however, nearby in his rooms at the Varangians' barracks. He was catching up on his sleep so that he would be awake all night while most of his axe-carrying men were, as they were every night, in the city's streets serving as the city's night watch and maintaining order.

The Regent's Varangian guards sounded the alarm when the first messenger arrived and one of them rushed to the Varangian barracks with the news. Erik gathered up all the available Varangians from their beds where they were sleeping after a night of patrolling the city, shouted orders that the requested barbering supplies of a needle and a roll of thread were to be fetched from the chest where the Varangians' barbering supplies were kept, and led all of his immediately available men at the double to the Regent's rooms.

When Erik and the now wide awake Varangians reached the Regent's rooms, they found the door to the tunnel open and the regent seriously distraught at the news about George and angry at being left with only a couple of Varangians to guard her when the handful of archers who had been left behind in her rooms rushed off to reinforce their mates in the tunnel.

There was an immediate problem—the Varangians who poured into the Regent's rooms did not know where to go in the tunnel. Indeed, it was the first time any of them except Erik even knew there was a tunnel. They also had no lanterns to light the way except the two the second messenger had left behind when he rushed off to fetch a sailmaker to sew up the wounded archer.

There was no question about it; the Varangians would have to wait for the messenger to return from the archers' concession with a sailmaker so he could lead them through the tunnel to the scene of the fighting.

Before the messenger returned, however, a totally out of breath Michael Oremus arrived. The major captain was soon followed by every archer who had been at the Commandry. He had brought them all.

The major captain himself was the first of the archer reinforcements to arrive. He had galloped back on the messenger's horse with his apprentice bouncing along behind him; the rest of the archers from the Commandry had to run all the way, and did so without waiting for even a second for those who fell out due to having weak legs and not being able to breath.

An equally out of breath Lieutenant Commander Lewes arrived at the palace at almost the same time along with the messenger who had been sent for a sailmaker. He brought with him his galley's entire complement of archers, about a hundred of them, along with two of his galley's sailmakers and their needles and thread.

Harold and his men had also run all the way. All an absolutely exhausted Harold knew as he and his men hurried through the palace gate was that George and some of the archers were fighting in a tunnel under the Great Palace and desperately needed reinforcements. That had been more than enough to get them moving.

It would be fair to say that the Empress's rooms and the hallway outside them were soon packed cheek to jowl with very excited sword and axe carrying men who did not know what to do or where to go.

"Quiet, Goddamn it. Quiet. Everyone is to go to the bailey and wait for orders."

****** *Erik the Varangian*

At first the only thing my men and I knew was that there was serious fighting somewhere near the Regent's room and that Elizabeth, the Emperor's Regent, was greatly distressed. My problem was simple—I did not know where the fighting was occurring and I would have no one to lead me there until the return of the messenger who had been sent to fetch a sailmaker to sew up the wounded. The messenger, it seems, had immediately gone on to the archer's concession at the harbour to fetch a sailmaker to sew up the archers' wounded.

I had no more than arrived at the palace with my men than one of Archers' major captains, a man I knew rather well, Michael Oremus, showed up with half a hundred out-of-breath archers from the Commandry. He too had heard about the fighting and also had no idea what to do or where to lead his men.

A few minutes later another hundred or so additional archers and a couple of sailmakers rushed into the palace from one of the galleys which were moored at the quay in front of the Company's concession. The messenger was with them.

The archers from the galley were led by a lieutenant commander I knew, Harold Lewes. All of them were carrying their longbows and quivers full of arrows and many of them were also carrying short swords and galley shields. My men and I had our great axes.

Almost immediately, and after more than a little confusion and shouting, the two archer commanders and I led our heavily armed men down the stone steps into the tunnel with the sailmaker's messenger carrying his original two candle lanterns and leading the way.

The two archer commanders and I were right behind the lantern carrier and had a relatively easy time of it because we could see where we were going. The men behind us, however, had to walk in the darkness. They had a hard time as they constantly stumbled in the darkness and hit their heads and equipment against the roof and sides of the tunnel.

It did not take all that long for those of us at the front of the relief column to reach a staircase and begin climbing. The rest of our force, however, was increasingly strung out far behind us and moving forward slowly, very slowly, in the tunnel's total darkness.

Our men made the best of their difficult circumstances. Each of the men behind the column's leaders walked in the total darkness using one hand to hold on to the tunic of the man ahead of him and the other held up in an effort to avoid banging his head and equipment against the rocks sticking out of the roof of the tunnel.

It was slow going in the darkness as shields, longbows, and heads constantly bounced off the low roof. The increasingly fearful men followed their orders and walked silently except for periodic mutters and curses when they stumbled or hit something.

The men walking at the front could see the lantern lights at the front of the column and moved right along; those walking in total darkness behind them, however, fell further and further behind. The column got more and more strung out. The one and only saving grace of the narrow tunnel was that it was so narrow that no one could turn off and get lost.

My place in the relief column was a good one. I was the third man walking behind the messenger carrying the lanterns. The two archer commanders walked in front of me and were immediately behind the lantern carrier.

It was difficult for me to keep up with the lantern-carrier because he was in a great hurry and I had to walk bent over because I was too tall for the tunnel. But I did. Even so, it was a great relief when we reached some stairs and began to climb them. It meant I could finally stand up straight again.

We followed the lantern-carrying messenger up the stairs, squeezed through a narrow door, and joined a number of men wearing archers' tunics in a large room at the top of the stairs—and my heart sank when I saw the tunics on the bodies and realized who they were and where I was standing.

Impossible. This cannot be. It is impossible.

****** *Commander Courtenay*

My prison cell seemed to a small room in an old and rundown daub and wattle building. I was in the home or work space of some sort of wainright or carpenter and his family and apprentices. At least that was my impression from what I saw during my short walk from the wagon to the building, and in the room when the young boy entered the room to retrieve his bedding.

Both before and after the boy arrived for his bedding I had flexed my arms and twisted my body and legs a bit to make sure I was not dizzy, in other words, to make sure I was fit enough to run if I had a chance.

I began exploring the room in earnest after the boy left with his bedding, and door was once again closed and barred. As my eyes adjusted to the dark I began to make out more and more of the bare outlines of the room by the light that leaked through the cracks and holes in the walls and its roof.

The pinpoints of light gave me hope that the walls were weak such that I might be able to escape by breaking through them or that I might be able to climb up through the thatched roof and jump down into the compound or into a street or alley.

It was not to be. I heard someone lifting the bar on the door and hurried back to slump in the corner as if I had been seriously injured and was harmless. It was, of course, a ruse; I wanted the door left open as long as possible so I could see more of the room and the roof over it.

"Are you comfortable, English?" My questioner spoke crusader French with a heavy accent and a satisfied, almost insulting, tone to his voice. He carried a sword but it was sheathed. Another man stood guard at the door. I could see him clearly because of the sun shining on him. He had a knife in his belt and was holding some kind of heavy club by his side.

"No," I replied very softly with a moan, and then told my lie as sincerely as possible. "I think something is broken inside my head. I cannot stand up without falling down." It was a believable lie because I had bled profusely from where I had been hit in the side of my head.

My plight did not impress him, but the door stayed open and he moved closer to listen. I was clearly not a threat. The man by the door was big and relaxed; the room was so small he could see my sad condition and hear everything that was said.

"Who are you? What do you want?" I asked very weakly. It was all I could do to get the words out.

He ignored my question and got straight to the point.

"I need to know the name of the man to whom we should send our ransom demands. Who should we contact?"

"Oh yes. A ransom. That would be good," I whispered even more feebly as I lifted my hand a few inches off the floor and weakly waved it to acknowledge his question. "You should go to the Company's concession and see ....."

I said it even more softly and mumbled the name as my head slumped forward a bit due to the seriousness of my injury. He asked me to say the name again. And since I was obviously not a threat, he leaned down so he could hear it. He had bad breath.

"His name is .. "

My questioner was still leaning forward and trying to hear my answer as my wrist knives came out their sheaths. He did not even have a chance to blink or make a sound as they both took him in the throat—one on the left side and one on the right.

I ripped both of my knives towards me as I leaped to my feet and, holding my knives out in front of me and ran straight for the man standing in the entrance to the room. *I had thought about screaming a battle cry to startle him, but decided against it because it might alert others in the bailey before I had a chance to get past them.*

"Hey," the man at the door said with surprise in his voice as I threw my questioner aside and ran at him with my knives outstretched.

He was a particularly big man, taller than me and he had a much bigger belly. My initial impression when I first saw him was that he was probably a gang member more used to intimidating people with his appearance than his ability to fight. I certainly hoped so since I was about to find out. I could see from the look on his face that he was more than a little surprised to see me coming straight at him with a knife in each hand.

My questioner's back had been towards the man in the door, and the light had been dim, so the big man probably had not seen my knives until he saw them coming at him. His mouth opened in surprise and he started to raise his club, but then he instinctively stepped back through the doorway and twisted away to his right in an instinctive effort to escape the on-coming knives—and partially succeeded.

Without slowing down, I went through the door and glanced off the big man as he was turning away. As I went past him, I dragged the knife in my right hand across his partially turned back, and then continued on past him and into the little courtyard where wagons were apparently being built and repaired. I did so without breaking my stride.

The compound's gate to the street was open, the man with the deeply sliced back began screaming in pain, and the sun was going down. Without slowing down, I ran right past two poorly dressed young men who were in the process of entering through the open gate, and turned right onto the street that ran along the front of the compound. They just stopped and gaped with their mouths open in astonishment as I ran past them.

    I turned to the right as I came out of the gate and continued running as fast as I could even though I had no idea where I was or how to find the Great Palace or the Commandry.

Chapter Sixteen
Confusion and suspicions.

The bailey in front of the substantial stone building where the attack had occurred was alive with lanterns and filled with armed men as the sun finished passing over Constantinople and darkness fell. It was the middle of September and the nights were already starting to get a bit chilly when the wind was blowing in from the sea.

"We are not doing any good here," Michael Oremus said to Harold Lewes.   There was resignation and bitterness in his voice. "I am going to take our dead and everyone except Peter Percy's men back to the Commandry."

"Aye, that is a good idea, Michael. Percy and his men can hold this place, and search it whilst Erik and his Varangians go off to spend the night in the city keeping order as they usually do.

But then Harold remembered something else.

"It seems to be the temple of some kind of religious order. We will need to find out more about it and question its members. Maybe they are a band of poisoners or hired killers like the assassins sent out by the old man in the mountains. If you remember, they tried to kill William once before in Alexandria."

"Aye, I remember," Michael said. "But I thought we made peace with them when we started buying their flower paste and selling it at our shipping posts?" It cannot be them. My God we have made them rich and us too."

Harold agreed.

"Aye, it is probably not true, Michael. Well, we will know soon enough who is using the building and have some questions for them, eh? In the meantime I am going to take the galley crews back to the concession and keep them there at a high state of readiness in case they are needed. We will moor our galleys up against the quay so their archers are instantly available as reinforcements."

"Excellent. And be sure to put a strong force on the Concession's gate so it cannot be shut to keep your men out of the city. And you best take a couple of the palace's horses and messengers with you in case you need to get word to me or Peter. I will do the same at the Commandry."

Harold Lewes smoothed his long white beard and, thought for a moment before he responded, and then said out loud what both men had been thinking.

"The city seems quiet. There is no sign that the murders and fighting that took Henry and George are part of an effort to raise the city against the Regent or weaken it for an invader. It feels more and more like the beginning of a coup by someone who wants to replace Elizabeth as the Regent. But who?"

Michael Oremus's response was what might be expected under the circumstances, and he said it with a great deal of intensity and emotion in his voice.

"Aye, Harold. It certainly does feel like a coup. I think you are right, by God. And when I find out who is behind it I am going to cut his guts out and hang his head from the city's main gate no matter who he is or his position. Prince or Patriarch it makes no difference. "

Michael continued after a pause.

"William and George were my friends, and every one of the others was an archer. We are going to see them properly revenged even if it is the last goddamn thing I ever do."

Harold grimly agreed. Even his apprentice, Archie Smith, instinctively nodded his head.

"Aye, Michael. And you can count on me being by your side and smiling when we do. But first we need to find George or whatever is left of him."

The men started to part, but then Michael spoke again.

"In the morning I am going to send a message to the merchants, churches, mosques, and Varangians asking them to announce that the Company will pay a thousand gold bezants for information about George that leads to our recovering him. Do you agree?"

"Yes, that is a princely sum and it is a good idea. But I think you should make a thousand if he if he is recovered alive, but only five hundred if he is not, eh?"

"Aye, you are right as usual. Consider it done."

****** *George Courtenay*

People walking about and cooking their evening meals on the street looked at me with a great deal of curiosity as I ran past them in the rapidly gathering darkness. But they ignored me, probably thinking I was running because I was either late for my supper or some kind of thief or robber making his getaway in the darkness.

From the voices I heard and the looks of the people's dress I could see by the light of the cooking fires in the street, I was fairly sure I was in one of the city's poorer Greek quarters. Hopefully it was one of the quarters where the Varangians kept the peace at night instead of the protection gang of the local Orthodox Church.

My problem was that I did not know how to gobble enough Greek to ask for directions. As I slowed down to a fast walk I reassured myself that my inability to talk to the Greeks should not be a problem because many of the Empire's Greek subjects also understand crusader French, the gobble that people were increasingly calling "English." The merchants almost all did and some of them were Greeks.

In other words, what I expected was that sooner or later I would come across someone who could tell me where the Hagia Sofia church was located. Once I knew the church's location, I would know how to get to everywhere else in Constantinople where I might want to go. Hopefully I would not be killed or recaptured before I knew where the church was located or step in a pile of shite before I got there.

Other things equal, I decided as I slowed down even more, the darkness was my friend and stepping in shite was an acceptable alternative to being recaptured because I did not run fast enough in the dark. My plan was simple—remain in the dark and lose myself in the city's crowded streets until I had put enough distance between myself and the wain wright's compound.

Only when I had put considerable distance from the wain wright's yard would I stop and ask for directions. And when I did I would only ask older people and women, never anyone where there was a man close by who might chase me.

So far only part of my plan was working. I had asked two women how to find the church, but both had merely shrugged and shook their heads. That was several cross streets back. It was time to make another attempt.

"Hagia Sofia? Where is it?"

I asked my question to a young woman, barely more than a child. She was holding an infant against her chest with one hand and bent over a cooking fire by the side of the street. She was poking at it with a stick that she held in her other hand. I put a questioning and friendly look on my face and waved my open hands in different directions in what I hoped was a friendly and questioning manner.

She was the third person I had stopped to ask, all women. The first two had merely shrugged, looked in surprise at my battered face when it was lit up by their cooking fires, and shook their heads in a manner that clearly indicated they wanted me to go away. After the second dismissal it struck me that my face was summoning fear rather than pity. I was a slow learner.

"Hagia Sofia?" I asked with a question in my voice and a questioning wave of my right hand. As I did, I used my left hand to cover the side of my face where it felt painful and turned it away from the flickering light of her little fire.

"Hagia Sofia?" she responded as she looked up quickly before returning to poke at her fire. The wood was clearly not fit for her purpose, but she was doing her best to get it going.

"Oui, Hagia Sofia," I said as I made the sign of the cross in the Greek manner and then held my hands together as if I was praying. *If anyone questions her, maybe she will say that the man who asked her for directions was a Frenchman.*

She looked up again at me, nodded her understanding, and pointed off to my left. "Hagia Sofia," she said. And then added some words I could not understand.

I smiled and nodded my thanks without saying a word, and made the sign of the cross to bless her. If my coin pouch had not been taken I would have given her a coin. She and her infant reminded me of the paintings of Mary and the infant Jesus that were in many of the Latin churches. She, of course, was not as beautiful as Mary and her infant periodically pooped and peed, something a God would never do.

She smiled up at me and went back to poking at her fire. I immediately began walking through the crowded street in the direction she had pointed. I could see where I was going because there was a half-moon above the city and the buildings along the street were not tall. It was light enough for me to see the outlines of people and carts in the street as I came to them, but not enough to see what was on the ground where I was stepping.

The evening was warm; the wind was not coming from the sea. If it had been I would have smelled the harbour and run towards it.

******

I had to stop and ask two more women tending their cooking fires before I finally saw the great church ahead of me in the moonlight. I knew I was getting close when the last woman I asked responded to me in crusader French. It was a great relief; I had made it to the Latin Quarter.

A pair of Varangians came into view almost immediately after I first saw the outline of the church against the moonlit skyline. They were identifiable by the distinctive turbans they wore on their heads when they were on patrol.

"Are you Varangians?" I asked as I hurried up to them. They heard me and saw me coming—and immediately moved apart and took up defensive stances with both hands gripping their axes. It seems that the people of the city rarely rushed up to them, especially when it was dark.

I realized what they were doing and immediately slowed down with my hands held high so they could see I was not carrying a weapon. At least I hoped they could see I was not. Getting chopped by an axe would have been a terrible ending after all my efforts to escape.

"Archer," I said as I came up to them. And I probably said it much too loudly because of my great relief at finding them.

"I am an archer. Can you take me to my friend Erik, your captain?"

It was about then that I realized I was both filled with joy at reaching safety and totally exhausted and thirsty beyond belief. One of them immediately spun me around and began patting me down to search for hidden weapons whilst his mate stood ready to chop me.

I held my hands as high as possible over my head whilst he searched me. As a result, he missed my wrist knives as most people usually did. It was when I was holding my arms up in the air that I first noticed I was trembling for some reason. Even so, I felt like laughing with joy; so I did.

Chapter Seventeen
What do we do next?

It was the middle of the night before a bloody-headed and exhausted George Courtenay walked up to the Great Palace's entry gate with two smiling and very hopeful Varangians holding firmly to his arms to help keep him upright.

Of course the two Varangians were smiling and hopeful; a few hours earlier they had been told about the huge reward that was being offered for George's safe return. They had not contributed much to his return, but they hoped it would be enough to earn at least some of it.

George's return resulted in almost as much chaos and confusion as had the first news of the fighting in which he and his fellow archers had been lost. The Regent rushed to his side and urgently summoned her Greek physician and a couple of spares, a Varangian guard ran to the Varangian barracks to inform his captain, and messengers galloped off to spread the word of George's return to the archers at Company's concession and the Commandry.

Numerous things immediately began occurring. The number of men leaving the Great Palace to spread the word was soon greatly exceeded by the number of men coming to see if it was true that George had returned alive and to find out from him what had happened.

Word quickly reached the Company's rank file archers and was particularly well-received. Their celebrations started immediately in the city's taverns.

As a result, there were dramatic increases in sale of wine and ale in the city and in the rental of women in the taverns, particularly those frequented by the archers. At the same time, the city's volunteer fire fighters left their wives and mistresses to turn out en masse with their buckets because they misunderstood the ringing of the church bells ordered by the Regent.

As might also be expected, a crowd of curious citizens, pickpockets, and small merchants selling food and drink began gathering at the gates of the Great Palace to see what was happening.

George missed most of the excitement. He was promptly honoured by the Regent insisting that he be carried off to a bed in the room next to her chambers "because the dear man is clearly too hurt and exhausted to go to his room in the Commandry."

A good night's sleep, however, was not in George' future. To the contrary, all night long he was constantly being awakened by new arrivals who wanted to see for themselves that he was actually alive and ask him what had happened, and by the poking and prodding and bickering of the learned Greek physicians summoned by the Regent. To the physicians he was just another lump of flesh to which they felt they had to do something to earn their coins from the newly established Regent.

It was not until the sun was almost ready to arrive that George was finally left alone to rest and recover. That was after George had become so angry at being constantly being poked and prodded and asked to pee and swallow potions that he pulled out his wrist knives and threatened to gut the next man who touched or talked to him.

More specifically, as a result of seeing George's knives and hearing about his reputation for using them, the Regent's physicians wisely decided he had been sufficiently barbered and would recover faster if they prayed for him and sacrificed a couple of chickens instead of constantly waking him up to take more foul-tasting potions and ask him how was feeling.

******

George finally woke up at mid-day. And then only because he had to pee because he had drunk a prodigious amount of water before he had finally been left alone to sleep. He found a number of archers waiting outside his door and was told the Regent herself had been in to look at him almost every hour since the sun arrived to light his room.

Harold was sitting in the room when George woke up. Michael Oremus and Erik the Varangian were with him. One look at Harold and Michael's sad faces and George did not have to be told if his fears about the fate of Henry and the other archers were true. He had asked about them when he returned, but his visitors and the physicians bustling about him had pretended not to know.

"All of them? Henry too?" he croaked.

"Aye. Henry and the others who went in with you are gone, may God rest their souls," Harold said mournfully.

"Who did it? And why, for God's sake?"

"We do not know, George, we just do not know. It is possible the attackers were members of a religious cult whose meeting place you entered.

"Inquiries are being made both by the Company and the Varangians, and there is a great deal of confusion and uncertainty, but it appears that the hall is or used to be the meeting place of the city's master masons and builders. Some sort of cult or secret organization apparently also uses it for their meetings. It is possible they thought you were entering it to attack them and they fought back. We just do not know.

"All of the city's wagon wrights were visited as soon as the sun arrived this morning. We think we have found the room where you were being held. There was blood on the floor, but no one was there to question and no one in the neighbourhood knows where the wright and his family are now. Is there anything else you can tell us?"

"I know very little other than what I told you last night when the Varangians brought me in. But the one thing I do know for certain is that the men who attacked us were not fighting back because we unexpectedly entered their meeting hall carrying weapons—the man I killed when I escaped said they had been paid to kill me, but they had decided to see if they could also get a ransom before they did."

"I know something important," said Erik the Varangian as he moved to close the door to the hallway so no one could overhear what he had to say. He had come into the room with Michael Oremus whilst Harold and I were talking.

"The killers had nothing to do with the Meeting Hall of the Master Masons where you were found. My men found the body of its caretaker this morning. He had been clubbed to death. And I personally talked to the men who meet there. They know nothing about the attack and swear they were not involved. They are among the most honest and reliable men in the city; I believe them."

"How can you be so sure?" Michael finally demanded. He and everyone else in the room had been surprised and quieted by what Erik had just told them.

"I know it for a fact because *I* am a member of the society that is lodged in the hall belonging to the city's master masons, and *I* know every single one of the men who meets there. They are all honest and reliable men and not a one of them has any reason to want you dead."

"But they were already waiting for us for in the hall of the Masons' when we got there," George protested as he took a drink of watered wine to relieve his wake-up thirst. It was quite tasty.

"Aye, they were waiting for you. That much is obvious. So whoever had them wait there for you must be someone who knew about the secret tunnel, and also knew you and your men were almost certain to be there sooner or later yesterday. And most important of all, it had to be someone who knew far enough in advance to be able to organize the ambush and kill the hall's caretaker so he would not be able to sound the alarm or identify them afterwards."

There was a long moment of silence. Then Michael spoke.

"You knew all that, Erik," Michael said quietly and ominously. "And you begged off and did not go out with George and his men on the second day. If you had not, you would have entered with them."

"Aye, I did know they would be in the tunnel," the Varangian admitted, "but so did half the city. The men who went with us on the first tunnel search spent the rest of the day and that evening in the taverns talking about the tunnels and how they would be exploring them again in the morning.

"So it could have been anyone who knew the tunnels were being explored and also knew that sooner or later that entrance would be found. And whoever it was, also knew that you, George, because of your position as the Company's Commander, would be amongst the first of the men to enter the room. All they had to do was get there early in the morning and wait for you to sooner or later show up.

"But they may have made a big mistake in using so many men to kill you. Men inevitably talk. So sooner or later one or more of your attackers will be overhead bragging or boasting about it. All my men need is to find one of them," Erik said grimly. "Then we will soon know the names of all the others and who hired them."

******

"Do you believe him?" Harold asked George after Erik left.

"I am not sure. Uncle Harold, I am not sure. He might fancy the Regent or the regency for himself. Or he might want me dead, in addition to my father and the Empress, so the Company would be less likely to support the Regent if he or someone else tries to replace her.

"On the other hand, he also knows the Company will continue to operate here and collect the Tolls even if I am replaced, and that I will sooner or later be gone to Cyprus and England. So why would he bother to go after me if the Company's next Commander might be even harder to deal with? It just does not make sense.

Michael made a helpful suggestion.

"Well, Erik is certainly right about one thing, Commander. There were a number of men involved in the attack. All we need is to get our hands on one of them to learn who the rest of them are and why they were supposed to kill you. And once we know who they are, we are likely to be able to learn who sent them.

George nodded his agreement, thought for a while, and then added another thought.

"You are right, Michael. The man who questioned me looked and sounded like someone who belonged to a gang of robbers or one of the church's protection gangs. All we need is one of them who can be made to talk.

"So how is this for an idea? We announce an offer that will be hard for a rank and file member of the attackers to turn down—the *first* man of the attackers who comes forward will receive a full pardon and a thousand gold bezants?"

"Aye," Harold agreed with his first smile in several days. "And we will hang the heads of all the others on spikes over the city gates, and our informant's as well if any of what he tells us turns out not to be true.

****** *Michael Oremus*

The announcement that a huge reward would be paid for information about the recent fighting that occurred when some archers were attacked caused a sensation in the city. It was accepted and believed to be true because a similar reward was immediately paid to the two Varangians who had helped rescue George and brought him to the great palace.

The Varangians received their reward coins in a hastily organized ceremony in front of the palace gate a few hours after George made his decision. It had been quickly announced by the city's criers and was such a novelty that hundreds of people turned out to watch.

They stood in a great throng, and many had their pockets picked, as they watched the gold bezants being counted one by one into the hands of the two Varangian guards. The two axe-carriers had not had much to do with George's return. Even so, paying them had been an easy decision.

George and his lieutenants had quickly decided that stiffing the Varangians on the reward was a very poor way to treat their allies and friends. More importantly, they knew that promptly paying such a huge reward would encourage others to come forward with information about both the attack in the masons' hall and the murder of the Empress and George's father.

Within hours of the reward coins being paid to the two axe-carriers and the announcement that another thousand gold bezants was available for information about the attack, everybody in the city knew about the new reward.

Even more importantly, the people of the city now knew what the Regent and the city's merchants and money lenders had long known—that the Company of Archers kept its promises and that providing assistance to the archers could bring a man or woman great rewards.

We met with the would-be informants at borrowed stalls in the market and at tables brought out from Commandry and set up in the shade of its walls.

Tips and accusations about the attackers and also about the killing of the Empress and the Company's former Commander poured in. Much of what we heard was gobbled in Greek and had to be translated by the merchants we hastily enlisted from the market to help us.

As you might imagine, the merchants all smiled a lot and claimed to have been pleased to be asked to help and provide space at their stalls. And they probably were—the Company, after all, was a very important customer.

Most of what we heard seemed to be wild shots in the dark or vengeful efforts to hurt someone the informant hated such as an abusive husband. Others were almost certainly deliberate falsehoods intended to remove a competitor or a rival for someone's affection.

And, of course, many were efforts to remove someone who stood in the way of the informant's advancement as was so often the case at the newly established monasteries and seminaries at the Ox ford near London.

Several of the leads we received, however, seemed promising. And the most promising of all pointed to Otto, the king of the Bulgarians, and his supporters.

Chapter Eighteen
Who can be trusted?

We were immediately overwhelmed with informants. The lines started forming as soon as the reward of a thousand gold bezants for "information as to who was responsible for a recent attack that killed some archers" was announced. The response began within minutes of the reward being loudly cried out on various street corners by the members of the city's Criers Guild.

Everyone in the city, or so it seemed, wanted to give us information and claim the huge reward. A few of those who lined up to come forward that afternoon claimed to been there as part of a band of robbers or a religious protection gang that had been hired to attack some archers. Even more said they knew or overheard someone who had been paid to join the attack.

Unfortunately, most of them did not even know that the fighting had occurred inside a building, others did not even know when it had occurred, and very few mentioned that spears were involved.

We listened to many reward-seeking stories all the rest of the afternoon and into the evening. Some of the story tellers sounded quite convincing even though they did not know where or when the fighting occurred.

Unfortunately, not one of the very few who correct said the fighting occurred yesterday and indoors also mentioned either the great eye that covered almost an entire wall of the Masons' meeting hall or the long wooden screen that the attackers had pushed over when they began their charge.

Our most promising initial lead came the next morning, two days after the attack, from one of the city's street women. She claimed to have been in a tavern in the Greek quarter on the afternoon of the attack with a drunken client who had boasted about having coins to spend for his drinks and access to her womanly pleasures because he had been on the winning side of a great fight the previous day.

What was significant was how he had described his role in the fighting to her, and the fact that he mentioned that it happened because he and his mates had been hired to kill someone, but had decided to try to collect a ransom for him before they did. He had carried a spear, the drinker told her, even though the fighting was indoors. All in all, it sounded very much like what we had heard of the fighting in the Masons' hall as it had been described by George and Andy Bishop.

The man who drank heavily while she sipped heavily watered wine and lifted her gown in the alley next to the tavern, she said, was a Bulgarian who wanted her company while he celebrated his last day in the city. He also told her, she said, that there had been some unexpected problems and he and his mates would be leaving as soon as it got dark to return to Bulgaria.

That evening she was questioned by three different archers and then by George himself. Her story was very convincing except for one problem—she claimed to have encountered him in a tavern in the Greek Quarter. That was a problem because Bulgarians looked to the Pope to tell them what God wanted them to do and, therefore, would have done their drinking in the Latin Quarter. *Or perhaps he was staying away from his normal haunts because he was supposed to hide?*

In the end, she was sent away with a gold coin and told to come back the next day for more coins if her story checked out. By then it was late in the evening. The Bulgarians would have been gone for more than a day if her story was true.

******

George and his lieutenants supped together late that evening to go over whatever had been learned so far as a result of the reward being offered. George himself was quite tired and had to struggle to stay awake, probably because the Regent had taken it upon herself to spend the previous night making sure he could still function after his recent ordeal.

"It could have been the Bulgarians, George," Harold said.

"The tavern girl's story rings true and it is well known that Otto the Bulgarian, him what fought with us against the Greeks, wants the throne for himself and does not think a woman should be the regent. I myself heard him say it and so did others."

"Aye, Uncle Harold, it could be. It could be. It would explain why he wanted to kill the Empress and ended up killing my father because he was with her, but why would Otto then risk everything by going to the trouble and expense of trying to kill me, eh?"

"Maybe he wants to take your .. uh .. place as the Regent's .. uh …friend and get power that way. He seemed to fancy her as I recall," Harold replied.

"Or maybe he wants his men and galleys to take the place of the Company as the Empire's toll collector and protector," suggested Michael. "Or he might even hope to become the next Regent or Emperor himself—instead of you."

George, as he had so many times previously, responded angrily.

"Not me, damnit Michael, and you know it. I am getting tired of saying it; I would rather be with the Company and spend my time in England and Cyprus than have to spend all my days in Constantinople dealing with the insipid arses that attend the court and pay for their rooms and food with flattery and meaningless gossip. So you two are never to bring it up again; and that is a goddamn order.

"In any event, we may find out more about the attack tomorrow. I have invited Erik to join us in the morning when we break our fast. He and his Varangians may have learned something from their inquiries."

****** *Erik the Varangian captain*

A messenger came late in the afternoon from George, the Commander of the English Company. He invited me to come to the palace in the morning to break my fast with him and talk about the attack and the current state of affairs in the city. I was not sure how to respond.

It was a worrisome invitation because the English suspect me of being responsible for both murders of the

Empress and their former Commander and the recent attempt to murder the archers' present Commander. Would they attempt to arrest me or kill me if I show up?

I merely nodded to the archer's messenger and said what he expected me to say.

"Of course I will come; I am honoured to be invited."

In fact, I was undecided as to whether or not I should attend. It would depend, I decided, on what I could learn of the archers' intentions before I was scheduled to arrive.

I immediately sent for both the captain of the palace guards and my first lieutenant to tell them what I wanted them to do.

The captain of the guards was told to watch the palace all night and, in the morning, question our spies among the servants. I wanted to know if there were any suspicious activities or preparations before I made a final decision about attending. If there were none I might show up. It was a decision I would make at the last minute.

My number two was told to stand ready to lead our men out of their barracks and launch an immediate massive assault on the palace with every available Varangian if the servants reported me taken or if I did not come out within one hour.

"The senior men of the English Company have always been trustworthy and dependable," I told my two lieutenants. "But now they suspect everyone, including me, and there is no way to know what they might do now that their Commanders have been attacked and some of them killed."

Erik the Varangian

The next morning the captain of the palace guard reported that everything seemed normal at the palace. He said he had personally questioned the guards on duty and our spies among the servants, and none of them had reported the arrival of any additional archers.

"So far as they know, the archers' Commander, Commander Courtenay, and two of his personal guards are the only ones who spent the night there.

"But the servants did say that two additional archers with many stripes on their tunics arrived separately early this morning, and that each was accompanied by a couple of guards and a young man who was some kind of an apprentice. They all said that it is quite common for the senior archers to break their overnight fasts together and talk in one of the private rooms.

"All in all, nothing has been reported that in any way suggests there might be a treachery underway. But those

English are tricky devils and I cannot be sure. And even just one or two of them can be quite dangerous as you well know."

In the end, I decided to walk over and meet with Commander Courtenay. I did so with my men ready to seize both the main entry gate and two of the doors into the palace, and lead a rescue through them.

George and his two senior lieutenant commanders were already in the room and sitting at the table talking when I arrived. It was a private room, as usual, because they did not want to break their fast in the great hall where the Regent's courtiers could listen to what was being said. *George seems to be tired. Perhaps he has not yet fully recovered.*

Several of the Company's apprentices were sitting and quietly listening at the end of the table. The guards that had accompanied George's senior lieutenants to the palace were nowhere to be seen. They were probably elsewhere breaking their fasts.

"I have news that might be helpful," I announced as I nodded to everyone with a smile and sat down.

"A party of Bulgarian merchants, about a dozen of them, left the city yesterday evening. They were on horseback except for a wagon that was carrying a man in it who might have been wounded.

"Also, one of our informers says that last week the protection gang from The Church of the Holy Apostles was hired to kill someone. It could have been you they were paid to kill, George, and your father and the Empress before that.

"What makes me think that they may be the people we are looking for is that, Gregorius Samaras, the bishop assigned to that church has also disappeared. He has gone off on a pilgrimage it is said. And some of the protectors and tithe collectors of the diocese are gone as well."

"Holy Apostles is a big Orthodox Church on the east side of the city, is it not, Erik?" George asked.

"Aye, Commander, it is. It is the city's biggest church in Constantinople other than the Hagia Sofia. And the missing bishop was one of the Patriarch's strongest supporters during the recent war. It was the bishop and the Holy Apostle's priests who tried to organize the city to rise up behind us and force open the city gate so the Orthodox army could enter and restore the Patriarch and Greek rule.

"That was not successful for them so perhaps they are now trying to get what they wish with plots and assassinations."

George nodded and asked me an important question.

"Do you think the Orthodox Metropolitan, I think his name is Andreas, has changed his mind and is involved in another attempt to return the Empire to Greek rule? If he is, it could be big trouble for the Regent, and thus for both your men and mine."

"I do not know, Commander, but I do not think so. According to the last I heard, and that was just a few days ago, he still enjoys living in the Patriarch's palace and does not want to give it up by helping the Patriarch return.

What I did not tell the Commander was it was not just something "I heard." Andreas himself told me that yesterday at our temporary meeting place when we met to discuss what those of us lodged with the Masons should do until the furore died down.

We would sooner or later return to where we were permanently lodged with the Masons. Of course we would. But there was no need to hurry. The hall would always be there because it had been made of stone by the city's master masons. Indeed, it would be there forever and so would we.

Chapter Nineteen
Surprising news.

Our morning meeting on the fifth day after the attack was held in an atmosphere of general disappointment for all of us. George was there along with me, Lieutenant Commander Michael Oremus, and Harold Lewes, the lieutenant commander responsible for all aspects of the Company's sea-going operations. Erik the Varangian captain was with us. He has begun joining us every morning so we could share the latest developments. *Or the lack of them.*

We were uniformly disappointed in that, despite the size of the reward on offer and the number of would-be informants it produced, there had once again been another day that yielded no useful information. We still knew next to nothing about either the murders of William and the Empress or the fighting in the masons' hall that cost us some of our best men and almost took George.

According to Erik, the wayward Orthodox bishop, Bishop Gregorios, has still not returned although some of his priests have done so. The priests said they had gone on a retreat to pray at a shrine in the mountains and did not know anything about the whereabouts of the bishop.

So far as they knew, or so the priests claimed, Bishop Gregorios had still been in his residence when they departed for the shrine, or so they claimed, and they had no idea where he might be. Erik said that he had several a couple of his men "talking to the priests" to check out their story, and that he expected to find it was true.

The only good news coming out of the meeting belonged to me and several men who were not present. I have been given another stripe and assigned to replace poor old Henry Harcourt, may he rest in peace, as the lieutenant commander responsible for preparing the Company's men to fight on land and keeping them ready to do so. I never thought it possible. Who would have thought a tavern girl's bastard such as me could rise so high.

George also announced what we had already known—that the Company would have to grow using our Venetian prizes so that it would not become overly dependent on the tolls we are collecting. Accordingly, the Company was somewhat reorganized and there were a number of promotions as well as some reassignments.

A captain by the name of Thomas Woods has been promoted to major captain and will report to me as the number two commander of the Company's foot archers and fighting on land. George's son, Young George, or George Young as he is now increasingly known, will be Wood's apprentice and scrivener just as he was mine when I was the number two. George's younger brother, John Courtenay, traded places with Harold's apprentice and will now go to sea to get sailing experience as Harold's apprentice sergeant and scrivener.

Also, it has been decided that each of the Company's lieutenant commanders, every one of them including me, will now have a lieutenant permanently assigned to assist him in his duties. Harold already had two on his galley, an experienced sailor man by the name of Johnny White and Jack Smith who commanded his archers.

George had decided, he told us, that an experienced man with the rank of lieutenant would be assigned to assist each of the Company's lieutenant commanders who did not already have at least one. The Company's lieutenant commanders were all already stretched thin and would need the additional assistance, he explained, now that it has been decided to grow the Company using our Venetian prizes. I, of course, enthusiastically agreed.

Sergeant Samuel Keene, him what told Henry to get a hold of himself and remain steady in the tunnel, has been promoted to lieutenant. Ordering Keane's promotion was the last thing Henry did before he was killed. Keene will be my personal lieutenant. Yoram, Richard, and Bishop Thomas will select their own lieutenants and apprentices.

George still has neither an apprentice nor captain major to take my place as his assistant, but he said he had someone in mind for his captain major and he will take the next apprentice Bishop Thomas sends out from Cornwall to help him with his scribing and run his errands.

****** *Michael Oremus*

Our meeting had no more than ended and we had walked out into the huge walled bailey of the Latin Empire's Great Palace, when an exhausted courier galloped into the bailey on a badly blown horse. He was carrying, the courier loudly announced, an important message for the Regent.

We were standing in the bailey saying our goodbyes to George when the courier arrived. Erik was with us. The messenger's urgency and the fact that he had staggered from fatigue and almost fallen when he dismounted, and also that had ridden his exhausted horse almost to death, caused us to linger to see what was up.

"For the Regent's eyes only," the courier said brusquely as he dismissed Georges offer to carry it to her and brushed past his outstretched hand. He hurried into the palace. As you might well imagine, all four of us turned around and followed him back through the door we had just exited.

The courier stopped to get directions from the servant at the door, and then hurried into palace's great hall where the Regent was socializing with the do-nothings of her court. She saw him enter and after a bit a dithering while she got rid of an elegantly dressed court dandy who was trying to toady up to her, the messenger extracted a parchment from his pouch and handed it to her with an elaborate bow.

Elizabeth Courtenay, George's "dear friend," who somehow had the same family name as George and was now the self-proclaimed Regent of her much younger brother, in turn, probably because she did not know how to read, broke the seal and handed it to her ever-hovering chancellor.

Years later I learned that the Courtenay's were an old family of very minor French nobles from Normandy. George's father, William, who had been born a serf without a family name, had liked the name and adopted it for his own after he took a castle from one of English offshoots of the French Courtenays.

William's taking Courtenay for his family name had apparently occurred after he and some archers killed one of the English line of Norman Courtenays and ended up with his castle at Okehampton. It turned out to be quite a good name because one of the Courtenays from France had gone crusading and ended up as the Emperor in Constantinople after the crusaders took the great capital city of the Greeks.

Now the two totally unrelated Courtenay descendants, one a descendant of an old French family and the other the descendant of an English serf, were periodically "knowing" each other in the biblical sense and the Company was protecting the self-proclaimed new Regent and her younger brother's Latin Empire in return for the Empire's toll coins. The world is small indeed and no one can deny that God's Will is truly great.

******

Elizabeth's elderly and very feminine chancellor, a Benedictine priest who had served both her mother and her mother's crusading brother who had been the first Latin Emperor, had seen the courier arrive and knew what would be expected of him. He had hurried to her side to read the message to her. He immediately opened the parchment and began whispering what it said into her ear as he read it.

I could tell it was important because her eyes widened and she had a shocked look on her face by the time he finished reading it to her the first time. By the time he had finished reading it to her a second time she had a very angry and determined look on her face. The Regent was, in a word, furious.

She grabbed the parchment out the chancellor's hand, motioned for George and Erik to follow her, and stormed out of the court. The courtiers gaped at her in silence until she was all the way up the stairs, and then they began chattering away in great excitement.

They were like me; they had no idea what the message said. But that did not hold them back from talking about it. All around me well-dressed fops and courtesans were everywhere gathered in small groups and feverishly speculating as to what might have happened to distress the Regent.

The Regent's boy husband and her even younger brother, Robert, the boy-Emperor, were nowhere to be seen. They were off somewhere playing together.

It was one of the few times I had ever been in the court when the courtiers were present. I wondered how things would have proceeded if either her husband or the young Emperor had been there. I decided to ask Erik when I had a chance. He would know if anyone would.

****** *Commander George Courtenay*

Elizabeth's imperious summons rankled me, but not much. I was, after all, greatly curious as to the contents of the parchment message and I knew I could put her in her proper place when she crept into my bed later in the evening.

Erik and I followed the Regent up the stairs to her private chambers. We knew it was serious when she strode right through her private receiving room and into her private room beyond it where she slept and pooped, the room that connected through a door to the adjacent room where I was, with her enthusiastic nightly assistance, still "recovering from the attack that almost took you from me."

Elizabeth was beside herself with rage as Erik shut the door behind us. She shook the parchment angrily as she turned back to look at us and give us the news.

"According to our ambassador to my Bulgarian subjects, their treacherous prince, that swine, Otto, has just renounced his fealty to my brother and proclaimed himself as the Emperor of the Latin Empire." *Our ambassador; My subjects*?

As Elizabeth angrily told us about the message, she had a look on her face that said "what are we going to do about it?"

"May I see it?" I asked as I held my hand out. She instinctively handed the parchment to me without thinking.

"Yes," I said as I read it. "That is what it says, alright."

"I want you to take your men and go north immediately and kill him. March or sail, I do not care how you do it. But he cannot be allowed to do this to me." She stomped her foot as she made her demands. *Me?*

"Whoa. Wait a minute. We need to think this through." I said. Erik nodded.

"There is nothing to think about, George. He killed your father and my mother and tried to kill you. If we do not kill him first, he will almost certainly try again and keeping trying until he succeeds."

I did not immediately agree.

"There is a lot to think about. We do not know if he killed your mother and my father or if he tried to kill me. And we do not know if he has the Pope's support or the support of any other of the Empire's princely states. All we know at the moment is that he wants to replace Robert as Emperor and you as Robert's Regent. We have always known that.

"And rushing off to fight a war before you are ready and know what you are getting into is not smart, not smart at all. In fact, it is damn stupid. And besides, there may be better and easier ways to bring him down or kill him if it really needs to be done to protect your empire and my company. I need to think about it and so does Erik."

And then, as she stood there glaring at me, I added my definitive response to her order.

"So cool your heels, goddamnit."

Erik looked away as we argued. I think saw him smile.

Chapter Twenty
Who is secretly seeking advancement?

Some of the courtiers saw Erik and me coming down the stairs after our meeting with the Regent. They hurried over to get the news. We waved them away and lied by promising to tell them all about it later. No words passed between us until we were outside and alone in the palace's great bailey.

"What do you really think about Elizabeth wanting my Company to go north and fight the Bulgarians," I asked Erik after we finally got out of the palace and walked out into the bailey so we could talk privately.

"I think she is mostly fearful about losing her new powers and determined not to go back to Epirus as merely the wife of a boy whose son may not even end up being the Epirus heir. I also think we both need to be careful, very careful, before we actually do anything she orders.

"For one, you and your archers marching or sailing north to Bulgaria would leave only me and my Varangians to defend the city against both an Orthodox rising from within and another attack on the walls. My men and I might be able to do one or the other, but not both at the same time.

"For another, we still do not know who killed your father and the Empress, let alone who tried to kill you. What if it was the Patriarch and he gathers another army? He very well might do so and order the city's Orthodox to rise against the Latins whilst you and your archers are gone north to visit the Bulgarians.

"For that matter, it could be the Latin archbishop or his priests who want a new Regent or an Emperor on the throne who will give them the city's Orthodox churches and tithes. Or it could have been the Moors or someone else who hates your father. We just do not know."

"Aye, Erik, you are right about the need to move carefully and think before we do anything, you certainly are. But if it is the Greeks, cannot your friend the Metropolitan stop them from rising against Elizabeth and Robert by telling them that God does not want them to rise?"

"Not if the Patriarch says God wants the Regent and her brother, Emperor Robert, replaced by a Greek prince or someone like himself. All Andreas can do if that happens is to try to weaken the revolt inside the city by providing it with bad leadership and reasonable-sounding orders that conflict with one another just as he did last time."

We talked for quite some time, ended up deciding to do nothing except fend off the Regent's demands, and agreed to continue meeting every morning at the Commandry to break our fasts together and talk. I had much to think about before I met Elizabeth again, as I almost certainly would later in the evening.

****** *Lieutenant Commander Michael Oremus*

George seemed very distracted and thoughtful that afternoon after he returned from the Great Palace. He had summoned Harold and me to a meeting at the Commandry. It was there, over a bowl of wine, with our apprentices listening, that he told us about Otto's decision to try to get the emperorship for himself.

Then he totally astonished us by telling us what the Regent wanted the Company to do because we collected her toll coins and kept them in exchange for protecting the city—sail or march north to attack the Bulgarians, and somehow get to Otto and kill him to remove the threat from Bulgaria once and for all.

And there was more.

"There is something else muddying the waters that we also need to think about. The Regent is pregnant from that Orthodox boy she married, the Epirus heir. If the thought of having another heir in his line pleases that old despot in Epirus, he might be willing to send another Orthodox army north against Otto to help her stay as the Regent until Robert comes of age. Or he might even bring his army here and try to replace her if we take our archers north.

"On the other hand, the poxed old bastard also might try to get rid of Robert and use the fact that Elizabeth is both in his family and the last living descendant of the old emperor as way to justify taking the emperorship for his son as her husband or for the new baby if it is a boy. Either way he could claim to be the Regent, though I doubt the Pope would agree unless he had enough coins to buy an enormous amount of prayers.

"Indeed, that sly old fox, Epirus, might even agree to become a Latin to get the Pope's approval, or even to make Epirus another papal state. I certainly would if I was him and wanted to be the Emperor or the Emperor's regent.

"But will Epirus wait to see if the baby is a boy and survives, or will he act immediately? And what will the Pope do when he finds out about Otto and worries about what Epirus or the Patriarch might do?"

I was surprised at what George said, particularly about Epirus, and said as much.

"One thing is certain, the Holy Father will never accept an Orthodox emperor for the Latin Empire. Never. He will almost certainly support Otto or some other Latin, *unless* Epirus converts or Elizabeth produces a boy who is raised as a Latin."

Harold was not so sure.

"It is always possible that nothing will happen. Epirus may decide to wait to make his move until he knows if his coming grandchild is a boy and he survives being born. But even if Epirus waits, the Company's contract to collect the tolls could still be threatened if Otto or another prince is able to takes over or there is a successful Orthodox rising."

"Aye, there is that," George replied. "There are so many possible threats to our toll-collecting contract that it gives me a pain behind my eyes."

We were all a bit tipsy from the wine by the time we finally quit for the day. When we finally decided to break-up and go to our beds for some sleep, at least so far as Harold and I knew, George was still undecided as to how the Company should respond to the Regent's demands for a war against her one-time supporter and only Latin ally, Otto.

The one thing we did agree to do turned out to be very significant—the Company would make a major effort to expand its other operations using our Venetian prizes so we would not be hurt too badly when we sooner or later lost the toll revenues for one reason or another. Although we did not know it at the time, it turned out to be an important decision.

****** *George Courtenay*

My meeting with Michael and Harold went well. Afterwards I walked back to the Great Palace and scribed messages to Richard and Thomas in Cornwall and to Yoram in Cyprus. I did so in order to bring them up to date on the situation here and to order them to do whatever they could to expand our various coin-earning operations. They were also told to send messages to their captains asking for their thoughts and suggestions.

The new orders would be a change of direction for them—they had been, or so I hoped, concentrating on recruiting and training men to replace our recent losses and provide crews for our recent prizes. Now it was time to put those prizes to work carrying more passengers and goods and clearing the Mediterranean of the pirates and our competitors. We especially needed to get rid of the Moors and the Christian and Jewish merchants who had stepped into our shoes whilst we were making the treacherous and ever-dangerous Venetians pay for the damages and trouble they had caused us.

It was time to go to the Great Palace for my supper by the time I finished scribing. And by the time I did finish I once again realized that I needed an apprentice sergeant to help me with my scribing and run my errands.

I thought about taking my younger brother or my even younger son as my apprentice, but promptly put them aside as still being too young and inexperienced. So I went back and added a few words to each parchment asking for recommendations for a useful apprentice.

Perhaps, I scribed to Yoram, my apprentice should be already be a lieutenant in order to be old and strong enough to fight by my side in addition to being able to scribe. It was about then, as I was finishing, that I remembered James Howard, the young sergeant who had done so well assisting me in Rome even though he could not scribe or do sums.

I had made James' promotion to sergeant permanent and sent him to Cyprus more than a year ago with a note to Yoram asking him to find someone to spend full time teaching him to scribe and a second note to Uncle Thomas asking him what he thought about setting up a Company school for such of our men. They had both responded that it was a good idea and agreed that the school should be started on Cyprus because most of our men were in the east. I had ordered it to be done but had not heard anything since.

In any event, I retrieved my parchments from both the primary courier pouch and the backup, and added another inquiry to Yoram who, the last I heard, had set up a small scribing and summing school for Company men with potential such as James.

"How is James Howard doing?" I inquired. "Is he or one of the others capable of serving as my scrivener? If he is, please send him to me; if James is not ready, please send me the best scrivener available."

When I finished and the messages were finally on their way, I walked briskly from the Commandry to the Great Place with my guards. The time I had spent scribing and the brisk walk had cleared my head of the afternoon's wine by the time I arrived.

******

Food was already being served to the court's usual mix of freeloaders and ambitious sycophants when I entered the hall. I was immediately accosted by a harridan with a white-powdered face and several of her simpering followers. *White face was both the latest fashion at court and made women look absolutely hideous and almost dead. Even Elizabeth had adopted it.*

It was a terrible inconvenience; I had to wash the ghastly tasting white stuff from all over me every morning to keep our relationship secret.

"Hoy, Commander Courtenay. There are rumours that you are an earl and the Regent is being challenged by the Bulgarian king. What can you tell us?"

"Why, a band of mummers?" I replied when I looked up and saw them. "How delightful. Giving us a play about dead people tonight, are you?"

The harridan was taken aback and quite aggrieved.

"I am not a mummer. I am Matilda, the wife of Lord Anthony." She said it with more than a little insulted outrage in her voice.

"Oh, you are with Lord Anthony and not a mummer? How disappointing. I heard a rumour he was ill of the French pox. Well, I am sure you will be joining him shortly. Please give him my regards and my best wishes for his recovery when next you see him." *I had not a clue as to who Lord Anthony might be or why he and his wife were attending the court, but I surely would like to be a mouse on the wall when they next spoke.*

Lord Anthony's wife, whoever she was, did not know whether to be insulted or pleased, so she curtsied and hurried away with some of her companions hurrying behind like a flock of white-faced crows. I felt much better as I sat down and waved at one of the serving girls to bring me some food and a bowl of wine. Elizabeth was nowhere in sight and neither was Erik; I was hoping to talk to him.

An Earl? My God, I suppose I am since my uncle bought the title for my father from old King John to keep him from sending one of his pompous-arsed favourites to lord over Cornwall and bother us.

****** *George Courtenay*

A parchment had come in from Uncle Thomas whilst I was meeting with Michael and Harold at the Commandry. I took it out while I waited for my food and began reading. I did so in the hope that by looking busy it would discourage anyone from sitting down and trying to talk to me before Erik arrived.

It was not to be. A party of self-important dandies marched up, flounced their lace cuffs to make sure they could be seen, and sat down around me without an invitation. Three sat themselves across from me and one next to me. *I knew I should have eaten in one of the private rooms.*

I made an effort to ignore my new companions even though one of them was somebody with whom I actually wished to speak, the Bulgarian ambassador. They were hard to ignore because they were all following the latest court custom by dousing themselves with the juice of fresh flowers instead of bathing. *At least they had not whitened their faces to look dead as Elizabeth the women of the court had begun doing; I suppose that is next.*

"An important message?" one of them inquired.

"No," I replied as I pulled the parchment closer and continued reading without looking up. Actually it was important. It was a message from my Uncle Thomas describing the latest conditions and events in Cornwall and in the approaches to it on the other side of the River Tamar.

Happily, none of my family had died and all was relatively peaceful except for a couple of highway robbers who needed to be hung and some priests that had to be turned away. Otherwise the crops were adequate and the recruiting and training of would-be archers at the Company camp near Restormel Castle was proceeding as expected. Another hundred or so archers would be ready to be sent east in the near future.

The biggest news in the message was about King Edward. According to Uncle Thomas either the queen had gone foul or his lice were acting up for he had announced another effort to regain the lands in Normandy that he considered to be rightfully his.

Whatever the reason, Edward had summoned his knights and nobles to bring their levies to Dover in preparation for being carried across the channel by the portsmen of the Cinque Ports to once again help Edward fight for his lands. They either had to report and carry out whatever duties the king demanded of them or pay a scutage to be excused. And they all would do one or the other—because failure to do so would result in them being stripped of their lands and titles.

Uncle Thomas, as usual, had regretfully informed the King of my great love for him and my temporarily absence in the east, and paid the scutage for both me and the only other knight in Cornwall, Richard, the Company's deputy commander. Richard had only recently returned from our war with the Greeks and was once again stationed with our horse archers just across the river in Devon.

We had to pay the scutage because Richard and I and several others, all now gone, had been unexpectedly knighted when we successfully destroyed an army trying to invade Cornwall. Apparently it had been led barons who were opposed to the king and he was pleased to have them defeated. It was an honour we could have done without because it cost us coins every time whatever damn fool was on the throne decided to go to war.

Uncle Thomas had promptly paid the scutage because it had long ago become Company's policy to always speak highly of whoever was on the throne, and never waste our men's time and lives fighting for him unless we were both very well paid and, because kings are kings and inevitably ignore their debts, paid in advance. Instead we would proclaim our undying loyalty to him, pay the smallest possible scutage, and lament our need to be away in the east to earn our bread because Cornwall was so poor.

Paying the scutages and doing everything possible to avoid taxes for the next thousand years, or until Jesus returns from heaven or the dragons return from the east, was in the Company's compact on which every man made his mark. Jesus, of course, is with God above the clouds and would be returning soon; it is only the dragons that are in the east according to the map makers and those who have been there and seen them.

******

I was thinking of Cornwall and my wife and family at Restormel when Erik arrived and sat down beside me. He did so after glaring and making a "move over" motion with his head at the lace-encrusted courtier sitting next to me.

The fragrantly scented fob hurriedly sidled down the bench to make room for Erik to sit next to me. He knew, Erik that is, what I thought of the useless layabouts who filled the Latin Empire's court and shared my contempt of them no matter how sweet they smelled.

"A hoy to you, Erik. It is good to see you."

"A hoy to you, George. It is good to see you too. We need to talk," Erik said softly as he put his axe-head on the floor and leaned on its handle as he straddled the bench and moved his head closer to mine so I could hear him and those around us could not. "But not here, somewhere private."

"Oh it is not necessary to move. I am sure these gentlemen will give us privacy. It is what one does when one is a courtier, eh?"

I leaned forward and said it with a great deal of certainty whilst looking directly and hard into the eyes of the courtiers sitting around me. Most of them got the message and promptly got up and moved. One tarried for a few seconds, but then hastily got up when Erik scowled menacingly and leaned towards him such that the head of the axe he was holding came off the floor.

When the last of the would-be listeners was gone, Erik leaned over and whispered some interesting news.

"I have just received word that Bishop Samaras has returned to his residence at the Church of the Holy Apostles. Would you like to come with me when my Varangians and I pay him a visit?"

Chapter Twenty-one
Something must be done.

The Church of the Holy Apostles sat at one end of a rather small square surrounded on three sides by decrepit daub and wattle tenements of two or three floors. The church and the palace next to it took up the entire fourth side of the square. The palace was the residence of the bishop and the church's priests and their families.

The ground floors of the tenements around the square were lined with small shops and merchant stalls. People were standing and squatting in them and in front of them. The remains of several of the mornings' cooking fires were smouldering by the side of the street. Narrow alleys for pooping and peeing stood between some of the tenements. Everyone else used the street.

There were people and horse carts moving on the street, and a few stationary merchant carts including a couple stacked high with some kind of melons. Many of the people on the street were children playing and women talking. Cats were everywhere. It was clearly an Orthodox quarter from the look and dress of the people. We were enough of an oddity that many of the people turned and stared at us as we walked toward bishop's palace.

A palatial-shaped residence and small cemetery stood immediately next to the rather large dome-topped church at the far end of the square. Between them they took up the entire fourth side of the square. A single low wall enclosed both the residence and the cemetery, but not the church. The door to the church was open.

According to what Erik told me as we entered the square, the palatial residence had at least two floors and the entire top floor belonged to the bishop. The church's priests and their families and a small chapel were on the ground floor. The bishop, he said, had a private entrance in the rear for himself and his family, if he had one.

Three Varangians and my four guards accompanied us as Erik and I walked on the cobblestoned street towards the bishop's palace. All of five of the archers were fully armed including me. We were carrying sheathed swords and galley shields, and each of us had our longbows strung and a quiver of arrows slung over our shoulders. Our company totalled nine in number including me and Erik.

The Varangians each carried a very large long-handled axe and had a shield slung across their backs. Their shields were interesting; they had strange animals and designs painted on them and were somewhere in size between our small round galley shields and the large infantry shields carried by knights and better-armed commoners when they fought on foot.

No one except me, so far as I could see, was wearing any armour. I was wearing a chain shirt under my tunic as I always did except when I was sleeping in my own room or with a woman. *It was something I promised my father and uncle I would always do, and it saved my life more than once.*

Erik had initially planned to send a couple of the Varangians around to the back of the bishop's palace in case the bishop decided to leave without saying goodbye. But he changed his mind when we saw a large number of men lolling about inside the little palace's walled-in bailey.

There were several dozen of them standing and sitting around the entrance to the palace and many of them appeared to be armed with spears. We nocked our arrows and continued walking towards them, but we did not draw our bows.

"Do you have any thoughts as to how we should fight if it comes to that and they decide to try us?" I asked Erik.

"How do *you* suggest we form our men?" Erik asked me as we continued towards the gate in the low wall without breaking our strides.

"You and your Varangian form a shield line and kneel. My men and I will stand behind you in a second line and push our arrows into the leaders and thrusters until they reach us. When they do, my archers and I will pull our swords or stick with our longbows, whichever seems best."

"Aye. That will work," he said. A moment later he gobbled something to the three Varangians that I did not understand.

A moment later he explained.

"I also told my men we needed prisoners to question," Erik said to me as we walked up to the gate in the wall and prepared to enter. But prisoners may be hard to take if this lot closes with us; a good axe chop usually finishes a man rather quickly."

"Not to worry. Some of those who go down with an arrow will be able to talk for a while. We will wait to pull or cut our arrows out until we are finished questioning them."

Erik grunted his acceptance, and then said something over his shoulder to his men.

Over the top of the low wall as we approached the entrance gate we could see the men lounging about in the courtyard get to their feet and start to move about. They had seen us coming. There were a number of women and children with them and at least one priest.

"They look like they might be the men of the diocese's protection society," Erik said as we walked toward the closest gate in the wall. And some of them are carrying spears—just like the men who surprised you and your men in the Mason's Hall.

"I hope that is not a coincidence and these are the men that we seek. It is also very interesting that they are carrying spears—because the hard men in the church gangs rarely carry spears when they are protecting their diocese's people and collecting their tithes and donations. In fact, I have never before seen one of them who did. It must mean something, but what?"

As he spoke, one of the men in the group facing us broke away and dashed into the bishop's palace. Obviously he was going to sound the alarm even though his warning was probably not be necessary. Faces had already begun appearing in the palace's wall opening both on the ground floor and on the floor above it.

Someone must have said something when we got close to the gate into the palace's low-walled bailey because the women and children suddenly began running to get inside and the men began gathering together around a man wearing a grey tunic. He was waving his arms and pointing towards us as he spoke with them. The priest went inside with the women and children.

Unlike the others, the arm waver who appeared to be their leader was wearing a sword. The rest of the men, we could now see, were carrying spears and clubs. I would have said they looked like the toughs of a church protection and collection gang if it were not for the spears.

"Erik, have you really never seen anyone in the city's church gangs carrying spears?" I asked as I reached the gate in the low wall and pushed it open.

"Never. It is something totally new. Perhaps this lot are something else, eh?"

"Well, we will know soon enough, I think; here they come."

Actually it was only the man wearing the sword and one other man who left the larger group and began walking towards us as we walked into the bailey of the residence. I held my bow and nocked arrow by my side as I moved forward and to the side a few steps to greet them. It might have been my imagination, but somehow the two of them looked different from the men in the group that were standing together behind them and staring at us.

"This is church land," the sword-wearer announced. "Visitors are not welcome, especially those who come bearing weapons. I regret that I must ask you to leave."

He spoke in crusader French with a heavy accent. I do not know why, but somehow he struck me as neither one of the city's Greek residents nor one of its Latins. It was also my impression that he spoke too smoothly to be the leader of the band of hard men who collected the Church of the Holy Apostles' tithes and protected its believers.

I moved forward with a hand at my ear to better hear him and get him closer. I also took a few steps forward and to the side to separate myself from Erik and our men. It seemed natural and unthreatening. He, after all, had done the same by coming forward with only one man and not drawing his sword.

"Hoy," I replied as the sword wearer stopped some ten paces or so in front of me.

"We come in peace. All we want to do is talk to Bishop Samaras about a matter of importance. We are not here to arrest him and take him away."

I told my lie as sincerely as I could manage. Unfortunately it was not enough. The man did not immediately send someone to fetch him. Some people are just naturally suspicious, and that is God's Truth.

"His Eminence is not receiving visitors today; he is praying and hearing confessions. You will have to make an appointment and come back later." He said it as if he was a young priest making an excuse for one of his betters."

"Tu es sacerdos in?" Are you a priest? I asked in Latin because I did not have Greek.

He understood my question. I could see the surprise in his eyes as he started to reply, but then he caught himself and merely grunted.

"You must go away and come back later," the surprisingly well-spoken man said again in crusader French. By then we were all through the gate and the Varangians were casually standing in front of the archers.

Although the men we were facing probably did not realize it, I was the only member of our party not standing ready to instantly move into a battle formation; I was standing by myself a few feet forward of Erik and our men and a couple of steps off to their right.

Of course I was not standing directly in front of the archers and Varangians whilst talking to the priest or whoever he might be; a man could get killed standing in front a Varangian swinging an axe or between archers and their targets.

***** *George Courtenay*

I turned my head and spoke quietly to my men and Erik.

"This is the man we need to keep alive for questioning. The others are no great loss. Does everyone understand?"

Erik immediately gobbled something to his men. "My men and I understand and are ready," he said a moment later with a big smile and a nod.

"Thank you," I replied with a smile and a bowing nod of my head to acknowledge him."

The man in front of me looked a bit uncertain. He may have heard what I said so there was no time to waste.

"Kill them all except this one," I said.

And this time I did not turn my head and try to speak so I could not be overheard. Instead, I fixed my eyes on the sword carrier and, as I spoke, I raised my bow and there was the familiar sound of my bowstring slapping against my wrist protector as I pushed my first arrow straight into the sword carrier's hip to the right of his dingle.

It all happened so fast that the sword carrier had no time to move. And he was so close that I could not possibly miss. The sound of my bowstring hitting the wrist protector and the "thud" as the arrow took him in the hip ran together as one sound.

All hell instantly broke loose and everything seemed to happen at the same time. All but one of the Varangians instantly kneeled and my archers raised their bows and pushed out their first arrows—and every single one of them had selected the second man as his target.

As you might imagine, the man who had come forward with the sword carrier was killed instantly. He went over backwards without saying anything except a loud "ooff" as three of the arrows hit him in the chest at almost the same moment and the fourth took him in the side a split second later as he was going down.

Within a few seconds my archers and I had each pushed two or three more arrows into the men gathered near the palace door. At that point I shouted "forward" and began moving towards them at a rapid walk whilst continuing to launch arrows as fast as I could. My men and the Varangians followed. Everywhere there was screaming and shouting and men running.

My archers and I moved forward at a fast walk whilst pushing out our arrows and taking a deadly toll from the bishop's spear carriers. Erik and the Varangians, however, were not slowed by the need to nock arrows and push them out accurately—they ran as fast as they could straight at the spear carriers shouting their battle cries and swinging their great axes.

Our unexpected and very ferocious and deadly attack caught the suddenly leaderless men in front of us totally by surprise. There was no resistance of any kind, just confusion followed by desperate efforts to escape. Their response was similar to ours when they surprised us in the Masons' hall—non-existent.

Some got away whilst their mates were being chopped down and shot down, but many did not. And the badly wounded sword carrying priest, for that is what he was, was one of those who did not get away. He was down and unable to move enough to get up. I stayed with him while Erik led our men into the palace.

"What is your name and who are you?" I asked the priest. "Tell me everything about why you tried to kill me and my men and I will give you some flower paste for your pain and have you barbered. And if you tell me something truly important I may even decide to let you live."

"You will not get anything from me," he said through gritted teeth as he looked at the arrow sticking his hip. It was little wonder that it pained him. It had obviously gone into the bone.

I responded to his refusal to talk by grabbing the shaft of my arrow and giving it a little shake to see if I could get it out without using one of my knives. It did not come out and the man who had killed my men screamed.

"Oh yes I will," I told him as I gave it another shake.

Chapter Twenty-two
It was the Bulgarians.

My conversation with the priest, for that was what he was, was both informative and disappointing. He was the member of an order of warrior priests that had been formed to protect the Bulgarian faithful from the Saracens and from the incursions by the horsemen from the east who had no religious beliefs whatsoever. He refused to talk at first, but then began babbling like a brook when I twisted the arrow and promised to do it again every time he told a lie or refused to answer a question.

"My order's father superior sent me and a couple of my men here to help the Orthodox tithe collectors kill you," he gasped. "Their bishop did not think his men had skills and ability to do it themselves. He was right, that much I can tell you for sure.

"It must have been important because I was told to help them even though they are heretics. I do not know why my order helped them, but it surely must have been for coins and promises for the Church and the head of my order. Why else would he have ordered me to help them?"

"Did you or one of your friends kill the Empress?" It was the first time I asked him.

He immediately denied knowing anything about the death of the Empress or my father. He had heard about their deaths, of course, everybody had. But he denied being involved in any way or knowing who was responsible. To the contrary, he said their deaths were a disaster for his order because it caused King Otto to start raising coins, including a demand for all of his order's, to buy God's acceptance of his claim to be the emperor's regent.

After a bit of digging, literally with the arrow sticking out of his hip, I was finally convinced that he was telling the truth—he did not know anything about my father's death. And he had only killed my men because he had been ordered to do so by the head of his order. What was interesting was that he was sure someone had paid his order to do so, but he did not know who.

I felt sorrow for his pain and lack of a future. The poor fellow was, or so it seemed, merely an ambitious priest trying to advance himself by doing murders or whatever else the head of his order told him to do. He would have been better off in some parish chanting prayers and selling indulgences.

But did I mind putting pains on him until I found out what I needed to know? Not in the least; the bastard killed my men and tried to kill me. He owed me and the Company more than his pain, his information, and his life even though that was all we would ever be able to collect.

******

Erik and I spent several hours questioning the priest. In between his moans and screams he admitted being in the Masons' hall when Uncle Henry and the others were killed and I was captured. He said that he and his sergeant had been met when they arrived in the city on a Black Sea cargo ship a week earlier and had immediately been led to a village near the city. He had waited in its tavern for orders.

His orders arrived late one afternoon from the same man who had led them to the village. He was almost certainly a Latin priest, even though he denied it, because he spoke both crusader French and Latin. The man had brought a horse-drawn cart full of firewood that carried them through one of the city gates without any questions being asked.

They had entered the city rode through it in the dark until they reached a merchant's building where firewood was stored. That is where he and his sergeant first met the leader of other men. He was fairly sure they were members of an Orthodox Church's protection gang because only one of them spoke crusader French and he met the rest of the gang at the nearby Orthodox Church.

Two nights later the messenger had come to them all excited and led them through the back streets and alleys to the big hall. When they got there he showed them the secret entrance and told them to hide themselves and wait because the man they were to kill would be there sometime the next day.

The messenger had showed them an archer's tunic before the left firewood warehouse and explained how the number of stripes would identify the man to be killed. The man wearing seven of them was the one they wanted. They were told he would be one of the first men entering the room through the secret entrance.

It was his decision to try to get more coins for his order, the priest claimed.

"You were the one we were paid to kill, not the others. But no one ever told me who paid my order to kill you or why. The sergeant and I were selected to do it because we could gobble crusader French and the head of my order thought that might be helpful.

"And we were paid so much to do it that I knew you would fetch a big ransom before we killed you. My order needs more coins because King Otto has "borrowed" all of ours such that we are penniless. *I did not know that.*

"Why did King Otto take your order's coins?"

"His Majesty took everybody's coins with a great scutage and a one-time tax on market stalls and all the land, even the land of all the monasteries and religious orders including mine. He also gathered up all the coins he could borrow. He even took the half-payment of coins my order was paid in advance to kill you.

"Stefan Kostov, the priest who heads my order, told me the king needed all those coins, and more, for the Pope's prayers so that God would choose him to be Emperor or, failing that, the new Regent.

"And with the help of Constantinople's Roman archbishop and Bishop Samaras, King Otto has arranged to borrow more from the money lenders here, both Orthodox and Latin, and even from the Jews. The priests have already begun collecting them."

"That is very interesting. Where are the coins from Constantinople being held and how will they be taken to Otto?"

The wounded priest initially swore in the name of God that he did not know. But after a bit more digging on my part, literally in his hip using the arrow, he told us more after he stopped screaming.

"King Otto's men will be coming on this year's grain fleet to get the borrowed coins from the Bishop Samaras and the Latin Archbishop next week. They will be added to the coins the grain fleet already has on board to carry to the Holy Father for his prayers," he gasped.

"A fleet of cargo transports will be coming soon with the first of this year's grain harvest for the city, but I do not know when. It all depends on the harvest along the Danube lands. It will be soon, I think.

"What I am sure is that it will be guarded by King Otto's galleys, probably all of them since he does not have many. Then part of the fleet, some or all of the king's galleys that is, will continue on to Rome to carry the coins to the Holy Father.

"The fleet is supposed to stop here to unload the harvest and take on water and supplies for the return trip to pick up more grain. But not all of the fleet will make the return trip. One or more of the galleys, maybe all of them, will pick up the coins collected by the bishops during their visit and continue on to Rome."

"How do you know all this?" I asked him.

"Because both the Latin archbishop and Bishop Samaras, the bishop who lives in this palace, were invited to Bulgaria to visit King Otto right after the Empress was killed. Bishop Samaras came himself, but the Latin archbishop was suspicious and sent a priest by the name of Mathias to represent him.

"King Otto had them come separately because he did not want each of the churches to know what he was promising to the other. I know what was agreed because I was one of the guards during the negotiations. That is where I heard with my own ears what each of the bishops was to get if he helped King Otto acquire the coins he needed to buy the prayers required for God's approval.

"The agreements themselves were very straightforward and perfectly reasonable. Bishop Samaras is to get one in five of the coins the Orthodox faithful and money lenders of Constantinople provide to the king and the Orthodox will get to keep their churches in the city when he is the Emperor or Regent. Similarly, the Latin archbishop will get to keep one in five of the coins that the city's Latin faithful and money lenders provide and the Latins will be allowed to take over the Orthodox churches in the city."

"They were invited separately so that each church could be promised what its leaders wanted and each of its leaders would get a share. I understand that. But why did they go to Bulgaria and do you know who killed the Empress?" *I asked once again just to be sure.*

"I already told you," he gasped. "I do not know who killed the Empress and my order has lost its coins as a result, so I am truly sorry it was done. But I can tell you that the representatives of both churches went to Bulgaria in order to negotiate directly with King Otto. Of course they did—because they did not trust the promises of King Otto's ambassador's or want to share the coins with him."

"I can understand why the Latin archbishop agreed to help the king. He wants to take over the Orthodox churches and their revenues. But why did the Orthodox bishop agree? Is he sharing the coins with the Metropolitan Andreas?"

"Oh no. Bishop Samaras intends to keep all the coins for himself and use them for his own advancement. That was part of the King Otto's agreement with him. The other part was that the Metropolitan is to be killed so Bishop Samaras can use his coins to buy the Patriarch's prayers needed take his place. That is why I was sent here—to kill you *and* him."

Samaras risking a trip to Latin Bulgaria to negotiate for his personal advancement was understandable and so was King Otto's duplicity. I immediately began thinking as to how we might turn that to the Company's advantage in addition to seizing the coins.

"Erik, I assume you will warn your friend, the Metropolitan, about Samaras?"

"Perhaps. But it may not be necessary if we take care of Samaras ourselves. Best to do it ourselves without letting Andreas know until the deed is done. He might get merciful or let the dog off the leash, eh?"

"You may be right, Erik. But might it not be better to wait until all the coins have been gathered so we can get those too?"

"Why should we wait? Bishop Samaras will know we are after him when he sees this so he is likely to run instead of sticking around to collect the Orthodox coins and pass them on to the Bulgarian fleet when it arrives."

"Not necessarily, Erik, not at all. All Bishop Samaras knows so far, and needs to believe, is that we have discovered and killed the men who tried to kill me. They fled here to the bishop's church because they were trying to reach a holy place in an effort to find refuge in a sanctuary. But they failed; we caught them before they could get inside and save themselves."

Erik smiled and nodded his agreement when I finished telling him what I thought we should do. Then he hefted his axe and went to settle Uncle Henry's account with the wounded priest and those of his followers we had captured.

The wounded priest saw Erik coming and knew what it meant. He tried to struggle to his feet and get away. He did not make it. Neither did those others of the priest's men we had taken alive. It was just as well; Samaras would be reassured that there was no one left to tell the Regent about him.

Did I feel troubled by the Varangians slaughtering them? Not in the least; it had to be done to prevent the bishop from finding out that we were on to him and knew about the coins being collected for the Pope's prayers. Besides, they deserved it and the Company's charter required that the men killed in the Mason's hall be revenged.

On the other hand, we still had not a clue as to who had murdered my father and the Empress.

******

I smiled sincerely and, with Erik translating for me, apologized profusely to the priest for soiling the ground near the good bishop's residence and his fine Holy Apostles' church. We would, of course, I assured the terrified man as I counted coins from my purse into his trembling hands, pay for the burial of the murderers we had just killed and compensate the church for any trouble they had caused.

"And they were murderers, Father," I said most sincerely to the Orthodox priest, "and Latins as well. Before he died their leader admitted to murdering some of my men in the hall of the Masons and that they came here to obtain sanctuary until they could make their escape. Fortunately, thanks no doubt to God, we were alerted to their presence by a reward seeker and were able to catch them before they were able to get inside and claim sanctuary."

"Well, what do you think?" I asked a blood-splattered Erik a few minutes later as we began walking back to the Great Palace. "Will Bishop Samaras buy my story?"

"Oh, I should think so. Giving them the coins and apologizing for causing the bishop trouble was a master stroke. It gave enough support to your lie to make it believable.

"Besides, it is likely the bishop will believe we chased the murderers here and they were killed for murdering your archers because that is what he will *want* to believe. He may not be sure, but he stands to gain so much that he is likely to convince himself that it is worth the risk for him to continue to collect the coins and turn them over to Otto's fleet when it arrives. That is particularly true because Bishop Samaras will think the men we killed were merely street scum who did not know of his agreement with King Otto."

"Aye, you are right my friend. Men like Bishop Samaras are so interested in themselves and their betters that they do not pay any attention to their servants and underlings when they are around them." *At least I hope so.*

Chapter Twenty-three
Coins are collected.

We never did see Bishop Samaras or even bother to try to find him, not that day nor in the days that followed. The recently-departed priest who had been employed to murder me said he had been told the bishop was in his palace only a few minutes before we arrived. But we never searched his palace or even inquired of his priests about him. It would have done no good. Besides, it is likely he fled our arrival either by running out the back door or by hurrying into a secret escape tunnel.

Erik's men made discrete inquiries in the days that followed and so did Harold and several of our captains who had close relations with the merchants that sold us supplies. We were able to confirm that the city's biggest money lenders and its richest merchants and families were all being approached by high-ranking churchmen from both the Latin and Orthodox churches for big gifts and loans "for the church and your future"

Every man who had been approached was promised many good things if he would temporarily part with some of his coins—big repayments in the years ahead, the Church's prayers for their health in the next plague, indulgences for their past and future sins, reduction in their tithes and protection fees, and the church's assistance in getting lower taxes. It was a long list with promises carefully tailored to fit each man who might be persuaded to part with some of his coins.

The result was inevitable—the coins rolled in and within days everyone in the city including Elizabeth knew that King Otto was raising money in the city for the Pope's prayers that God recognize him as either the Empire's emperor or as young Robert's regent. Which position he sought was not clear; probably the emperorship with a fall back to being the Regent if he could not buy enough prayers to immediately get the emperorship away from Robert.

As you might imagine, Elizabeth was beside herself with rage when she found out that the city's churchmen and Otto's representatives were already doing what she herself was just starting to do—raise money to buy enough prayers from the Pope so God would choose her to be Robert's regent. She immediately began working through her chancellor to discourage the city's money lenders and merchants from making gifts and loans to anyone except herself. She even made a list of people she thought were helping Otto despite her efforts and got quite angry with me and Erik for not immediately leading our men out to kill them.

Elizabeth was also now visibly pregnant and increasingly spent her time with her courtiers extolling her wonderful young husband as "a true son of his great father." She was probably hedging her bets in case she was not able to stay on as Regent and had to run for her life back to Epirus. She was also spending a lot of time at court dropping veiled threats as to what her confessor suggested would be the fate of those who "do not support the family chosen by God to sit on the throne."

Erik and I were met with Elizabeth almost every day. When we did, we attempted to placate her by telling her we were constantly and systematically contacting Otto's potential coin suppliers among the merchants and moneylenders and warning them not to help him. I also did what I could to calm her along the same lines at night when we slept together.

It was a lie, of course; Erik and I were doing no such thing.

We did not tell Elizabeth what we were planning, let alone why, because we *wanted* Otto's coin collecting to proceed—so we could take *all* the coins whilst they were being carried to Rome. We dared not share our plan with her because she, being the woman she was, was prone to gossiping and sharing secrets with the courtiers who pretended to be her closest and dearest friends.

Elizabeth, by Erik's count, had over a hundred people in her court with whom she regularly talked and gossiped as she whiled away her days. In other words, we had good reason to fear she might say something and inadvertently give our plans away.

I said "our plans" because the Company and I had promised Erik one coin in ten of any coins the Company ended up taking off Otto and his coin providers. As you might imagine, Erik had come around to thinking that taking Otto's coins was a splendid idea.

Our basic plan was simple—we would practice "benign neglect" by patiently waiting while the city's two traitorous churchmen collected coins for Otto. And then we would continue to wait patiently until the coins from Constantinople and Otto's lands were all together and on their way to Rome to be delivered. Only then would we seize them. And, even better, we would pretend to be pirates from various different countries when we seized them so the Pope and Otto would be uncertain as to who to blame.

More specifically, our plan was to intercept Otto's coins when they exited the narrow Dardanelles Strait on their way to Rome. After we had the coins in hand, would we return to Constantinople and, if we could, put paid to the accounts of the traitorous churchmen by quietly killing them and trying to get our hands on the coins they had held back "to cover their expenses."

So far as I was concerned, it was a good plan and the Christian thing to do since Elizabeth's family had been awarded the throne by God himself.

That we were going to try to intercept the coin carriers and seize the coins was a closely held secret known only to Harold, Michael, Erik and me. And, of course, Harold's and Michael's apprentices also knew because they had overheard us. Elizabeth did not know; she could not be trusted to keep her mouth shut.

Despite our optimism about the plan in general, my lieutenants and I understood that had a major problem—we were short of both the time and men needed to accomplish it. Since we returned from Venice we had recruited enough sailors and pilots to replenish our losses and crew our prizes.

Sailors and men who claimed to be pilots were, as always, a copper a dozen, particularly in a major port such as Constantinople. It was useful fighting men,

English and Welsh archers who knew how to use longbows, where we were short-handed.

Indeed, the Company was so short of fighting men that Harold, Michael, and I seriously considered trying to borrow some of Erik's Varangians. But I decided against it because, as I told myself and later explained to Erik, his men were not used to fighting at sea and might get in the way because they used different weapons and did not fight as we did. Also they were In and might be too sea poxed to fight.

The big problem, of course, was that Erik would almost certainly demand an even bigger share if his men helped with the fighting at sea.

There was also a rumour, and I believed it likely to be true because it sounded reasonable, that the galleys delivering the prayer coins for Otto would also stop in Athens to pick up more coins. It suggested that we might be able to enrich ourselves even more if we waited to take Otto's coin carrying galleys until the Athens coins were added to the total.

After a lengthy discussion over several bowls of ale, and remembering the bible's adage that a squirrel on a spit is worth two in the trees, Harold and I decided *not* to be greedy and wait for the Athens' coins to be added to the shipment. We would attempt to take them as soon as the coins being collected in Constantinople were added to the shipment.

Besides, greed is not a good Christian thing to have. It says so somewhere in the bible. On the other hand, neither is sloth so we decided to think of other ways by which we could also get the coins being collected for Otto in Athens.

Could we send a galley to Athens pretending to be from Otto? Would we have to give a share to Erik? Would the Pope be angry if he knew the Company had taken coins raised by the moneylenders and merchants of mostly Orthodox Athens and we did not tithe some to his private purse? There were many important questions that needed to be answered before we could finalize a plan.

****** *George Courtenay*

We did our best to get ready in the days that followed. The first thing we did was send one of our faster galleys, Captain Jackson's Number Forty-six, into the Gulf of Varna in the Black Sea. It would be our spy picket and watch the grain fleet that assembled in the Gulf each year after buying up the grain that was sold off the riverbanks and out of the towns and villages along the Danube River and its tributaries.

Jackson's galley would hurry back and report when it appeared the grain fleet was ready to sail for Constantinople with the grain for this year's bread. We needed to know because it would be escorted this year by galleys carrying King Otto's prayer coins. At least that was what several of the merchants who enjoyed our customer told us—and they would know because they had each been tapped for contributions "for the church" and had it explained to them when they inquired before parting with their coins.

In other words, that the coins would be carried safely to Rome by the galleys had become an open secret, probably because so many people were involved who had big mouths and no common sense.

Otto's plan was for his galleys to arrive in Constantinople as part of the great mass of the grain fleet. Then, unnoticed in the annual hubbub that always accompanied the arrival of the grain fleet, they would pick up the coins collected in the city and proceed on to Athens and Rome instead of accompanying the grain fleet back to the Black Sea.

After consulting a map and some merchant sailors, Harold estimated that with hard rowing Jackson's picket galley would be able to reach Constantinople about two days ahead of the grain fleet depending on the weather.

Harold's lieutenant, Jack Smith, and his sailing sergeant, Johnny White, agreed with Harold—and, because they were both good men, they agreed because they really did agree with him.

Whilst we waited for the picket galley to return, Harold worked diligently to gather up every available archer including almost all those who had arrived on the skeleton crews of our Venetian prizes. He also took most of the men serving on the crews of our toll collectors and at our local shipping post. He even taxed the two Company transports that arrived that week for the half dozen or so archers each carried to protect its captain in the event of a mutiny and to fight off any pirates who tried to take it.

By the time the hastily dispatched picket galley returned and reported that the transports in the grain fleet had set their sails and were on their way to Constantinople, we had enough archers to fully crew six galleys, including the picket.

It was late on a Tuesday morning when the picket galley, its crew exhausted by two days of non-stop rowing, returned with word that the Danube grain fleet forming up in the river' Bulgarian estuary appeared to be on its way and the galleys thought to be carrying Otto's prayer coins were escorting it "to keep pirates from getting the grain" as an excuse to bring the galleys to the city.

We immediately announced a similar lie to our men and the city's merchants—that we would be sailing first thing the next morning "because we had just received word that our fortress on Cyprus was about to be attacked by the Moors."

And to make sure the word got out of our immediate departure and that we would be gone for many weeks and the coast was clear for the galleys coming to pick up King Otto's coins, we made sure every captain gave his men liberty coins that night so they could rush to the taverns and street women for one last bowl or poke.

Getting to Cyprus and fighting to defeat the Moors would take time. We would obviously be gone for months, at least so far as everyone in the city and our men knew. The traitors were suddenly free to finalize their betrayal of Elizabeth by adding the coins they had raised in and around Constantinople to those that were already aboard King Otto's galleys.

We reinforced the idea that the traitors could safely deliver their coins by spending the rest of the day hastily loading our Cyprus-bound galleys with the live cattle, sheep, and poultry that would typically be carried on a long voyage. They would go overboard if we had not finished eating them by the time King Otto's coin-carrying galleys reached us where we planned to intercept them—on the far side of the narrow Dardanelles strait.

Travelling through the strait was the only way to reach Rome from Constantinople and King Otto's lands at the mouth of the Danube without going by land through many kingdoms. Going by land would take months with so many dangers along the way that it would be total folly for King Otto's prayer coins to be carried overland. They would be robbed ten times over before they reached Rome.

There was no alternative. King Otto's prayer coins would have to be carried to Rome by sea—and that meant the galleys or transports that carried them would have to pay their tolls and pass through the extremely narrow Dardanelles strait.

****** *George Courtenay*

Elizabeth was furious at my suddenly need to hurry off to relieve Cyprus "when I am with child and need you the most." She was so angry that she threw a bowl at me and was heading for the piss pot when I ducked out the door. That last night before we sailed I moved back to the Commandry and slept alone.

Truth be told, being away from Elizabeth was a great relief since she had begun constantly barfing. It puts a man off when he is in bed with a woman who barfs, yes it does, even if she washes her mouth out with wine immediately afterwards.

Although we did not know it at the time, the grain fleet and its escort of galleys was about two days out when our six galleys and their hungover crews cast off the next morning for our long voyage to Cyprus. Numerous people, mostly lamenting women, were on the quay to see us off along with the usual fortune tellers, pickpockets, and small merchants selling last-minute bowls of wine and the religious icons needed to guarantee that a man would have a safe voyage.

We were already through the Dardanelles strait by the time the first of the grain fleet's ships and cogs began arriving in Constantinople along with King Otto's coin-carrying galleys that were ostensibly guarding them. By then five of our galleys including the picket from Varna were already tucked away out of sight in a protected anchorage near the exit from the strait.

Our sixth galley, once again Captain Jackson's Number Forty-six, was at the entrance of the strait. It would hurriedly row through the strait and sound the alert as soon as its lookouts sighted the coin carriers.

In order to avoid anyone in the constant stream of inbound transports warning off the coin carriers, Captain Jackson's galley was moored alongside old Galley Number Twenty-nine which was acting as the Empire's toll collector for the inbound traffic even though it now had no archers aboard. A galley or two waiting at the entrance to the strait to collect the tolls from inbound transports that had just finished passing through the strait was so normal that it would attract no attention or comment.

A close watch would be kept from the very top of Forty-six's mast. Any outbound galleys that they sighted coming towards them from Constantinople would almost certainly be King Otto's coin carrier or carriers. As soon as the first galley was sighted, Captain Jackson would put everyone on his oars and hurry through the strait to alert us that the coins were coming.

The rest of our little fleet of Company galleys waited just out of sight at the other end of the strait. While we waited the men practiced with their longbows and with their galley's pikes and short swords. It felt good to get the archers back to soldiering again as Marines.

While the men were practicing, the captains and lieutenants of the waiting Company galleys met with Harold and me to discuss the finer points of fighting and boarding another galley, and especially what each captain might expected to do under various circumstances. As you might imagine, there was much uncertainty because we neither knew how many galleys would be guarding the coins nor whether one carried them all or if they had been divided up to insure that as many as possible reached Rome. We tried to think of all the possibilities and what we would do to respond to each.

And whilst we practiced and talked we prepared our galleys to mislead the coin carriers when we met them—we began by flying the three-pointed oriflamme pennants of the French king on our masts and having the men turn their tunics inside out to hide the front and back stripes that would identify them as Company men.

I myself had an additional minor personal decision to make—what name to use if we took the coin carriers and I met their captains. It was an important decision for it is always better to have someone else blamed if the Company ends up with something whose ownership might be claimed by others.

After giving it some thought, I finally decided to trim my beard very short and introduce myself as a French cleric with a common French name. I would, at least initially, be Father Maurice Lemieux from Anvers. Harold would be the fleet's commander; I would be his translator and the cleric who did his scribing and summing.

It would be easy for me to take off my archer's tunic and become a priest. There was a priestly robe and large wooden cross at the bottom of my wooden chest for me to wear when I thought it might be helpful. Indeed, Latin was the language of the Company's school and every boy passing out of it was ordained and provided with a priest's robe. It gave him something to do to earn his bread if he was not up to making his mark on the Company's roll.

Our captains were, I initially informed them, to claim that our galleys were Burgundians sailing under a contract to help protect a French fleet that had carried crusaders to the Holy Land. That would be believable because it would tie into the story we put out about our being part of a French fleet when we raided Venice earlier in the year.

But then I changed my mind about the story—I decided that I would keep my French name and priestly position as Harold's cleric and translator, but our galleys would be independent galleys of lowland pirates, Burgandians from Holland, men whose galleys had remained behind to seek their fortunes independently when the French fleet sailed back to France to pick up another cargo of crusaders.

The oriflamme pennants on our masts were quickly replaced by hurriedly sewn flags with the saw-toothed cross of Burgandy. If adding Burgandy and pirates to the list of those who might have taken the coins did not confuse and mislead everyone, I did not know what would.

Our problem, of course, was that our own men would sooner or later be in a tavern or whorehouse somewhere and let the rabbit out of the sack such that the Company would be blamed for the loss of the prayer coins. So our men and their captains had to be misled so they would tell a different story. In fact, as many different stories as possible in order to cause the greatest confusion and uncertainty.

Accordingly, I explained to the captains what they were to tell their men and how they and their men were to behave when dealing with the men and galleys we hoped to capture "for the Duke of Burgundy."

"Each of you is to tell his men that your galley will be sailing independently under a French flag as part of a fleet of Burgundian pirates searching for some enemy galleys that are reported to be carrying a treasure in coins.

"Tell them that you were given a choice, that if you did not want to help the Burgandians take the coins and get a share of the prize money, you could sail away and return to Malta to await further orders. Tell them that you want the prize money so you have decided to stay.

"As a result, for the next few days they will be sailing under the flags of France and Burgundy. They will do so as part of a fleet of galleys from many states that is under a contract with the Duke of Burgundy to help him take some enemy galleys that are reported to have several crates of coins on board. The Company of Archers is not involved.

"So the first thing you must do when you return to your galley is assemble your crew, point to the Burgandian flag on your mast, and tell your men that you have accepted a single one-time independent contract for your galley that should not last more than a few days.

"And here is something for you alone and not your crews—since the Company is not involved, Harold will be posing as the commander of the Burgandian fleet and I as his priestly clerk and translator. We will claim to be Burgundian mercenaries who had been under contract to help defend the French fleet of crusader-carrying transports, but are now pirates taking prizes for ourselves."

Spirits were high and our men were pleased at the prospect of prize coins even though no one had any idea as to how many galleys we would face or who they would face when we closed with King Otto's Rome-bound fleet. They did not fully understand the need to turn their tunics inside out or why we were flying new flags, but they were truly elated to learn that there was the possibility of prize coins and that a Moorish invasion force was no longer gathering to invade Cyprus.

Captain Jackson and his men of Galley Forty-six would be particularly pleased when they re-joined us and learned that we were going after coin carrying galleys. They had remained behind to collect the Empress's tolls and help defend the city when most of our galleys sailed to Venice and the men in their crews earned fortunes in prize coins. Jackson and his men, I was sure, would be excited by the prospect that their turn to collect significant prize coins might have finally come.

Chapter Twenty-four

My epiphany.

That night, alone at last in my cabin, I was unable to sleep for some reason. Instead, I began worrying. At first I worried that I should have left a galley other than Jackson's with the archer-less toll collector, and tried to decide which of the other galleys I should have chosen. Then, for some reason, I began reflecting on my life and the Company.

Why was it, I asked myself, that we always seemed to be competing with the Churches for people's coins? That was when it first dawned on me that the two great Churches, Latin and Orthodox, were really just companies of men very much like the Company of Archers. The only difference being that the Churches were older and bigger and providing different services to earn coins and provide advancement for their men.

Our companies were similar in many ways. For one, we all three employed men who had volunteered to made their marks on our rolls in order to earn their daily bread and get ahead in life. The Churches' men made their marks as priests and as members of the gangs that collected the tithes and sold protection in each diocese; the Company's men made their marks as archers and sailors. Indeed, those were about the only choices a man had if he wanted to better himself.

There were many other similarities as well. In all three companies the higher a man's rank the more coins he earned and the better he lived. The priests and monks worked out of churches and monasteries; the archers and sailors worked out of transports, galleys, and shipping posts; the Churches had priests and bishops and cardinals with Pope or Patriarch leading them, and we had sergeants, lieutenants, and captains with a Commander leading them.

All this, I decided, was in great contrast to the princely companies such as those of the Venetians, French, and Moors whose men stayed forever with the rank at which they were born. That was because they were all the vassals of a prince who was himself born to lead them no matter how weak and stupid he might be. As a result, good men *could not* rise and the princely companies were riddled with weak and incompetent leaders at all levels because they had been born into their positions rather than acquiring them with accomplishments.

In contrast to the princely companies, companies such as ours and the two Churches tended to be relatively well-led because good men *could* rise to leadership positions including to the very top if they had family connections or could acquire enough coins. Accordingly, it was inevitable that companies such as ours and the two Churches would end up larger and last longer than the princely-controlled companies such as those of Venice, the Moors, and the French whose incompetent leaders would sooner or later bring them down.

Once I began thinking along those lines I could not sleep. I realized there were other fundamental similarities between the men of the Churches and the men of the Company of Archers. For example, the men of all three companies wore clothes that identified their ranks. The main difference being that we identified our ranks with stripes running across the fronts and backs of our tunics and the two Churches identified their ranks with different types and colours of hats and robes.

Similarly, the two Churches took people's coins to save their souls and answer their prayers; we in the

Company of Archers took people's coins to save their lives and move their cargos and money orders.

In essence, I decided as I rolled over yet again in my bed, the Holy Father and the Patriarch were the heads of companies of priests and monks just as I was the head of a company of archers and sailors. We were mostly similar because, I decided as I sat up and took a slurp from a bowl of morning ale to moisten my mouth, at the end of the day both they and I were leading coin-seeking companies filled with men trying to advance themselves in order to get better food and shelter for themselves and their families.

Where we differed, I realized, was that we provided people with different services in order to get them to give us their coins. One would think, because we provided different services, that there would be no reason for us to ever be in conflict. But that was not the case and never would be—the Churches and the Company of Archers were doomed to be forever in conflict, even after Jesus returned in a few years and peace finally arrived. I reached that sad conclusion because there were only so many coins in the world and we all three wanted them.

Being in constant conflict with the two great Churches in the years ahead until Jesus returned and everything was peaceful was not a pleasant prospect even though we were often allies when we could get ahead by assisting each other.

It helped, I realized, that the leaders of Churches did not yet appear to realize that we were competitors for the available coins, and that we only pretended to be submissive to them because it suited us not to get into an open conflict with competitors we could not yet easily defeat. Even so, and despite the future appearing to be brighter for us because of our inherent advantages, there were serious problems and potential conflicts between the men of the Company and the men of the two Churches.

The Company's basic problems at the moment, I decided, were that the men of the two Churches had God's ear, outnumbered us greatly, and its men were allowed to put some of the coins they collected directly into their pouches to enrich themselves. The men in the Company of Archers, on the other hand, had a fixed annual pay based on their ranks, the possibility of periodic prize monies and promotions, and we used weapons and specific contracts requiring our performance whereas the priests only had to use words and promises.

One great advantage the Company had over the two Churches was that it did not take as long to teach a man to push arrows out of a longbow and step down on a foot to a beat of a drum as it did to teach a man to gobble Latin or Greek and memorize the prayers and chants needed to get God's attention. That was significant; it meant we could recruit men and expand more quickly when an opportunity arose.

Another great advantage was that we had a better reputation for honouring our promises and agreements than did either of the Churches. People could count on us to do our very best without crossing our fingers behind our backs or mumbling disclaimers in Latin or Greek which people could not understand. Also, and unlike the churches and all the others, we neither held nor bought and sold slaves and serfs; instead, we freed them and many asked to join us so they too could get ahead in life.

Yet another great advantage was that we could immediately kill our enemies and send them off to purgatory and God's judgment instead of having to employ others to do it as the priests were required to do. That was because the bible said "thou shall not kill" and the churchmen had to pretend that there was a difference between killing someone and ordering it done. We, on the other hand, did not have to wait; we could get on with eliminating our enemies when it was necessary.

All in all, I decided as I shook my head to clear out some of the thoughts that were swirling behind my eyes, my priestly Uncle Thomas was probably right: the future was ours and two Churches were only larger than the Company because the churches had started providing their services to people long before the Company started doing so.

And that was certainly true—the Church, before it split into two separate companies of men, had started many years ago right after Jesus came back alive a few days after the Romans killed him. The Company, on the other hand, only really started coming into our own a few years earlier when my father and uncle used the coins they got off the murderous archbishop of Damascus to buy a boat to carry the Company's survivors back to England. That was when my father and my Uncle Thomas discovered they could also use the boat to earn coins by carrying refugees to safety.

Actually, they started out by buying three boats, a cog and two galleys, because their poxed owner would not sell just one of his boats; it was, according to my father and uncle, all or nothing—they had to agree to buy all three before their poxed owner was willing to sell his little fleet and go ashore.

According to Uncle Thomas, our Company had already passed the biggest princely-led companies, those of the Venetians, French, and Moors, in terms of our ability to recruit useful men and earn coins. And sooner or later, he said, we would catch up with the two Churches. It was hard for me to understand, but he truly thought the Company had a bigger and brighter future even though he himself was a priest who had bought a bishopric and was already doing well for himself in the Latin-gobbling Church.

We would end up bigger than the Churches, Uncle Thomas always claimed, because people would always prefer to give their coins to the Company so they could live longer and better today instead of giving them to one of the Churches because its priests promised that if they did they would sooner or later come back to life after they died just as Jesus had done.

In other words, our Company was more in tune with the realities of the modern and civilized world in which people actually lived. For example, we did not chase after young boys; our wives and the street women were more than enough. Besides, giving coins to the Company in order to live better and longer today was a better result than giving them to one of the Churches in return for its priests' promises of being resurrected in a few years, particular since no mortal man or woman had ever made it back.

In essence, I decided as I lay in my bed sleepless, the Company's future was brighter because more people desired to live better today, and continue living in the case of refugees, instead of dying today and coming back sometime later in the future. That was especially true since people were not fools. They knew that only Jesus had made it back so far. And he did not last very long when he did.

All things considered, according to my priestly Uncle Thomas who knew about such things because he had read so many books, it was inevitable that the Company would sooner or later overtake the Churches in terms of both the number of coins in our chests and in the number of men who made their marks on our respective rolls as priests and archers.

In other words, the day was coming when the Company would have more earners on its rolls and more coins in its chests than the Churches. *Would we make the priests kneel and kiss our hands and get our blessings when that day arrived? I did not think so even though I could not speak for all of our men when it came to having women on their knees in front of them; some of the men seemed to enjoy that sort of pleasure.*

It all seemed very reasonable to me as I turned over once again in my narrow bed and the galley rolled back and forth from gentle motion of the sheltered waters around it. Even with my eyes closed I could see that sooner or later in the years ahead there would likely be more archers delivering cargos and passengers than priests delivering another life after someone died.

Today, however, was another story. We were only number three and would have to try harder to stay in the running if we wanted more coins. Our being smaller and having to try harder was understandable—the companies of the Pope and the Patriarch had been around longer and were much larger than ours in addition to being more blessed by God and having someone who could talk to God to find out what he wanted people to do.

The lessons to be learnt by comparing the three companies were clear to me, or so I thought as I rolled over in my bed once again in an effort to get more comfortable—it pays for a company to be the first mover and get an early start; a Commander or Holy Father and his men have to try harder if their company is number two or three. In other words, your men need to be better trained and have better weapons and provide more valuable services if your company is to whittle down the other big companies and replace them as the biggest and most powerful.

   I had never truly understood why Uncle Thomas bought his diocese and bishop's mitre until I had experienced the Church's ambitious and treacherous priests for myself and realized we were competing with them for coins and men. Now I finally understood—he bought them so he could keep priests and monks out of Cornwall. If he had not, they would have competed with us in the pursuit of coins and people to work for our company's prosperity and advancement.

   On the other hand, and despite all that, was it somehow significant and right that he taught me and the other lads in his school how to gobble Latin and ordained as priests? Yes, I decided, because it gave his boys something to fall back on if he was wrong about the Company being the wave of the future. But it raised questions even so.

   My thoughts were just turning to the Moors and Venetians and other free companies as possible competitors of ours for the world's coins when the next thing I knew it was morning and I could smell the pleasant smell of newly burnt bread. As I did, I was instantly aware that I desperately needed to pee and that I knew for sure who had killed my father and the Latin Empress.

Chapter Twenty-five
Chasing the coins.

"Hoy the deck," the lookout shouted from the very top of the mainmast where he was perched, "a galley be coming and coming fast."

Everyone everywhere stopped whatever he was doing and listened. A few moments later the lookout added more information.

"It be Forty-six and she be waving her enemy in sight flag."

The lookout's cry ignited a long-awaited frenzy of activity on our galley. Harold began roaring out orders. This immediately led to his archers hurrying to their rowing benches and his sailors to begin hoisting the anchor that had kept us from drifting ashore. The sounds of similar activities could be heard all around us on the four Company galleys anchored around us.

Harold and I immediately began climbing the mast to see for ourselves. Harold shouted "stay here" to his apprentice and went up first.

It was an impressive sight—Harold literally ran up the rope ladder with his long white hair streaming out behind him in the wind. I went up behind him, but moved very differently; my fears about once again being on a falling mast kicked in and I went slowly up the mast and only part of the way. *I did not have to climb it and I certainly did not want to do so, but the men expected it of me, at least, I thought they did.*

Everything began according to our plan. I looked around for a minute or two before I began climbing down whilst Harold remained aloft and gave his orders from the top of the mainmast based on what he saw.

Our galley's rowing drum was loud and beating faster and faster as we began rowing to get closer to the distant entrance to the strait. We were moving to get into a position such that we would be able to see the enemy coin carriers coming out of the strait from the very top of our mast.

The other four galleys in our little fleet were holding back, way back, also as planned. It was about then that I realized Captain Jackson would *not* know where to position his rapidly approaching galley or what to do when he joined us. That was because he had not been present when I gave my orders to the other captains.

It took me a while, but I was still on the mast ladder when I finally realized that Captain Jackson would have to be told what his galley was to do, I shouted down an order for a "form on me" signal flag to be waved at Jackson's galley. I wanted his galley to come alongside so he could be told where to position it and what its role would be after he did. When he got close enough I would use our galley's loud talker to shout my battle orders across the water to him.

My order was instantly carried out. A wide-eyed two-stripe sailor with a determined look on his face and carrying the "form on me" flag quickly came up the rope ladder and scurried on past me to the lookout's nest atop of the main mast and began waving it—and that was the moment when everything started to go wrong.

******

I resumed my slow and careful climb down the mast and returned to my position on the roof of the forward deck castle a minute or two later. Climbing down was a reasonable thing to do and would not distress the men, at least that is what I hoped. Besides, Harold could see well enough for both of us. He did not need me up there pointing things out to him.

When I finally reached the deck, I breathed a sigh of relief and looked towards the north where the four galleys that had been following us were supposed to be waiting—and my heart sank when I realized what had happened; they had seen the "form on me" flag intended for Captain Jackson. As a result, they had abandoned their assigned out-of-sight positions behind us and begun raising their sails and rowing hard in order to move forward to join us.

My carefully constructed plan to take the coin carriers was starting to collapse before it even began.

Our carefully conceived plan had been for *only* Harold's galley to be in view to north of the strait's entrance when the coin carrier or carriers came out of the strait and entered the Aegean. My thinking was that we only needed one set of eyes on the exit from the strait to know when the coin carriers were starting to enter the Aegean, and that if the enemy lookouts saw just the top of one mast off to the north, the enemy galleys carrying the coins would not be discouraged and would likely keep on coming out of the strait and into the Aegean.

Moreover, even if Harold's galley inadvertently got close enough to the enemy coin carriers such that they could identify the mast as belonging to a war galley, all they would see would be a single galley that was not using its sails to close on them. What they would *not* see, and thus would *not* be alarmed by, was the rest of our galleys. They would be staying far enough back so they too could only see the top of Harold's mast, and thus, not even the top of their masts would be seen by the more distant coin carriers.

Once Harold saw the coin carriers were out of the strait and into the Aegean Sea beyond it, he would order the attack flag waved. Then and only then would the rest of our galleys, which had heretofore been staying back so as to be unseen, raise their sails and row hard in order to come charging up and join us in engaging the enemy.

Each one of the Company's galleys was supposed to chase after one of the enemy galleys and stay with it until it was taken. Harold's galley would wait off the mouth of the strait and take the sixth coin carrier as it came out of the strait. Alternately, he and I would decide which of the potential coin carriers his galley would go after if there were more or fewer than six.

Waiting until our would-be prizes and the coins they were carrying moved out of the strait and into the Aegean's endless miles of open water before they were engaged was the most important part of the plan.

It was in the endless miles of open water in the Aegean where our archer-crewed galleys would be most effective. The open water and the strong arms of the archers doing our rowing would allow us to stand off and use the superior range of our longbows to harass and weaken the men on the enemy coin carriers. And we would continue to do so for each of them until it crew was either willing to lower their sails and surrender or were weakened enough such that we could come alongside to grapple them and fight our way aboard.

It was a good plan—and it immediately fell apart. A couple of unknown galleys came out of the strait and into the Aegean. They may have been the coin carriers we expected or, perhaps, they were scouts or an advance guard. It did not matter—whoever and whatever they were, they spun around and re-entered the narrow strait as soon as they saw our entire fleet coming over the horizon towards them.

Turning around and running was a reasonable thing for the coin carriers and their escorts to do and it was probably pre-planned. For all they knew, there were even more of our galleys behind those they could see.

The coin-carrying rabbits were out of the sack and running; there was nothing we could do but go into the long and narrow strait and chase them down before they could get away. We had lost our greatest advantage and we still did not have any idea as to how many enemy war galleys we faced or how hard they would fight.

For that matter, we did not even know if they were carrying coins. Perhaps they were decoys or just some poor dorks who had somehow ended up in the wrong place at the wrong time.

****** *Lieutenant Commander Harold Lewes*

I could see everything from where I was perched at the very top of my galley's main mast. The lookout's nest where the "form on me" flag had been waved was about ten feet below me. The lookout was long gone and it was now crowded with three of my best archers.

Several sailors were squatted down and waiting at the foot of the mast. They would carry additional arrows up to the archers whenever more were needed. There was another similar nest about ten feet below the one near the top. It also had room for three archers but was not yet manned.

Similar empty nests were on the slightly shorter stern mast. Also mostly empty were the roofs of my galley's forward and stern deck castles. The castle roofs and mast nests were good positions for archers to stand because from them the archers could push arrows down on to the decks of an enemy galley without being charged and chopped by enemy swordsmen.

As you might imagine, when the fighting began the roofs and lookout nests would be occupied by my galley's best archers. At the moment, most of our fighting positions were not manned because the men assigned to them were still rowing.

We were traveling at a dangerously high speed as we followed what we assumed were a couple of our coin-carrying prey into the narrow Dardanelles strait. It was a normal day and the weather was good, meaning that the strait was crowded with boats and barges of all types and sizes going in both directions one right after the next. Our sails were quickly lowered as soon as we entered the strait. Oars were more than enough and using them exclusively made my galley much more steerable.

Collisions constantly threatened and had to be avoided as we threaded our way through the traffic in the narrow strait in pursuit of what we hoped were the carriers of King Otto's prayer coins. As a result I lashed myself on to the very top of the forward mast so I could see what was coming and call my orders down to my lieutenant and my sailing sergeant, both of whom were standing on the roof of the forward deck castle with George.

Being able to see everything was quite useful. Everyone below me was on high alert and I was constantly calling out descriptions of impending problems and minor course changes for my lieutenant and my sailing sergeant to pass on to our rudder men and the rowing sergeant.

The slightly smaller enemy galleys were in the strait up ahead of us and desperately attempting to escape. I could see the flashes as the sun glinted off the water being thrown up by their oars as they weaved in and out of the shipping that clogged the strait—sometimes the flashes were on both sides, sometimes on only one, and sometimes on neither when they pulled in their oars to squeeze through a narrow opening.

We were doing the same as the galleys we were pursuing, but moving slightly faster, probably because our galley was in better shape and we had more and stronger rowers because we did not use slaves. There was no question about it, sooner or later our galleys would catch up to theirs unless we suffered a mishap.

About a mile ahead of the first two I could see at least two more enemy galleys, and God alone knew what or how many were beyond them. The far two must have also spun around and begun rowing to escape in response to seeing the first two spin around and start to run when they spotted us.

We still had not a clue as to whether any of the four I could see were actually being used to carry King Otto's prayer coins to Rome; but they certainly were acting as if they were carrying something of value. Otherwise, why did four war galleys immediately turn back and start running as soon as they saw us? We were all very excited and optimistic.

George was standing on the roof of the forward deck castle with Johnny White, my sailing sergeant and Jack Smith, my lieutenant, a smith's son who hailed from a village near Stratford. Standing just behind them was my newly assigned apprentice, George's younger brother John. All four of them were looking up at me and listening carefully as I constantly shouted out to describe what I was seeing ahead of us and the changes in direction that would soon be needed.

Johnny was the son of a Deal smuggler and fisherman, and Jack had made his mark on the Company's roll as Jack Smith number three, meaning he was the third smith or son of a smith to use the name Jack Smith. His predecessor had been promoted to captain on one of the two fine Venetian galleys we took. Jack had made his mark on the Company's roll as an archer and he was a good lieutenant. I had both him and Freddie in my mind as future captains.

Johnny, based on what I shouted down to him, and what he could see for himself, was constantly calling out rowing and ruddering orders as we moved back and forth to avoid colliding with the boats and barges coming towards us and to get past those that were heading in the same direction but moving slower.

George stood silently between Johnny White and Jack after having shouted an important order up to me. My apprentice, George's younger brother John, stood quietly behind him.

"Do not slow down when you reach the first two enemy galleys, Lieutenant Commander Lewes. Go right past them and past the next two as well. We will rake them with arrows when we go past them, but do not slow down. We need to know if there are any galleys beyond these four. If there are, they are probably the coin carriers."

"Aye Commander, we are to go past the first four without slowing and rake them as we do."

I repeated the order back to George so that he would know that I understood it. In so doing, of course, my entire crew would know what was happening and be prepared for whatever we were going to do. Similarly, George and I speaking formally to each other and my repeating back of his orders told my crew that things were deadly serious and that every man would be expected to look sharp and move fast when he received an order.

A few minutes later we were coming up on the first of the fleeing galleys and I shouted down an order I probably should have given earlier.

"Lieutenant Smith, I would be obliged if you would order all of your mast and roof archers to report to their arrow pushing positions for a chase."

My words, and Jack Smith instantly repeating them at the top of his voice, created what would appear to an outsider as a lot of shouting and confusion as the archer sergeants loudly repeated them and the designated men abandoned their rowing benches and ran to their new positions. In fact, it was actually quite orderly. Archers moving from their rowing positions to their various battle positions for a chase was something that was constantly practiced on every Company galley.

****** *George Courtenay*

Harold had our archers more than ready by the time we got close enough to the first galley to begin pushing arrows at it. And the range got shorter and shorter as we began slowly pulling up alongside it. Every archer pushed out arrows as we close on the first galley, including me and John.

By the time we got alongside and began moving past it there was no one left alive on the enemy deck except wounded men who were playing dead next to those who had already died. Even so, the enemy galley was under control and continuing to move through the strait. Its rudder men and rowers were obviously responding to sailing orders coming from someone sheltered on the far side of one or both of its deck castles.

In fact, our men had been pushing out arrows at the enemy galley from aloft and from the roofs of our castles long before we actually caught up to it. And, for a brief while the Bulgarians or whoever they were, had been shooting back from behind their stern railing with crossbows—something that is hard to do for very long when twenty or thirty expertly pushed arrows immediately begin being pushed at you every time you raise your head to take aim and loose a bolt.

The coin carrier, if that is what the enemy galley was, was flying no flag when we caught up with it so we were still not absolutely certain what it was or why it was running; we, on the other hand, were flying Burgundian flags on both of our masts as were the five Company galleys rowing through the strait behind us.

I think the crew of the enemy galley was quite surprised when we rowed right on past them despite the fact that it veered off to starboard as we came alongside and its bow ploughed into the side of a barge coming downstream. The barge, in turn, was driven into shallow water and when last seen was sinking rapidly from having its side stove in by the stricken galley's bow.

We continued on past the enemy galley at the highest possible speed Johnny White thought our rowers could give us under the circumstances. Whilst we were passing it the archers on our castles and masts were pushing out arrows at such close range whenever they saw someone that it was hard to believe any missed.

And obviously some of our arrows had not; there were five or six dead and wounded men clearly visible on our enemy's deck as we went past with barely ten feet of open water between our hulls. Our victim had been rowing hard and trying to escape when it hit the barge; so most of its crew were probably still safely below deck on its rowing benches.

Although the enemy crew did not know it yet, everyone who might be alive on its deck, or anywhere else where they could be seen by one of our archers, would be receiving another hail of arrows each time one of our galleys came past. It would be boarded by the last galley of ours to reach it. At least that was what was supposed to happen. Hopefully, the enemy crew would not have any fight left in them by the time it was boarded.

The enemy galley we passed was not the only one with casualties. We had several wounded men and at least one fatality. I assumed our man was dead because he had fallen out of one of the lookouts' nests and landed hard on the deck with a crossbow bolt in his chest.

It was our men up in the rigging and on the masts that were the most vulnerable because the enemy crossbowmen huddling for safety up against the side of their galley's hull could see them—and be seen in return.

******

We showered the second galley with arrows as we caught up to it and slowly moved past it. It was rowing hard and going fast, but we were going faster. And once again we took casualties from crossbowmen before the men we could see on the enemy dec either went down under a hail of arrows or took cover behind something so our archers on our galley's masts and castle roofs could not see them.

Harold was almost one of the casualties; a bolt with his name on it hit the mast behind which he had the presence of mind to hide behind when he saw someone on the deck of the second galley start to aim a crossbow at him.

"The bastards have crossbows," Harold shouted down unnecessarily as our galley suddenly turned hard to port in response to a cog that appeared to be drifting towards us. We were closing in on the two remaining enemy galleys.

"Do you see any more enemy galleys up ahead of the two in front of us, Lieutenant Commander?" I shouted.

"No Commander. None in sight."

"Keep your galley moving forward, Lieutenant Commander. Pass the two ahead of us and keep going.

We are not going to take any chances on the coins being ahead of us and getting away."

It was both an order and an announcement to keep our crew informed—and it did not happen.

******

The strait was wider where we overtook and passed the third galley with a storm of arrows and crossbow bolts going over the water between us. And then it was on to the fourth.

There may have been more galleys ahead of us, but we would never know; we never got past the fourth galley. We were behind it and showering it with arrows, and taking periodic crossbow bolts in return, when it suddenly used its oars to swing around and came straight at us. Clearly its captain had given up on trying to escape by outrunning us and was now trying to either ram us or scrape off enough of our oars that it could get away. Probably the latter.

Our sailing sergeant, lieutenant Johnny White, knew what to do. He kept our bow pointed straight at the on-rushing enemy so that we would be hit head on instead turning away and being rammed in the side.

Both galleys pulled in their oars just before they collided and scraped along each other's starboard side.

"Repel boarders. Everyone on deck. Repel boarders," I shouted at almost the same moment as Harold and Johnny White.

"Throw your grapple; throw your grapples," Johnny White ordered a moment later.

There was much shouting as the archers who had been rowing poured on to our deck with their assigned weapons and our sailors threw their grapples and began pulling the hulls of the two galleys together. The enemy galley did not throw its grapples; its captain had obviously realized he could not outrun us and had been trying to get away by scraping off some our oars so we could not keep up the pursuit.

It did not happen. Our oars survived by being pulled at the last moment and our grapples held. A horn sounded and the men of the enemy galley charged up on to its deck to engage us. They met a storm of arrows and there was great confusion on the enemy deck as many of the survivors responded to the arrows by turning around and trying to get back to the relative safety of their galley's rowing benches.

I saw it all from where I was standing on the roof of our forward deck castle. At first I thought some of the enemy galley's fighting men were staying below to continue rowing. But then I realized that those who had tried to come up on deck to fight were all the fighting men that the other galley had available.

"Of course," I said out loud without thinking. Then I began bellowing "It is slave-rowed. We outnumber them, lads, we outnumber them."

The fight did not last long. The bladed pikes of our boarders and the storm of arrows coming from our masts and the castle roofs did for most of the enemy galley's men before they could even bring their swords into play.

One of the Company galleys came alongside as our men were climbing over the hull railings to board the enemy galley. I was afraid it would stop and try to assist us.

"Continue on into the Marmara," I roared at its captain as I used my bow to point up the strait towards Constantinople. "Hurry, Robert. Do not let the others get away."

The captain of the new arrival, a Yorkshire man on our roll as Robert from Towns End, saluted and began shouting orders. His rowing drum began beating even faster as I turned away. I had more immediate things to think about; we were lashed to the enemy galley and slowly drifting towards the shore without any rowers to keep us away from the strand.

Did I know that there were other enemy galleys in addition to the four? No. It turned out there were only four. Robert rowed hard towards Constantinople for several hours before he concluded as much and turned back.

******

You would have thought that Harold would be ecstatic at our taking some of King Otto's prayer coins, for that is what we had done. Not so; I had to endure a tongue whipping from him as soon as he came down off the mast. He was very irate.

"I saw you and John standing near each other on the roof. If one of you had been hit the other might have done something stupid and we would have lost both of you. Your father's ghost would never forgive me and neither would your mother's.

"John needs experience at sea, but not on the same galley with you, George. I never should have agreed.

When we get back to Constantinople I am going to find another berth for him and take back Archie Smith as my apprentice."

"Yes, Uncle Harold I agree," I said. *I did not think it was the right time to mention that we would not be going back to Constantinople for quite some time and I had other plans for my brother.*

Chapter Twenty-six

What now?

It took all the rest of that day and much of the next to sort things out. The first big problem was that our prizes and the chests with the coins they were carrying were in four different locations along the strait. The second was that Harold's galley had not taken the galley carrying the prayer coin fleet's commander and his assistants; and they were the men we particularly needed to question. The third was that we had taken a lot of prisoners and freed a number of slaves, and the fourth was that there were a number of seriously wounded men at each location who needed immediate sewing and barbering.

The good news was that we soon learned that the four galleys were the entirety of King Otto's Black Sea fleet and all four were carrying a portion of the king's prayer coins. Their captains had wisely divided the weight of the coin chests so that they would not break through their hulls in heavy weather.

From questioning the captains of our prizes and King Otto's representatives, an arrogant nobleman and a couple of priests who were his clerics, we learned many important things. For one, they confirmed that Athens was to be their next and final stop prior to sailing for Rome. For another, and more importantly, they gave us what we needed most—the names of the men in Athens who had been collecting coins for King Otto.

There were three coin raisers waiting for them—a Bulgarian nobleman who was King Otto's ambassador to the Duke of Athens, the papal nuncio who was the Pope's ambassador to the Duke, and the city's Orthodox Metropolitan, the Patriarch's man in the city.

Interestingly enough, the Latin archbishop collecting tithes, selling indulgences, and running the gangs that "protected" Athens' relatively small Latin community was never mentioned. That was a little surprising since both Otto and the Duke of Athens were Latins in the sense that they looked to the Pope to tell them what God wanted them to do and were guided by Latin gobbling priests to do it.

On the other hand, perhaps it was understandable the Latin archbishop was not involved—there were very few Latins in Athens except the Duke and his men who had been forced on the Greeks when the crusaders took Constantinople and assigned the various states of the old Byzantine Empire to the crusade's captains.

******

An arrogant and self-important young nobleman was in command of the galleys we captured. His name was Tarnovo. I never did find out if that was his family name or where his lands were located. Who he was and where he came from, of course, did not matter. What did matter was that his next stop was to be the port of Piraeus to pick up the coins that had been collected in Athens for King Otto. From there he was to carry them to Rome and deliver them to King Otto's ambassador.

Lord Tarnovo and his entourage of friends and servants were on the third galley. He was apparently the second or third son of one of the king's brothers and wore a gorgeous uniform to indicate his rank. It was immaculate, probably because he and his friends hid in one of the deck castles and barred its door during the fighting.

I put on my priestly robe and wooden cross and questioned Lord Tarnovo after introducing myself as a

Burgundian priest from Toulon by the name of Conrad. Why Conrad and Toulon? Because those were the names I wanted him and his friends to spread about after, or perhaps I should say if, we released them. We would use other names elsewhere.

Tarnovo was a classic insignificant prince in that he had an exaggerated sense of his own importance, an extremely fancy sword he had never used, and could neither read nor scribe nor gobble anything except Bulgarian. But he was a Latin and had brought a couple of priestly Latin clerics to assist him and translate for him. As a result, we were able to conduct our "negotiations" in Latin with his priestly clerks doing the translating.

Questioning Taranov and the priestly members of his entourage did not take long. They all three became very talkative when their choices were explained to them, especially after Tarnovo became Bulgaria's first nine-fingered nobleman. It soon became apparent that Tarnovo was a meaningless figurehead; it was the older of the two priests who was really in charge.

I made things very clear from the beginning.

"If you tell us everything and do not lie, we will take you three and the prince's friends with us to the Holy Land. When we get there, we will free you all so that you can make your way back home or join the crusade, whatever you wish.

"But if you do not truthfully answer ever question immediately, or if you lie and tell us something that differs from what we hear from one of the others when we speak to them privately, we will cut off your fingers one at a time until you tell us the truth."

One of the things I wanted to know, of course, was what arrangements had already been made with the Pope and what King Otto had been promised. We needed to know that so we would have some idea as to how much of our prize money we would have to "donate" to the Holy Father to keep him sweet.

The other important thing we needed to know was the names of the man or men in Athens who had the coins they were to pick up there. "And, by the way, have you ever seen any of them?" *Which was another way saying "would any of them recognize you if they saw you?"*

Our archers and sailors worked all the rest of that day and part of the next to move our galleys and the two usable prizes to one place, a wide section of the strait, and to redistribute their coins, slaves, and crews into the six galleys, four of ours and two prizes, that would be leaving immediately for Cyprus.

It was a happy time and our men were cheerful, and rightly so despite our casualties. They instinctively knew that we had taken an unexpectedly large amount of coins such that many a man's share might well be enough for him to buy himself out of the company and retire—twenty-one chests of gold and silver including a surprising number of gold bezants.

The surviving able-bodied and lightly wounded common sailors and soldiers of the four captured galleys took the place of their slaves and were chained to the lower rowing benches of two of the captured galleys. The two galleys were given very strong prize crews and immediately set their sails for Cyprus with some of the captured coins and a few of the slaves.

Jack Smith and Johnny White were each immediately given an additional stripe and appointed as the two captured galleys' prize captains with a couple of senior archer sergeants as their lieutenants and a couple of newly promoted sailors as their sailing sergeants. They were all quite pleased since it doubled their pay and prize shares and greatly improved their sleeping quarters.

My brother John went with Johnny White as his apprentice sergeant. I thought about promoting John to lieutenant but did not; he was still much too young and inexperienced to take over if Johnny went down, and the men would know it and be concerned.

We freed the slaves on all four of the captured galleys because they posed no threat as there were not nearly enough of them to have any chance of overcoming the archers with whom they would be sailing. They were scattered about all six galleys that would be sailing to Cyprus. Besides, they had no reason to rise against us. They would help with the rowing and be allowed to go ashore and begin making their way home as soon as they reached Cyprus. The captured galley crews would be released somewhere in the Holy Land.

Two of the enemy galleys were burned after the supplies they were carrying were removed. One because its hull was too badly damaged from colliding with a northbound barge to be quickly repaired, and the other because it was so decrepit and its hull was in such bad shape that Harold thought it would likely give way and the galley would sink if it encountered heavy seas.

All the captured coins were distributed among our four Cyprus-bound Company galleys along with all of the captured captains and sergeants to help them row. They too immediately set off for Cyprus.

The six galleys of our Cyprus-bound fleet, four of ours and the two prizes, would attempt to stay together all the way. It was a formidable force, both individually and as a fleet, such that it had more to fear from foul weather than any Moorish or Venetian pirates it might encounter. At least that is what we all thought.

Harold's galley and Captain Jackson's Number Forty-six did not sail with our Cyprus-bound fleet and did not take on any of the coins or slaves or prisoners. We would end up in Cyprus, but first we were going to Athens—to see if we could gull the Athenian supporters and financiers of King Otto into giving us the coins that were being assembled there for Lord Tarnovo and his men to carry to Rome.

Everyone in the crews of our six galleys who understood and gobble Greek was going with us to Athens, both of them. So was the nine-fingered leader of the Bulgarians and the two priests who were his clerics—they were in chains on the lower rowing bench in case we needed more information or their "assistance" when we reached Athens and had to deal with King Otto's coin collectors. In the meantime they would help with the rowing.

******

Our eight galleys were full of happy Company men as we sailed out of the strait and into the Aegean, and rightly so—we had captured a lot of coins such that there would be substantial prize money for everyone.

There was certainly more coins than I expected. That was because, according to young Lord Tarnovo, who had become extremely cooperative after our initial discussions, one of the great lords of the Eastern Rus had provided King Otto with several chests of coins in exchange for some disputed lands along the Danube. Otto had, or so his nine-fingered lordship claimed, accepted the Rus coins in order to reach the total that the Pope's nuncio, the Holy Father's ambassador to King Otto, said would result in the Holy Father's prayers being successful.

Did the nuncio actually know how much it would cost to get sufficient Papal prayers to have God decide that King Otto should be the Latin Empire's Regent or Emperor? Probably not: There had not been enough time since the Empress was murdered for the nuncio to be informed of her death, and then for a messenger to then carry an inquiry to Rome and carry the Pope's answer back to Bulgaria, and then for all the required negotiations and necessary arrangements to be made.

No, I decided. It would have been impossible for the nuncio to tell King Otto how many prayer coins would be needed and all the necessary arrangements made to get them *unless* the inquiry had been made and the negotiations started *before* the Empress died. As you might imagine, that interested me greatly even though I now knew who had killed her and my father.

On the other hand, at least so far as I was concerned, it was reasonable for the nuncio to tell King Otto a specific number of coins that would be required and for King Otto to begin raising them—it was reasonable for Otto because there was always the chance that the Pope would accept whatever Otto ended up being able to pay such that Otto's dreams would come true.

It was similarly reasonable for the nuncio to tell Otto a specific amount even though he had heard nothing from the Pope. He almost certainly been in Rome long enough to know that there was such a number and to have some idea as to what it might be.

More likely, however, was that the nuncio claimed to know the precise number to encourage Otto to obtain as many coins as possible—because he knew some of the coins would inevitably stick to his fingers even if the total ended up not being enough for the papal prayers needed to get a positive response from God.

I especially understood, or at least thought I did, why Otto had done everything possible to get enough coins to buy the necessary prayers—because even having a longshot chance of getting his hands on the entire Latin Empire was better than having a few more fields along the Danube. Besides, if he really missed his lands he could take them back by decree if he did become the Empire's Regent or Emperor, or by force if he did not.

And how much would Otto be willing to pay the Company to help him get his lands back if the Holy Father did not pray hard enough to get God to accept him? Hmm.

In any event, based on what I now knew about the Empress's death, Otto's odds of success at becoming the Empire's Regent or its Emperor were probably better than he thought even though he would almost certainly have to raise more coins and try again to get them to Rome.

That led me to begin daydreaming behind my eyes about how we might be able to get some or all of the next chests of prayer coins in addition to the current chests. It could be done, I decided. For example, we could carry them to Rome for a fee as we did for the Empress when she bought the regency. Or we could once again intercept them and take them all.

But how could we get away with them without making the Holy Father angry or risking the loss of the toll coins?

Stop thinking so far into the future, I told myself as I shook my head to clear it; we have not yet even taken all of the currently available prayer coins nor even safely reached Cyprus and Cornwall with those we have already taken.

****** *Commander Courtenay*

After we cleared the Dardanelles strait I sat alone on the roof of the forward deck castle with a bowl of wine and turned my thoughts once again to King Otto's coins—both those we had already taken that were disappearing over the horizon on their way to Cyprus and those we might be able to get our hands on when we reached Athens. What I was mostly thinking about were the coins that were thought to be waiting for Otto in Athens.

In the normal course of such events, the Holy Father's ambassador to King Otto, the papal nuncio, would get some of Otto's coins "for his services" and be able to use them to advance himself. The nuncios and ambassadors in Constantinople and Athens would similarly expect a share of whatever coins they helped to provide—and I wondered if they had already gotten them.

And that led to another thought.

Nuncios and ambassadors always expect to end up with some of the coins that pass through their hands. And "intermediaries" and "agents" almost always do. That raised the interesting question as to how they might be made to shoulder the blame for the loss of the coins.

Could it have been, for instance, that one or more of the papal nuncios or Otto's ambassadors tipped off an agent of the Moorish or Burgundian pirates, or some other pirates for that matter, as to the fact that the coins might be successfully taken when they came through the Dardanelles Strait?

I knew that was not the case, of course, since we were the ones who took them. But it *could* have been a nuncio or ambassador who told the Moors or the French or the Venetians or someone else about the coins in exchange for getting more of them.

And if it had been someone like that, or if everyone just *thought* that might be the case, it would certainly be helpful because one or more of them would be suspect in the coins disappearance so that less attention was paid to the Company.

It was a gambit I decided to try—nothing would be lost if providing more suspects did not work. But if it did, the list of those who might have been responsible for the coins going missing would get much larger because it would not be limited to the Burgandians or the French or, God forbid, the Company.

Suggesting that one or more of the nuncios or ambassadors tipped off one or more of the pirates who infested the Mediterranean in order to get a larger share of the coins was an interesting idea. It would, at the very least, make the disappearance of the coins even more confusing and the source of their loss even harder to pin down. The more the merrier so to speak. *Hmm? Yes, that would be a fine move to make.*

Thinking about how to get others blamed for the missing coins got me to thinking even more, which is always a good thing to do when one is trying to decide what moves to make to get his hands on more money. And then it came to me how we might be able to get the coins waiting in Athens and get someone else blamed for their loss.

We had a shipping post serving Athens, so once we cleared the strait and were underway I got to work scribing an important message for our post captain and his men. I decided to send it to Lieutenant Edward Sparrow at our Piraeus compound instead of to Robert Archer, the captain of our Athens shipping post which included Piraeus. It ordered Edward to deliver a second message which would accompany the first, a message that would already be written and sealed. It would go to the papal nuncio in Athens

I decided to use Edward as the messenger because Robert Archer was *not* the man to do what needed to be done. Edward was smarter; he was more likely to read between the lines and understand both what needed to be done and what must *not* be done.

Besides, Edward was literate and Robert was not, meaning Edward could read the first message with my instructions and Robert could not. If I sent Robert a message ordering him to secretly deliver the second parchment to the Athens nuncio, someone else, almost certainly an Athenian employed as a scribe, would have to read the delivery order and explain it to Robert.

Involving someone from outside the Company would not do. We had already suffered from one disloyal scribe in Athens; allowing his replacement to also hurt us would be unforgivable. And it would also be dangerous since it might lead them to be waiting for us with swords instead of with coins.

With that in mind, I scribed the second parchment that I wanted Edward to deliver to the nuncio in Athens. I did not suggest how Edward should accomplish the delivery of the second parchment to the nuncio, only that it be done without anyone being able to find out where it came from or who sent it. Edward was smart and knew the local situation; he would figure it out.

This is what I scribed in the message to be delivered to the nuncio. It was, of course, scribed in Latin.

"Excellency, we are here to collect King Otto's prayer coins and we are concerned because there are reports that the French and Moorish pirates and the Duke of Athens know about the coins and have spies in the households of the ambassador and the Metropolitan. The risk is too great that the coins will be intercepted. So please make the necessary arrangements to meet us without informing either of them as to when and where we collect the coins.

"We will bring one or two of our galleys to the north end of Piraeus's north quay on Wednesday evening just as the sun goes down. Please be there with the coins and as many guards as possible one hour after dark. I will try to be there, but I am in my bed with a terrible coughing pox and may not be able to come myself. If I cannot be there, our man will be one of my clerics,

Father Mathias. He will accept delivery and sign for them.

I signed the parchment as if I were a cleric writing for "Lord Tarnovo" and sealed it with his lordship's ring. I felt good about the message because it was not entirely a lie—I was not Father Mathias, of course. But I was probably close enough since I was a priest and could gobble Latin. And if I had even the smallest of opportunities, I would let it be known that I was from Constantinople.

There was, I knew for sure, a Father Mathias in Constantinople—he was Elizabeth's confessor. And from what Elizabeth had told me about the various penances and indulgences he had required of her as a result of her knowing me, I knew he was a greedier and more devious priest than most, and thus a worthy scapegoat whose elimination would benefit everyone.

Indeed, the more I thought about it, the more I was sure that no one was more deserving of the Holy Father's and King Otto's anger for the loss of the prayer coins than Father Mathias. And if not Father Mathias, then the other nuncios or any of the many others whose names I intended to suggest took whatever blame and penalties resulted from the loss of the coins.

Blaming anyone except the Company was quite acceptable so far as I was concerned, especially if they were like Father Mathias and deserved it. I know he did not alert any pirates about the coins, but he probably would have done so if he thought he could profit from it and that was close enough.

After I sealed the parchments with Lord Tarnovo's ring, which he had eagerly provided when I sent for it, my thoughts turned to the fact that I spent so much of my time trying to get more coins for the Company. I wondered if the Pope and Patriarch spent as much time thinking about coins as I did.

Probably not, I decided. They had other more important things to do. Why at this very moment the Holy Father might be standing at the top of the great stairway that leads up to the church that is the Holy Father's private chapel, the newly rebuilt ones the Spanish prince donated to the Church a few years ago, welcoming Jesus back and the dead people he had brought back with him.

Surely the Holy Father would not be thinking of coins at a time like that. He would be distracted the same way I was when I was fighting with someone who was trying to kill me or poking Elizabeth.

There was no doubt about it behind my eyes—we who were the commanders and captains of the still-growing companies of coin collectors like the archers were all alike. We had to work harder than the churchmen because our companies have not yet collected enough coins to see us through the peace that would occur when Jesus returned and brought some of the good dead people back with him.

Of course, like the Pope and Patriarch, we archers also wanted Jesus to return and bring the dead people who paid their tithes back with him as the Pope promised. Hopefully, however, that would not happen not until we had enough coins in our Restormel and Cyprus strongholds to see us through lean days of peace that are sure to follow Jesus's return and continue until he decides to go back to heaven again. Only then, when Jesus leaves again, would men turn on each other once again and we could get back to earning our daily bread by carrying refugees to safety and the like.

Is it possible Jesus has been periodically returning to see how we are doing? Uncle Thomas says it is possible because there have been several brief periods of peace when there was no fighting and we could find no mercenary contracts on which to make our marks and there were no refugees to carry to safety.

But who really knows if he did, return that is. I certainly did not. In any event, I had things to do until he decided to return and bide with us for a while—there were coins to fetch and blames and revenges to shift on to others, preferably those who deserved them.

Chapter Twenty-seven
A delivery is arranged.

We raised our sails and rowed hard in order to get to Athens before the news of the fighting in the strait could reach the Greeks' great city and alarm the coin collectors. We hurried because we were afraid that news of the fighting would put the gatherers and holders of coins for King Otto on guard and hamper our efforts to get our hands on them.

Fortunately, the weather was good and the winds fair so we made good time. The men were even able to take turns practicing archery and sword fighting when they were not rowing. Captain Jackson's galley kept up with us and did the same.

Perhaps even more important, we were also able to do what we could to make our two galleys look as much as possible like the Black Sea galleys we had taken a few days earlier. We would, of course, fly King Otto's pennants from our masts, the ones we took from the galleys we burned.

But merely flying King Otto's pennants was not enough, not near enough. The problem was that Harold's galley had forty-four oars to a side and Captain Jackson's had forty. All of the Black Sea galleys, on the other hand, were slightly smaller with a unique and noticeable thirty-six oars to a side that was common to the Black Sea. Accordingly, if there were any seamen amongst those who had gathered the coins or were guarding them, they might spot the difference and sound the alarm.

We responded to the problem by keeping our galleys' carpenters and their mates busy doing whatever they could to convert both of our galleys into what Harold and I hoped would look like Black Sea thirty-sixes. They mostly did it with hull patches that covered some the holes in our galleys' hulls where their oars were poked through to row.

The covers looked false when one got close enough, but we hoped they would pass at a distance. Even so, we decided not take any chances when we reached Piraeus—we would come in just as the sun was finishing its daily voyage around the world and anchor far enough out in the harbour that the number of oar openings in our hull could barely be counted by someone standing on the nearest shore.

As you might expect, our men would *not* be given a shore leave and no supplies would be purchased. Our plan was for Harold's galley to come in alone at the very end of the day to land the message telling King Otto's men that we were there to pick up the coins the next night at the far end of the north quay, and then, as soon as the messenger returned the next morning, immediately go back out to sea to re-join Number Forty-six.

Both galleys would then return together the next day, once again at the last minute just as it was getting dark, to pick up the coins. It was a reasonable plan. It was also the only one I could come up with that had any chance of success.

****** *Commander Courtenay*

The rain squall and its sudden winds hit us as I was being rowed ashore in the galley's dinghy. Harold's galley was anchored somewhere behind us with its archers almost certainly having been called to begin rowing so that it would hold its place against the gusting wind. The fading light of the day had suddenly turned into darkness and there were waves in the usually calm and sheltered harbour. It would pass.

I was being rowed ashore by two sailors so I could deliver my parchments to Edward Sparrow personally instead of sending them via a messenger. Why I was doing it myself? I was not sure. I told Harold I was going to go ashore and deliver the messages myself because I was afraid they would fall into the wrong hands, and also that I wanted to make sure that Edward Sparrow knew exactly what I wanted him to do.

What I told Harold was not exactly true, and I think he knew it. A better explanation was probably that I suddenly had an urge to get off the galley and walk on dry land. The big problem at the moment, of course, was that the land we were approaching was anything but dry.

Whatever the reason, I seemed to have made a mistake. The quay where the Company's shipping post had its Piraeus compound was quite a distance from where our galley was anchored. That was by design in case someone was watching. But it increasingly looked like it was a bad decision not to drop me off closer to our shipping post, or so it seemed to me now that I was sopping wet and my teeth were chattering from the cold wind.

One of the two sailors rowing me ashore in the gathering darkness was Anthony Thatcher, a two-stripe chosen man from Walmer whose father was, he claimed, the best roof thatcher in all of Kent. According to Harold, Anthony understood Greek and could gobble it fluently due to having a Greek wife on Cyprus and six children. I wanted him with me in case we ran into any Greeks and needed to talk or bribe our way out of trouble.

The other rower was Edwardo. He had no second name on the Company roll, probably because he was the only Edwardo in the entire Company. Edwardo was from a little fishing village somewhere on the Spanish coast. Apparently he had somehow joined the Company years ago when my father's galley put in there whilst searching for some missing relics. He was particularly good with a dinghy and was known as the best cook in the fleet.

Edward had always been favoured by my father because he too, like my father, had a bad leg and walked with a limp. Edwardo had been a fisherman as a boy but broke his leg when he fell off a mast. It had been set badly and Edwardo had walked with a limp ever since. That is what apparently caught my father's eye and caused him to be accepted as a recruit. Or it may have been that Edwardo was a very good cook and my father liked to eat. It was probably both.

My father, of course, had limped for another reason—he had taken a sword run all the way through his leg in a fight with some Moors. I was not sure how it happened as he never talked about it.

******

Water had to be constantly bailed out of the dinghy and I was wet and shivering by the time we finally made it to the strand next to the quay used by the Company's transports and galleys. The quay was empty except for a forlorn-looking three-masted ship and a couple of cogs. I did recognize any of them. And to make things worse, a wave came in and washed over me all the way up to my knees as I climbed out to help my two rowers pull the dinghy above the water line so it would not be caught by a rogue wave and float away. The water was cold and so was I.

Pulling the dinghy high enough on to the strand turned out to relatively easy even though we had to haul it quite a distance before we reached a large number of similarly stranded dinghies and small fishing boats. Most of them were turned over so they would not fill up with rainwater. Some, however, were tilted on their sides and there were men sheltering under them from the rain. They just looked at us in the dwindling light.

A couple of men sheltering under one of the fishing boats had somehow gotten a little fire going and were warming their hands on it. They looked up and one of them said something to us as we pulled the dinghy up next to them and turned it over.

Anthony, our Greek gobbling sailor, responded with a smile and they smiled back. One of them lifted his hand in acknowledgement of whatever it was that Anthony said. No one seemed to notice that I had a messenger's leather message carrying pouch slung over my shoulder and that all three of us were wearing sheathed swords.

After we got the dinghy placed amongst all the others pulled up on to the strand, and turned it over so it would not fill with rain water, we sloshed through the rain and mud to the Company's nearby compound—and damn near walked past it because of the darkness.

The compound's gate was already closed and barred for the night because the sun had finished passing overhead and night had fallen. I was exhausted and cold even though I had not had done any of the rowing, just the bailing which had been bad enough; God only knew how Edwardo and Vincent felt.

The walking helped but my teeth were still chattering and I was shivering as I pounded on both the gate and the little door in the gate with the handle of one of my wrist knives. It seemed to take forever until there was a voice on the other side. *Finally.*

"We are closed. What do you want?" a voice on the other side asked in crusader French. He sounded quite aggrieved at being out in the rain.

"We are archers. Let us in," I shouted.

"I cannot let you in without the lieutenant's permission," was the reply. The man was clearly quite suspicious about who we might be and our intentions. It was understandable; only fools would be out and walking about at night in such foul weather. Hopefully the city's night watch believed that and was staying in their guardroom.

"Well go get Lieutenant Sparrow and get permission. And run, damn you. It is wet and cold out here."

******

A few minutes later we were in the relative comfort of the Company's unheated post and being attended to by a very surprised and concerned Edward Sparrow and his wife. His little file of four long-serving Company veterans and their wives and a couple of children gathered quietly and looked on from the room beyond the post's reception area where they lived in separate tented spaces.

Normally I would have made straight for the archers and greeted them. This time I did not. What I hoped, instead, was they would not recognize me because I was wearing a one-stripe tunic, had cut my beard almost down to my skin, and was totally bedraggled from the our trip in the rain. If they recognized me they or their wives might talk.

Edward, however, had instantly recognized me and understood that I was there incognito. He was, however, visibly concerned about my unexpected arrival and worried that I would be angry about being kept out in the rain.

"Please excuse me for not letting you in right away, Commander," he said quietly so that no one else could hear what he was saying. "Charlie is a good man and he was following my orders not to let anyone in after dark."

"I agree with you totally, Edward; I only would have been unhappy if Charlie *had* opened the gate without making sure it was safe to do so—especially today."

And then I told him why I was there in a quiet voice so that once again no one else could hear.

"There is an important message from King Otto of Bulgaria that must be delivered to the papal nuncio in Athens as earlier as possible tomorrow, and it must be done without anyone knowing it was the Company that delivered it or ever finding out that we did or that I was ever here to help deliver it."

Edward thought about what I said before he replied.

"The nuncio will almost certainly be at the Duke of Athens' hall in the morning to get a free meal. If we walk fast it will take us three hours to get there. We could start before dawn and be there whilst he and the members of the court are breaking their nightly fasts in the Duke's hall."

"Aye, that would do." ... "But there is more. No one must ever know that I have been in Greece and I have to leave first thing in the morning at dawn's earliest light. So *you* will have to arrange the delivery of the message parchment to the nuncio. Can you disguise yourself and do it without anyone knowing that you did the deed, not even Robert Archer or your men or wife?"

"Aye Commander, I can do it. What should I tell my men and my wife?"

"Tell them that I am merely a messenger who brought rumours that the post might be attacked and robbed such that the men must be prepared to fight on a moment's notice and everyone must remain inside for their own safety. And starting now you are not to let anyone, not even the wives, leave the compound or talk to anyone for any reason for at least the next four or five days, not even to go to the market.

"Moreover, the Company's involvement in delivering the message must never be known and neither should it ever be known that I am the one who brought it to you. That is very important. So for the next week or so you and you alone are to do the Company's business by meeting with anyone who comes. You are to handle everything all yourself without any of the men or wives being present or allowed to talk to any visitors.

"And you are especially *not* to tell anyone, not even your wife, that you are going to Athens to deliver a message. I will also be leaving as soon as it is early light so you can tell everyone here that you will be accompanying us to the quay to bid us farewell and wish us a safe voyage.

"Now here is the thing, Edward, and mark it well. It may well be that the message you deliver to the nuncio will cause something to happen that will cast suspicion on the Company. I do not think it will if you disguise yourself properly before you deliver it, but it might despite your best efforts.

"If it does, men might come here and make inquiries. So stay on your guard and keep your gate and doors barred. Try to keep everyone out by claiming you are all down with the spotted pox. And, if you must, only let one or two visitors in at a time and make sure they have no weapons and that yours are at hand. Explain that the Company requires that no armed men be allowed to enter because the post has coins and other valuables here that must be guarded.

"Alternately, you might be summoned for questioning. If you are, plead a serious case of the pox and also that you must stay here to guard the post because of the coins and valuables. But keep up the appearance of being innocent and knowing nothing by saying you would be happy to talk to anyone who wants to visit and is willing to risk the pox.

"Can you handle all that?"

"Aye, Commander, I can handle it. You can count on me. But can you tell me what the message is about?"

"I can, but it is best that you not know so that you remain innocent if a problem ever develops. Even so, I want you to put your post on high alert. Make sure your men have their weapons at hand at all times and your emergency escape routes are ready for immediate use. Tell them that we brought word a possible robbery.

******

We spent the night at the post and returned to the dinghy as soon as the sun came up the next morning. We immediately launched it and rowed back to the galley. The weather was good and our clothes were dry because we had traded our wet tunics with three of Edward's men for their dry tunics.

Our stomachs were full as Edwardo and Anthony rowed me back. Edwardo and Edward's wife had arisen before dawn and used the kitchen in the courtyard to make what has become my favourite meal to break my nightly fast—"donkitos."

At my suggestion, Edwardo had brought a sack with the ingredients with him and enough additional food so that no one at the post would have to go to the market for three or four days. I asked him to bring the food because I knew we would have to break our fasts early and I did not want anyone going to the market and mentioning that the Company's shipping post had unexpected visitors, not until we were long gone.

Donkitos for breaking one's nightly fast are typically a combination of cheese, eggs rumpoled by being burnt on a piece of metal after being rapidly beaten with a wooden spoon, and sliced onions and peppers, and all of them then rolled up together in a soft flatbread such that nothing can fall out before it is eaten.

Edwardo had long ago told me he called it a "donkito" because it is like a little donkey that can carry a great load of many different things at the same time." He sometimes cooked other donkitos such as those with beans and slices of meat for my suppers or to carry about in my coin purse to eat during the day.

In any event, in the morning after the donkitos were properly burnt over the cooking fire, Edwardo covered them with the juice and seeds of the hot pepper juice that the Company's galley cooks sometimes put on meat when it is starting to smell. As a result, they were quite tasty and went down into my belly surprisingly well with a bowl of the post's morning ale despite the fact that I was coughing and sneezing and ached all over.

******

The early morning food was good but I had slept poorly and not enough. By the time we climbed back on to Harold's galley my face was red and I was coughing and sweating. I was poxed for sure.

Chapter Twenty-eight
The Athens coins.

Harold took one look at me as I climbed on to the deck of his galley and ordered me to go to the forward castle and get in bed. Then he began giving orders for the galley to begin rowing out of the harbour. The anchor had been hauled up as soon as the dinghy was sighted so we left immediately.

For a while I could feel the hull move each time the oars bit into the water. Then I did not remember anything until I woke up all wet from being drenched in sweat.

****** *Ten hours later*

"You look like shite. Are you sure you want to do this tonight? I can go to the quay and stand in for you if you would prefer to go back to bed."

Those were Uncle Harold's cheery words some hours later when I emerged coughing and sneezing from my berth in the galley's forward deck castle and made my way across the deck to the shite nest hanging over the galley's stern.

I was in a foul mood and very hungry. It was late in the afternoon. It was almost time to row back to Piraeus and, hopefully, pick up the coins. We were wallowing in small waves outside Piraeus's harbour with Captain Jackson's galley off to our starboard waiting with us. It would take us about an hour to reach the quay.

"No damn it, Harold. I will do it myself. I must; I am the only one other than your apprentice who has the Latin that will be needed to talk to the nuncio. And he would not be useful if something went wrong and you had to fight your way out, would he? So it must be me."

A few minutes later, and much relieved, I returned to Uncle Harold where he was waiting on the roof of the forward castle. I was still sneezing and coughing, but even hungrier. The roof of the forward castle was a captain's proper place when his galley was about to enter a harbour. His lieutenant, sailing sergeant, and apprentice had already been sent away so we could talk privately.

"Is everything ready for tonight?" I asked as one of the cook's helpers approached with a warm flatbread, a piece of beef that had been left on the fire so long that it was so over burnt and hard, and some cheese and morning ale. *I wonder how Edwardo is doing. He is obviously not doing the cooking this morning. That was the thought behind my eyes as I reached for the food.*

"Everything is as ready as it can be," was Harold's reply. Then he explained.

"We will arrive just as it gets totally dark and use our oars to hold our galley against the quay without using our mooring lines. Captain Jackson and his Number Forty-six will come in right behind us and do the same.

"As soon as we arrive you and I will climb up to the quay along with some sailors to help lower the coin chests down to our galley's deck. All the rest of our galley's men except the rowers will be armed and on the deck as a boarding party. They will be ready and waiting in case a rescue is needed.

"The boarding party will be up the ladders and on the quay in a lightning flash if everything turns to shite. The men know you and I will be carrying candle lanterns to identify us if there is fighting. So whatever you do, do not drop your lantern until you jump down to the deck."

"And the sailors will be ready to stow the chests? Do they know they will be heavy?"

"Aye. Robby Morgan, Johnny White's replacement, knows how to lower chests from a quay to a galley's deck. He has been doing it for almost twenty years. He will be on the deck sergeanting the sailors and archers who have been assigned to receive the chests and stow them.

"You and I will stay on the quay and see that the nets are loaded and lowered, and to make sure all the sailors doing the lowering get safely back on board. Jack Smith's replacement, William Castle will stay on deck with the boarding party and be instantly ready to lead the boarders up the ladders and on to the quay if a rescue is needed. I will already be there with you, of course.

"Captain Jackson will bring his galley up to the quay alongside us at the same time we get there. He and his men will also be instantly ready to join in the rescue if we need one. But he will do nothing unless William Castle leads our boarding party on to the quay."

******

There were already men waiting on the quay as we slowly approached it in the dark. We knew there were at least three because we could see the lanterns they were carrying moving about. There may have been more men and, hopefully, coin chests or carts carrying them. But if there were, it was too dark to see them as we slowly and silently rowed up to the quay and used our oars to hold our galley against it.

And it was too dark to see. The storm had passed while I slept but there were still a lot of clouds in the sky and only a partial moon.

Not a word was spoken as we approached the quay and the light of day totally disappeared. The only noise was the sound of our oars, the creaking of the hull, and the crunch of the twigs and branches in our hull bumpers as they were pushed up against the stone side of the quay. Even the harbour gulls were quiet; they had gone off to sleep away the night.

The silence was understandable—the men had been ordered to maintain total silence at all times; any man who spoke so much as a single word would lose all his stripes.

"Who are you and where did you come from?"

A voice in the darkness asked in Greek and then in Latin as the boarding ladders were put in place and Harold and I began to climb them.

I answered in Latin as I began slowly and cautiously climbing the six or seven feet from the galley's deck to the quay.

"We are King Otto's men and we have just arrived from Constantinople to collect some chests that belong to him. Is everything ready? Is there any danger?"

I gave my answer and then coughed such a great rasping cough and sneezed that I would have become overbalanced if I had not grasped the ladder tightly with my one free hand.

There was no doubt about it, I decided; climbing even a short distance on a boarding ladder set on a galley's slightly bobbing deck is not the easiest thing to do when you are carrying a lighted candle lantern in one hand and have a big wooden cross hanging from your neck and a sheathed short sword hanging down under an ankle-length priest's robe.

My rusty chain shirt and wrist knives, on the other hand, did not bother me, probably because I was so used to wearing them at all times except when I was sleeping or with a woman.

"There is no danger." ... "Where is Lord Tarnovo?" a man asked as he held his lantern up for a moment so he could get a look at my face as I swung my leg from the ladder to the quay.

"He is greatly poxed and may be dying even though he has not yet made his final confession and received his last prayers. Many of us are poxed. It is God's Will and cannot be changed. I am Father Mathias, his cleric." ... "Do you have the shipment ready?"

"Two carts with the chests are waiting nearby, Father. A man was sent to fetch them when we saw your galleys approaching. They will be here in a few minutes."

A minute or so later we could hear distant voices and the wheels of the carts as they clattered over the quay towards us. A few moments after that we could see the very dim outlines of carts and the horses pulling them.

There were two carts and they seemed to be surrounded by a large number of men on foot. We could hear them talking quietly and moving about. The men appeared to be carrying weapons but I could not make out for sure what they were carrying because of the darkness. Spears and clubs I later realized when the clouds parted for a moment. A church's protection gang for sure.

"Here they are. You can start unloading them. Best you hurry so we can get out of here before the Duke's night watch sees the lights and comes for a visit."

I waved my lantern back and forth.

Waving the lantern was the signal for the loading to begin. Silent figures immediately began climbing up the boarding ladders. They were carrying the galley's loading nets with them.

Within seconds the loading nets were being spread out along the edge of the quay. Not a word was spoken as the chests were hurriedly unloaded from the horse carts and placed in the middle of each net. The chests were heavy. It took two men to carry each of them. The guards appeared to be gathered in a great semi-circle around the carts but did not volunteer to help.

Ropes attached to the corners of the nets were then used to lower them down to the men waiting on the galley's deck a few feet below. There were dozen or so sailors and archers assigned to the task, three for each net on the quay and three more on the galley below to receive them.

It went smoothly despite the darkness, and there was no surprise in that; not only were Harold's men experienced at loading a galley, they had spent most of the previous day practicing climbing up to a quay and lowering heavy chests down to the galley's deck. They had used chests full of ballast rocks for the coin chests and the roof of the stern castle for the quay.

Then it happened. Someone held a lantern up to my face and looked at me closely.

"You are not Father Mathias from Constantinople," he said accusingly in Latin. I did not know who it was but I suspected the nuncio.

"Well you are certainly right about that," I whispered in reply with an unfriendly laugh and a cough that bent me over and sprayed him. "I am Father Mathias from Burgundy. Who are you?"

"Your men are strangely quiet," he said venomously in Latin instead of answering my question. "Why is that?"

"It is probably because they were told that any man who uttered a word would be hung," I replied in a hissed whisper. "Piraeus has an active night watch, or so we were warned in Constantinople, and we do not want to attract their attention. Is it true or not that the city has a night watch?"

"Well, yes it does. But I do not …."

"Then kindly lower your voice and get that light out of my eyes so I can see what King Otto's sailors are doing, eh?"

I whispered my order with an arrogant snarl and pushed away the lantern. He stepped back and obeyed. I was relieved—and he would have been too if he had realized how close he had come to getting one of my wrist knives in his throat.

Chapter Twenty-nine
Another deception.

Both of our galleys remained at anchor near the quay all night and for most of the following morning. The sun was high overhead and the sky was only partly cloudy when we finally rowed out of the harbour and set our course for Cyprus. It was a brisk day in late October.

Originally we had planned to leave quietly in the night as soon as we finished loading the coin chests. That was changed after we finished loading them when Harold and his new sailing sergeant decided that leaving the harbour that night would be too dangerous because it was too crowded and visibility too poor.

"Why take a chance when it is not necessary, eh?" was how he put it.

Harold and his sailing sergeant were right, of course. There was no need to risk a collision in the dark now that we had the chests on board. And the idea that there was a fighting force in the harbour, let alone anywhere in the Aegean, that could take two fully crewed Company galleys was just plain absurd. At least that is what we thought at the time. Accordingly, when we finished loading the coin chests we merely moved about an arrow's flight away from the quay and dropped our anchors to spend the night.

And after thinking about it whilst we were hoisting a few bowls of ale to celebrate our Company's newest fortune, I decided to change our departure time again—we would, I announced to everyone's surprise, remain in the harbour and close to the quay for most of the next morning because "there are changes that have to be made."

Our galleys would continue to be on alert, of course, but they would remain anchored off the quay such that everyone on shore would be able to see them quite clearly when the sun returned on its daily trip around the world.

******

Our galleys spent the night together just off the quay, and then continued staying there throughout the next morning whilst they were implementing my new plan. It was actually quite simple.

We had used King Otto's pennants and the hull coverings over some of the oar ports to gull the coin collectors into thinking we were Black Sea galleys so they would turn the coins over to us. Now it was time to shift the blame for the theft of the coins and further increase the confusion and uncertainty as to who had taken them.

Accordingly, we did *not* sail away in the dark towards Rome as the nuncio and other collectors of King Otto's coins had undoubtedly expected us to do. To the contrary, we remained in the harbour near the quay in plain sight of everyone on the quay and aboard the nearby boats in the densely packed harbour.

About two hours after sunrise, when the quay was crowded with people going about their normal activities, I ordered the Burgundian flag with its blue and gold stripes hoisted on the masts of both galleys to replace King Otto's pennant and the fake covers removed from our oar ports.

As I expected and hoped, the changes were seen and noted as soon as they began being made. The quay soon became more and more crowded with onlookers. Most of the onlookers did not know what had happened or why, but they did know that it was significant and worth talking about when war galleys suddenly changed their flags and altered their appearances.

There was no question in my mind; it would soon be the talk of both Piraeus and Athens that a couple of galleys that initially looked as though they belonged to King Otto had suddenly changed their flags and appearances to become Burgundians.

There was no way to know if the nuncio and his fellow coin collectors actually came to the quay in time to see for themselves that they had probably turned the coins over to the wrong galleys. It did not matter; word would sooner later reach them about the galleys fighting in the Dardanelles strait, about the coins not reaching Rome, and about the strange happenings in the Piraeus harbour the morning after the coins were collected by Lord Tarnovo's galleys.

Sooner or later King Otto and his coin collectors would put things together and understand that the coins had been turned over to someone other than Lord Tarnovo and had promptly disappeared. And that raised a number of questions as to what everybody involved would then think and do. Perhaps, for example, Lord Tarnovo and his men had sailed off with them. Or perhaps it was the Moors or French or Venetians or the English archers. It was impossible to know for sure. *We hoped.*

The immediate questions, of course, were whether King Otto would blame the Burgundians or Lord Tarnovo or someone else for their loss, and what would happen to Father Mathias and those of King Otto's supporters who would be suspected of helping them or were guilty of letting them get away with the coins. I myself really did not care who was blamed or what happened to them so long as there was enough uncertainty and confusion about the loss of the coins and their whereabouts such that nothing bad happened to the Company.

A much more important question, at least so far as the Company was concerned, was how King Otto and the Holy Father would react to the loss of the coins and how their loss would affect the current and future regents and emperors of the Latin Empire. Specifically, did Otto's inability to pay for enough of the Pope's prayers mean that Elizabeth and her young brother would still be in those positions when I returned to Constantinople in the spring?

I certainly hoped they would be able to hold on to the throne and be there when I returned to Constantinople next year, and not just because I wanted the Company to continue collecting the tolls and keeping them.

Chapter Thirty
Return to Cyprus.

Our voyage to Cyprus turned out to be quite uneventful. We encountered one storm that blew us slightly off course and separated us from Captain Jackson for a day, but otherwise we had a rather pleasant time of it with plenty of archery practice and moors dancing.

We reached Cyprus and came around the island to Limassol on a fine October day. There was great happiness aboard the galley as we did. It was understandable. This was the galley's home port and some of the men had families here. And most of the rest had their favourite taverns and public women.

What really had everyone excited, however, was that Harold's crew would soon be receiving their prize coins for both Venice and for the more recent fighting in the Dardanelles. It would be a huge amount for every man and they knew it. Harold was concerned. He thought that as many as half of his crew would take their coins and retire, even the young one-stripers.

I was much less concerned about it.

"Yes, Uncle Harold, you are right. We will lose some good men. But think of what it will do for our ability to recruit good men to replace them when they return to England with their prize money and begin buying land and hovels in their home villages!

"Besides, serving in the Company is a good life compared to living in a village or the foulness of London. In the end I would wager that less than one in five of your crew will take their prize coins and leave us. The rest will either leave their prize money on the Company's books until they have even more, or they will take their coins and squander them on women and gambling—and I will wager you an amphora of good Italian wine on it."

"Less than one in five, you say. And for an amphora of wine? Done, by God, even though it is the first time I ever made a bet I wanted to lose."

We smiled at each other and laughed as we spit on our hands and bumped our fists to seal the bet.

"I know they are good men, Uncle Harold, I truly do. And I hope you are wrong about so many of them leaving. I would be as surprised and unhappy as a fish out of water, or perhaps I should say out of wine, if more than one man in five leaves.

"Now how about we get out of the wind and have one last game of chess and a bowl of ale before we go ashore and have to face Henry's widow?"

******

Yoram and a large throng of people came hurrying down to the quay to greet us as we rowed into the harbour. The six galleys from the Dardanelles strait fighting had arrived safely some days earlier so everyone had heard about the fighting in the strait, and the new additions to our fleet and coin chests that came of it; what they wanted to know now was where the galleys of Harold and Captain Jackson had gone afterwards and what they had done and who had been lost.

Harold and Captain Jackson and their sailing sergeants knew where we had been, of course, and so did their lieutenants. They had to know so they could get us to Piraeus. But it was a Company secret for obvious reasons and they had been sworn to never mention it to anyone, not even their wives.

Our men, however, were not entirely sure where we had been or what we had done. Some of them thought they had sailed to Piraeus after the fighting in the strait, because that was what a few of the sailors were claiming to be the case. But most of the sailors were not absolutely sure since they were never allowed to go ashore and everyone had originally been told that the port we would be visiting was Thessaloniki.

Even more importantly, only Harold and I knew for sure what we took aboard when we crept to the quay as the light was fading and loaded a dozen heavy chests in the dark. The men thought it might be coins because the crates were heavy and because of the great care that was taken loading them. But they were not certain because Harold and I had deliberately confused things by allowing ourselves to be overheard calling such things as "are you sure the flower paste has been stored where it will not get wet, Sailing Sergeant?"

Yoram, of course, wanted an immediate report as to what was in the chests and what losses we had suffered getting them. I put him off.

"Their contents are valuable and that is a fact. But it is a long story. Tonight at supper Harold and I will tell you all about buying the chests of flower past in Thessaloniki. But first I want to know about the men who were wounded fighting the French galleys in the Dardanelles Strait, the ones that raided the grain fleet."

I said it loud enough that the people walking around us could hear. If the past was any guide, it would be repeated in the taverns that night, known to every merchant in the Limassol market before noon tomorrow, and talked about in every port of the civilized world within the month.

That was all I told Yoram about the chests as we walked from the quay to the Company's fortress. We did so, walked to the Company's fortress that is, leading a grand procession of several hundreds of people including Yoram's wife and children and a horse-drawn wagon on which the chests had been loaded.

We passed through the familiar gates and bailies of our fortress's four curtain walls and kept walking until we reached the citadel in innermost bailey. The chests were immediately unloaded from the wagon and stowed away in one of the two rooms on the upper floor of the citadel.

The room where the chests were taken was the most secure place in the entire fortress. And rightly so because it was where Company's coins and the priceless pain-killing flower paste were stored. And the chests certainly were safe once they were in it. It was a room with no wall openings whose only entrance was a door in one of the walls of the room where Yoram and his family lived and slept.

Yoram's room, in turn, had no entrance door at all, just an opening in the floor through which a ladder poked up from the hall below, the hall where I and the Company's visiting lieutenant commanders and major captains ate and slept when we were ashore. The ladder was pulled up at night and whenever else Yoram wanted to further isolate himself and the Company's treasures.

The citadel, and thus the chests stored in it, would be extremely difficult for invaders or robbers to reach. It was in the centre of a fortress with enough water, food, and firewood to withstand a three year siege. It was also a particularly powerful fortress because it was ringed by no less than four separate tall and thick curtain walls that an attacker would have to fight through to get to them and their defenders.

Each of the walls that ringed it had only one entrance gate and enclosed a bailey where the men with certain ranks and their families lived. And each of the stone walls had periodic towers along it that were within arrow range of the towers on either side of it. Each bailey's wall was longer than the one it surrounded and housed more people.

The innermost of the four baileys and the towers of its wall were inhabited by the Company's Cyprus-based men with the rank of lieutenant or higher and their families. The next innermost bailey and its towers was home of the men and families with the rank of sergeant and higher. The third was inhabited by the Company's one and two-stripers, and the fourth by the Company's servants and workers.

A fifth wall was under construction to keep everyone busy and out of mischief. It would circle the outermost of the existing four and enclosed an area so large it would almost reach the Limassol city wall when it was complete. Passengers waiting for passages lived in the immediately adjacent city of Limassol or in cell-like rooms in the fifth wall's partially completed bailey.

Each bailey had at least one kitchen and a well. As you might imagine rank had its privileges. Accordingly, the baileys got larger and larger and the living quarters of the men and their families living in them got smaller and smaller the further out they were from the citadel where Yoram and his family safely lived in splendid isolation.

Taken all together, the Company's fortress on Cyprus was probably the strongest fortress in the world. It certainly needed to be in view of the state of the world and its location.

So how would we take it if we were on the outside instead of the inside? It was a question we constantly asked ourselves when we were drinking. Trickery or starvation or hostage taking seemed to be the only answers. And hostage taking would not work because anyone in the Company who was taken or compromised would be immediately replaced by someone being promoted into his position.

The Company, in other words, would not be going away if someone killed or captured its Commander and his heirs.

******

Harold and I visited Henry's widow as soon as the chests were safely stored away. I brought her a coin pouch full of the latest prize coins Henry had earned and assured her of what she already knew—that she and the Company's other widows would always get their husband's half pay until they remarried.

The widow's name was Jeanette and she was French. She had met Henry years ago whilst the crusaders were preparing to assault Constantinople. My father had recruited her as a spy when she was a forlorn and starving widow in the foetid crusader camp across the water from wall that circled the city. Henry had met her and gotten to know her when she came to the Company's little strip of neutral concession land next to the wall to make her periodic reports.

I told Jeanette what I knew of how Henry died even though I really did not see him go down or how it happened. And, of course, I lied and said it all happened so quickly that he probably never felt a thing. It was what we always said when someone fell.

Jeanette's eyes teared up and she wept for a while as I hugged her and patted her on her back. Then she listened carefully whilst I told her why we were in the tunnels and how I had been knocked on the head and played dead after Henry and I entered the strange room and were almost instantly attacked and overwhelmed.

"He is buried in Constantinople, George. Is there any chance my daughter and I could go there to visit and pray for him? He would like that, I think."

"Of course, Jeanette. I know he would. You just say the word when you want to go and Yoram will arrange everything.

Damn I hate it when someone weeps and sobs for a good reason. It makes me want to weep and sob too. So we all did, even crusty old Harold.

******

We talked of many things that night whilst we sat in Yoram's little hall and ate our supper of freshly burnt fish and lamb with the new-style round bread loaves with balsamic vinegar and olive oil. Yoram was absolutely delighted when we explained what had really happened at Piraeus and why we were deliberately spreading confusion such that others might be held responsible.

Yoram, in turn, told us how the Company's regular custom and shipping posts were doing and explained the numbers to us. They were very encouraging. It seems the renewed fighting between the Crusaders and the Saracens was causing more desperate passage-buying refugees and the renewal of charters for standby escape galleys at Alexandria and several of the Syrian ports.

Also up were our revenues from money transfers and general cargos. There was no doubt about it; we would have a large number of coins to send to Cornwall as soon as the winter storm season passed.

And send the coins we would. According to Yoram, a total of eleven different galleys and eight transports were already scheduled to sail for England in the spring and many more were expected to follow them. They would be carrying everything from spices and flower paste to passengers such as returning crusaders and pilgrims. And every one of them would be carrying a chest or two of coins. Some of the cargos and passengers would continue on to France and the Low Countries; the coins would not.

Another bit of news was that our relations with Cyprus's King and his regent remained cordial and were expected to continue that way just as they had for many years. That was understandable since the current king was two years old and lived on the far side of the island with his mother who was his regent.

It also helped that his mother was quite young and very much under the control of her chancellor, a minor lord and distant relative named Phillip Ibelin. According to Yoram, Ibelin was smart enough to recognize that the Company was far stronger than the kingdom. Accordingly, he was apparently afraid, and rightly so, that we would throw them out take over the entire island if they bothered us in any way.

At some point in the evening, I asked Yoram about the Company's relatively new scribing and summing school for men with potential who are already archers. I particularly wanted to know about the progress of Sergeant James Howard who had been in Constantinople as the assistant to the Company's late and greatly lamented alchemist.

James had been sent here to the new school to learn to scribe. He needed to be able to do so in order to write reports and keep records as he tried to perfect the man-made lightning and the "ribaldis" that the Company's alchemist he had been assisting in Constantinople had built—and died when he used them against the Greeks.

What really got to me and that I remember most from that evening was seeing Yoram surrounded by his loving family and suddenly realizing how much I missed my wife and children. In the spring I would definitely return to Cornwall to spend the summer.

Chapter Thirty-one
Homeward bound.

Time flew by and the beginning of spring in the year 1220 arrived before I knew it. It was time for my annual voyage back to Cornwall. This time would be a little different in that I was adding Constantinople to the stops I would make along the way to visit our shipping posts.

Harold and Yoram were greatly fluxed by my decision. They pointed out that a visit to Constantinople would definitely involve a major detour that would add weeks to the voyage.

I had a reason for going, a very good one so far as I was concerned, but I did not share it with my lieutenants. Instead, I reminded them that the Company's biggest single regular source of coins were the tolls we collected from all the shipping that used the Bosporus and Dardanelles straits.

The tolls, of course, being the tolls the Company collected and kept in exchange for helping to protect the Latin Empire's great capital city by keeping pirates and enemy fleets out of its waters and helping to man its wall when it was attacked. The waters being the Marmara Sea and the Bosporus and Dardanelles straits at either end of it.

I expected my return to England would involve an interesting and comfortable voyage on Harold's galley. For one, James Howard, the Company's only expert on turning lead into gold would be sailing with us. He did it by using the man-made lightning that occurred when a flame was put to a proper mixture of powdered sulphur, charcoal, and bird shite.

James had just been promoted to Lieutenant to give him the rank and authority to get it done. He also played a good game of chess. I was looking forward to learning more about his progress whilst we played.

Hopefully James will sooner or later be able to make gold by focusing sufficient amounts of the man-made lightning on pieces of lead. In the meantime he has been told to concentrate on making better ribaldis for the Company, the hollowed out logs and strapped together horse watering troughs that can be used to throw stones long distances when fire is put to a mixture of the powders and causes the thunder and lightning to occur.

James was sailing with me because Uncle Thomas wanted him to make both the gold and the ribaldis in Cornwall so he, Uncle Thomas, himself can learn how to do it and be able to teach it to the boys in his school at Restormel. Accordingly, Cornwall is where I am taking James. Moreover, and even though James is only a new lieutenant, he will be accompanied by a young apprentice sergeant from Uncle Thomas's school by the name of Alfred Hayward.

Alfred was an orphan lad from a village of royal heath wardens and deer hunting guides in Sussex who was spotted by the village priest who called him to the attention of Uncle Thomas. He was successfully learnt to scribe and sum and gobble Latin in the Company school at Restormel, and came east with the early leavers from the Company school for the Greek war.

Initially Alfred was one of the lads assigned to assist Yoram as one of his clerics. Yoram, in turn, determined that Alfred was good at thinking behind his eyes and assigned him to work with James. His assignment was to assist James in the making of gold and ribaldis, and to help James improve his scribing and summing—and in the process learn and scribe all he can about the making of gold and ribaldis in case James goes down.

Having men in the Company who know how to make gold would be very useful when Jesus returns. For when he does our coins from carrying refugees and cargos will almost certainly dry up because peace will break out and everyone will have enough to eat and not have to worry about such things as invaders and pirates.

In the meantime, until Jesus does return, knowing how to make and use ribaldis would help the Company earn coins by killing invaders and pirates, particularly if we can figure out how to use them on our galleys and transports.

In other words, and despite the uncertainty surrounding Jesus's return, it would clearly be a win-win situation and guarantee the Company's future if the secret of making of both gold and man-made thunder and lightning could be perfected and known only to the Company—and that explained why the Company was putting so much effort into it.

******

It was a brisk spring morning when we threw off our mooring lines and began rowing out of Limassol's harbour to begin our long voyage to Cornwall via Rhodes and Constantinople. Gulls were circling overhead and several hundred people were on the quay to see us off and have their pockets picked.

Harold's galley was prepared for every eventuality. Our hold was full of food and water and our deck was covered with struggling birds and beasts to be killed and eaten along the way. Every man aboard was either an experienced archer or sailor. In other words, we would be virtually impossible to catch or take.

We were carrying parchment orders and offers for merchants and also parchment money orders directing our shipping posts to provide certain amounts of coins at one post as a result of larger amounts of coins deposited at another post. What we were not carrying were passengers and cargos.

As the highest ranking man on board I was living alone in the galley's forward desk castle. And I was living luxuriously with my own bed and sleeping furs that I did not have to share with anyone else. I also had two wooden stools in case I had a visitor I wanted to sit with, and a flat wooden board with raised sides fixed to the wall such that it would not slide about and could be used for scribing or playing chess or holding a bowl of ale or wine if the sea was not so rough as to cause sloshing.

An amphora of wine was lashed securely into the far corner of the little castle. I had won it in wager with Uncle Harold because fewer than one in five of the galley's crew had run. He had paid under protest because some of his crew had their prize coins with them and were likely to leave the Company as soon as they reached England.

On the other hand, there had been no problem about the collection of my winnings. I promised Uncle Harold that we would drink it up together during the voyage and that, because he might still win the wager, I would pay to have the amphora re-filled in Lisbon for our trip across to England and back.

There is never any need to wait when good wine is involved.

******

Harold's galley called in at the island of Rhodes even though we had enough water, food, and firewood supplies on board to reach Constantinople without stopping. We did so at the request of Rhode's self-proclaimed Caesar, Leo Gabalas.

A few weeks earlier his chancellor had used our little four-man shipping post to send a message to Cyprus requesting that Company have someone call in at Rhodes for a visit—someone of high rank who was "authorized to discretely negotiate a matter of mutual interest and make his mark on a contract related to it."

It was an intriguing message and I decided to follow up on it. As a result, less than an hour after we arrived in Rhodes' harbour Harold and I were being ushered into the court of the island's self-proclaimed Caesar. The ushering was done by a very officious and highly costumed courtier who tried to tell us how we were to behave when we met "Caesar." I nodded my head in agreement and told Harold to ignore him and copy me.

We were led into a great hall that was conspicuous by being empty of everyone except two men—one sitting in an elevated chair with a golden ring atop his head and the other standing next to him. Being quick witted and intelligent, I quickly deduced the "Caesar" was the man sitting in the chair and no one else was present except his advisor because he did not want anyone to know about our conversation.

I walked up to them and gave a great sweeping bow to convey great respect, even if I did not particularly mean it. What I did not do was what the flunky pointedly told me was expected and appropriate—bang my head on the stone floor as my father told me old King Guy used to require on Cyprus before his death and

Elizabeth had recently begun requiring new arrivals to do when they first came to her court.

In fact, I would have banged it if I had thought it would improve my bargaining position for whatever the island's Caesar wanted, but I did not bang my head for Elizabeth and was not about to begin for this one just because he wanted everyone to think he ruled his island with a strong hand. It probably meant he felt as insecure as Elizabeth.

The Caesar of the island motioned for me to come forward, and then surprised me by gobbling to me directly in crusader French instead of using a translator.

"Thank you for coming, Commander. We asked you to visit Rhodes because the Venetians are sniffing about and *We* have heard many good things about the Company of Archers, including that it honours its mercenary contracts. We would like to negotiate such a contract with you to help protect our island against the Venetians."

Ah, so he is a "we" and a contract is what "we" wants.

"That would require many men and galleys to be available on relatively short notice, Caesar. It is possible, of course, but only if there are enough immediately available coins to pay them and buy their food and shelter."

Of course, I pretended he was a Caesar and addressed him as such; a coin is a coin no matter the name of the man who hands it to you. Besides, anything we received for keeping the Venetians out of this corner of the Aegean would be found money as we were not about to let the Venetians or anyone else bring galleys into the waters between Cyprus and Constantinople.

"Ah, there is something else, Commander. We will also require a galley to be stationed here that is instantly available carry messages in the event the Venetians or any other enemies arrive and infest our waters. We have a galley of our own, of course, but it may be away sometimes when a message needs to be sent quickly for some reason or another.

"We understand that your company has contracted to provide such messenger galleys elsewhere. Is that true?"

"It is true, Caesar. You are indeed well informed. Our Company presently is providing standby messenger galleys at Alexandria and Acre and several other ports. They are immediately available to instantly take whoever contracts for their use to wherever he wants to go."

He kept calling them messenger galleys, but they were really instantly available escape galleys. He obviously wanted one in case his people rose against him or the Venetians or the Nicean king who was his overlord or anyone else came for him. I immediately began wondering what was worrying him; just about everything from the sound of it.

"Caesar, the cost of a fully crewed and provisioned galley for a year depends on how many of our archers and sailors must be instantly available to launch it and to work its sails and do the rowing. And they must be fed and have a place to live in addition to being paid and there must be a place where the galley can be pulled ashore and quickly launched whenever it is needed."

Caesar and his chancellor, who turned out to be his brother, nodded their heads and we commenced to bargain. It is always necessary to bargain when dealing with Greeks.

******

Harold gave his men liberty coins to spend in the handful of taverns in the little island's one walled city that night. In the morning I made my mark on a two-year contract and we rowed away with another chest of coins. The chest had enough coins in it for two years of the Company of doing whatever was necessary to keep the Venetians out of the waters around Rhodes and half of the coins for the first year of a two year contract for a crewed "messenger galley."

The rest of the first year's coins were to be paid upon the arrival of a seaworthy galley with no less than twenty able-bodied archers and sailors to crew it. The Caesar of Rhodes would keep it stocked with supplies and provide the rest of necessary rowers, no doubt from his loyal servants who were running away with him.

"It is not just the Venetians he is worried about, is it?" Harold had asked as we watched the chest with the coins being stowed away.

"He is probably worried about everyone. Nicea even more than the Venetians I would wager and the Hospitallers more than the Niceans. And also, or so it sounds, he is worried about the loyalty of his galley's crew or that it might not be seaworthy. Probably both.

"What he knows most of all, I would think, is that his enemies are quite likely to go after his galley and are not likely to risk of attacking one of ours."

Harold reflected on my words for a few moments, and then nodded his head.

"Well, at least the coins are right and we have found employment for one of the Black Sea galleys we took last year. Now if we could just find another dozen or so archers to serve in its crew."

Chapter Thirty-two
The end of an affair.

We reached the company's concession next to Constantinople's great city wall on a windy and rainy day in middle of April. "It is good to see our concession," I said to James Howard as we stepped ashore.

"This little strip of land between the sea and the city wall has been the Company's ever since my father and his men defeated the Byzantine Emperor's army when the Emperor was foolish enough to send it out from behind the city walls to fight them. I would hate to be known as the man who lost it."

A messenger had been sent to fetch Michael Oremus as soon as our galley was sighted as it rowed toward the quay. Michael showed up immediately and gave me a brief report of the state of things in the city. Then we started off so I could pay my respects to the Empress and gage the state of her feelings toward me and the Company.

Harold remained behind with the captain of our shipping post to deal with the inevitable minor galley matters such as arranging the delivery of new supplies and finding a barber for an archer who had broken his arm the day after we left Rhodes.

People and wagons of all types filled the streets despite the rain that was causing some people to run from one place of shelter to the next. The only things that had changed in the city in the months since the sunny day I sailed away were the absence of the city's numerous cats and the increased need to be careful where you put your sandals down, particularly in a puddle of water because you had no way of knowing how deep it was or what was in it.

Of course we did not see any of the city's many cats as we walked to the Great Palace; they were too smart to be out in the rain. We, on the other hand, were getting wet and chilled from the driving rain despite the hooded wool-covered rain jackets we were wearing over our tunics. What we needed were some of the little leather tents on the top of poles that some of the gentry-dressed people on the street were carrying.

Michael brought me up to date on the various things that had happened whilst I was gone as we splashed our way through the streets to the Great Palace. I listened carefully even they were things I already knew about from the parchment reports he had sent to Cyprus some months earlier.

"The Regent delivered up a boy while you were away, Commander. So far as I know it is still alive and healthy. The merchants say the young lad from Epirus who is her husband is amazed and his father is ecstatic because there is another boy available if her husband should be lost. Rumour has it that her husband does not know enough about his wife or his father to be worried."

Michael looked at me out of the corner of his eye after he delivered the news. Then he continued.

"I also received your message and did what you suggested Commander—I had an audience with the Regent and reported that King Otto's efforts to buy the Pope's prayers had been totally nobbled and his prayer coins lost. As you suggested, I spoke with her privately when I told her and did *not* tell her who did it or how it was done.

"She asked, of course, but I said I did not know the facts, only that I was sure that King Otto's ability to buy the necessary prayers had been ended. She said she was pleased but I got the feeling that there was still some kind of problem."

My only response was to nod to Michael and say "thank you." I did not tell him that it would not make any difference.

******

Michael and I handed our dripping wet sheepskins to a servant as we entered the Great Palace's hall. There were courtiers everywhere and the smell of people and the rose juice they sprinkled on themselves was intense. Overlaying it all was the faint smell of wood smoke from the fireplace at the far end of the hall. It was not cold enough for a warming fire in England, but people here seemed to need them more.

A number of conversations suddenly stopped as we entered. As a result the noise level in the hall dropped noticeably and almost faded totally away. The courtiers looked at us with great interest as Michael and I walked into the hall.

I had no illusions of being important. We were of interest primarily because our arrival gave the courtiers something new to talk about instead of how many buttons or feathers someone was wearing.

My nagging fear that Elizabeth would refuse to see me, or reject me when she did, was soon put to rest. She saw me enter and immediately sent away those with whom she had been chattering so I could approach.

Michael hung back as I walked toward her and gave a great sweeping bow when I reached her.

"Your Highness," I said with a smile. "I have returned."

"I have missed you," she said very quietly as she nodded her head to agree with herself. "We have much to talk about."

"Indeed we do," I replied in a similar whisper. "But not here."

"Stay here tonight in the room next to mine and come to me after supper. And please feel free to visit the baths before you do." *The invitation was clear and reminded me that I had just come ashore after spending weeks on a galley.*

I gave another sweeping bow and withdrew. Before I did, however, I smiled and quietly, very quietly, said "Your wish is my command, Your Majesty. However, people word might get back to your husband's father if we are too blatant. I will come to you using the tunnel."

She smiled and nodded her head in agreement. I gave her another grand bow and withdrew. My head remained unbanged.

Two minutes later Michael and I were back in the rain with our little guard of archers and Elizabeth's courtiers, with nothing else to do, were no doubt feverishly gossiping about the purpose of my visit and the things that were important at the Empress's court—such as the cut of my clothes and the length of my hair.

"I am going to visit the city baths, Michael. Please send one of your guards to fetch a new tunic for me from the Commandry's slop chest. Tell him to bring it the baths and not to worry if it does not have any stripes on it."

******

Elizabeth had been waiting impatiently and opened the door to the upright clothes chest quickly when I tapped lightly on the inner door of the upright chest that served as the entrance to the tunnel. I used the rhythmic little knock on the wood that had somehow become a tradition between us. It felt like old times—except it was not.

She seemed initially to be rather tense and, for that matter, so was I. It was understandable; we had not been alone together for many months. We could see each other clearly because the room was well lit by six or seven lanterns and candles. She was certainly thinner than the last time I saw her.

"I am told you have a fine new son," I said. " Where is he?"

"No need to worry. A wet nurse has him. He will not bother us?"

"Well that is good to know. Having someone walk in on us is not at all what I have in mind." *That is the understatement of the day was my thought at the time.*

"My brother does not want me to be his regent," Elizabeth announced as I sat myself down on her bed and looked at her. She remained standing. "Some of the people in my court have been telling Robert that he is ready to rule the Empire without a regent."

"It will happen sooner or later," was my response.

"He is like my mother; he is not strong enough to rule by himself," she responded with a strange tone of anger in her voice. And then she added somewhat ominously, "and he never will."

"King Otto, on the other hand, is strong. Did you know that he is once again gathering coins? This time so the Pope would pray for God to recognize Him as the Emperor and me as the Empress? I have agreed by the way.

"Otto is the one who tried to kill you," she said. "He said he needed to kill you if we married so he could use the toll coins to hire mercenaries to replace your archers."

I looked at Elizabeth closely, and then took our conversation in a different direction instead of replying to her comments.

"I know it was you who told Otto that I would sooner or later be in the Mason's hall whilst searching the tunnels. Do you intend to kill your brother just as you did your mother and my father?

She ignored my question and answered with one of her own, and rather sternly at that.

"I know the Company's concession is important to you, George, and so is the contact to collect the tolls. But surely you know that you are not the only one who wants the toll coins and can use them to hire men to defend the city?

"So if you want to keep your concession and the tolls you will have to defend me and marry me. If you will not, then I will have to find someone else; probably Otto since he has already asked me and thinks I have agreed.

"On the other hand, if my brother is removed you could be the Emperor and I the Empress. What say you to that?"

I looked at Elizabeth a long time before I responded.

"I am sorry Elizabeth, truly I am. It is an interesting proposal but there are several reasons why I cannot agree. One is that you killed my father. The second is that I would prefer to be the Commander of my company rather than tied down here with your insipid courtiers. *I did not mention the third reason, that if I was foolish enough to give up the Company she would probably end up killing me so she could rule alone.*

"I knew you would say something like that." She said with a touch of exasperated pity in her voice.

"Besides, some things are more important than money," I said as I stretched out on the bed. And then I asked her the question that had brought me back to Constantinople instead of sailing directly to Cornwall.

"I know you killed your own mother and my father with her. But why?"

My questioned surprised her. She reacted as if the answer was obvious and I should have already known it.

"It was necessary. My mother was not strong enough to be my brother's Regent. She wrote to the Pope saying she wanted Otto to become his regent if anything happened to her. She did not want her own daughter to rise. Can you imagine how I felt?"

I shook my head and waved my hand to indicate she should continue.

"I knew I had to act when I found out about her letter to the Pope. I did not trust her to protect me. She might have sent me back to Epirus."

Then she asked me the inevitable question.

"But how did you learn that it was me who killed them?"

Elizabeth asked the question with a degree of surprise in her voice as she turned away and began unrolling a roll of linen she had been holding ever since I arrived.

"I knew last year when you told me about meeting Helen when she was at the church saying the prayers for my father. That was when I knew you had lied to me about rushing to the city as soon as you got the news of their deaths. There was no way you could have been there for the prayers unless you were already in the city.

"It is a long way from Constantinople to Epirus. It would have taken a couple of days for a galloper to reach you with the news and more than a week for you to return. There is no way you could have talked to my father's wife in church a couple of days after the murders unless you were already here in the city.

"I also knew it was you because I saw a candle lantern and the tunnel dust on your sandals when I searched the room you used before you moved into the Regent's chambers. You had already explored the tunnels.

"That was when I realized you had only pretended not to know about the tunnels and the door in the upright chest. And also that you were only pretending when you helped me discover how to open the door. You found it so quickly because you already knew.

"I know you killed my father and your mother, and probably intend to do your brother as well. But why did you and Otto try to have me killed?" I asked.

"Because Otto said he needed the tolls to hire mercenaries and to pay for the prayers so I could get divorced and marry him. I knew you would never give them up. Father Mathias said it was the only choice I had and that God would understand."

"So was it you or your confessor who told Otto's men about my exploring the tunnels and that I would sooner or later be in the Mason hall?"

She ignored my question.

"It does not have to be Otto I marry in order to become the Empress, George. Your Company has the toll coins and I have the Empire's taxes and fees. We could buy the necessary prayers for us to marry and be the Emperor and Empress."

I, in turn, ignored her suggestion.

"So there it is –you came through the tunnel and killed my father and your mother in order that you could take her place as Empress.

She stiffened at my words and began shaking her head. Finally, after a pause, she spoke.

"Silly man. I did *not* have to use the tunnel to get into her room. I talked with her in her chambers until late in the afternoon when the servant brought in the bowl of watered wine she kept by her bed in case she or your father became thirsty.

"It was easy. I just poured the poison into the bowl next to her bed when I went in to use the piss pot. They both most have drunk out of it."

Then she looked over her shoulder at me and told me more.

"It is your father's fault for being where he should not have been. So you should not blame me. That is what my confessor, Father Mathias, says."

"But I do have a surprise for you, think of it as a gift from Otto," she said as she turned to unfold the linen she was carrying and then turned back to lean over me—and pushed the blade she had unwrapped straight into my chest. Her eyes widened in surprise as she did.

There was a slight scratching and scraping sound when her blade hit my chain shirt. She had never known I wore it because I always took it off before I went to her or was waiting in bed for her to arrive.

I did not hesitate. I did what I had come to Constantinople to do—my wrist knives went into both sides of her throat without making any sound at all.

"Well, one thing is certain; your brother is either going to need a new regent or he is going to have to rule without one."

I said it rather viciously as I used the knives in her throat to pull her face towards mine and hold her there.

By the light of the rooms candle lanterns I watched Elizabeth's panic-stricken eyes as she realized what had happened, and then as they dimmed when she finished her struggling and trembling.

I left by the tunnel and was wearing a new tunic without blood on it and enjoying a bowl of wine in the Commandry by the time her servants found her.

Epilogue

Erik was very serious as he sat down across from me. I thought he was there to ask me if I knew anything about Elizabeth's mysterious murder two days earlier. I was wrong.

"George, when the war with the Greeks was over you asked your father how it was that he knew the Orthodox Metropolitan, Andreas, and why he thought the Metropolitan could be trusted. Do you remember?"

George nodded warily at the captain of the Varangians.

"Your father, and Andreas *and I* were all part of the same fraternal brotherhood that meets in the Hall of the Masons under the eye of the all-seeing God who watches over everyone no matter who we are or what our earthly religion might be.

"People think we are just another drinking and social club, because that is the part of us they can see. But we are much more than that. We are a group of men who believe in one God and are sworn to always honest with each other and to do what we can to make the world a better place for everyone.

"We would like you to take your father's place. Would you like me to tell you about us?"

The end

There are more books in *The Company of Archers Saga*.

All of the books in this exciting and action-packed medieval saga are available on Amazon as individual eBooks, and some of them are also available in print and as audio books. Many of them are available in multi-book collections. You can find them by searching for *Martin Archer Stories*. The first book in the saga is *The Archers* for those who wish to start at the beginning and read the stories in order.

A bargain-priced collection containing all of first six books of the saga is available as *The Archers' Story*. Similarly, a collection of the next four books in the saga is available as *The Archers' Story: Part II;* the three novels after that as *The Archers' Story Part III;* and the four after that as *The Archers' Story: Part IV*. There is also a *Part V* with the next three.

A chronological list of all the books in the saga, and other books by Martin Archer, can be found below along with a few sample pages from the first book in the saga.

Finally, a word from Martin:

"I sincerely hope you enjoyed reading the latest story about the hard men of Britain's first great merchant company as much as I enjoyed writing it. If so, I hope you will consider reading the other stories in the saga and leaving a favourable review on Amazon or Google with as many stars as possible in order to encourage other readers.

"And, if you could please spare a moment, I would also very much appreciate your thoughts and suggestions about this saga and its stories. Should the stories continue? What do you think? I can be reached at martinarcherV@gmail.com."

Cheers and thank you once again. /S/ Martin Archer

Books in the exciting and action-packed *The Company of Archers* saga:

The Archers

The Archers' Castle

The Archers' Return

The Archers' War

Rescuing the Hostages

Archers and Crusaders

The Archers' Gold

The Missing Treasure

Castling the King

The Sea Warriors

The Captain's Men

Gulling the Kings

The Magna Carta Decision

The War of the Kings

The Company's Revenge

The Ransom

The New Commander

The Gold Coins

The Emperor has no Gold

Protecting the Gold: The Fatal Mistakes

The Alchemist's Revenge

The Venetian Gambit

Today's Friends

eBooks in Martin Archer's epic *Soldiers and Marines* saga:

Soldiers and Marines

Peace and Conflict

War Breaks Out

War in the East (A fictional tale of America's role in the next great war)

Israel's Next War (A prescient book much hated by Islamic reviewers)

Collections of Martin Archer's books on Amazon

The Archers Stories I - complete books I, II, III, IV, V, and VI

The Archers Stories II - complete books VII, VIII, IX, and X

The Archers Stories III - complete books XI, XII, and XIII

The Archers Stories IV – complete books XIV, XV, XVI, and XVII

The Archers Stories V – complete books XVIII, XIX, and XX

The Soldiers and Marines Saga - complete books I, II, and III

Other eBooks you might enjoy:

Cage's Crew by Martin Archer writing as Raymond Casey

America's Next War by Michael Cameron – an adaption of Martin Archer's *War Breaks Out* set in the immediate future when Eastern and Western Europe go to war over another wave of Islamic refugees.